Nikki Gemmell writes novels, memoirs, essays and columns. She is the bestselling author of some twenty books, including *Shiver*, *The Bride Stripped Bare*, *After*, *The Ripping Tree* and *Dissolve*. Her books have been translated into twenty-two languages. She was born in Wollongong, New South Wales.

Also by Nikki Gemmell

Shiver

Cleave

Love Song

The Bride Stripped Bare

Pleasure: An Almanac for the Heart

The Book of Rapture

Why You Are Australian

With My Body

I Take You

Honestly: Notes on Life

Personally: Further Notes on Life

After

On Quiet

The Ripping Tree

Dissolve

As N.J. Gemmell

The Kensington Reptilarium

The Icicle Illuminarium

The Luna Laboratorium

Coco Banjo is Having a Yay Day

Coco Banjo Has Been Unfriended

Coco Banjo and the Super Wow Surprise

NIKKI GEMMELL
WING

FOURTH ESTATE

Fourth Estate
An imprint of HarperCollins*Publishers*

HarperCollins*Publishers*
Australia • Brazil • Canada • France • Germany • Holland • India
Italy • Japan • Mexico • New Zealand • Poland • Spain • Sweden
Switzerland • United Kingdom • United States of America

HarperCollins acknowledges the Traditional Custodians
of the lands upon which we live and work, and pays respect
to Elders past and present.

First published on Gadigal Country in Australia in 2024
by HarperCollins*Publishers* Australia Pty Limited
ABN 36 009 913 517
harpercollins.com.au

Copyright © Nikki Gemmell 2024

The right of Nikki Gemmell to be identified as the author of this work has been asserted by her in accordance with the *Copyright Amendment (Moral Rights) Act 2000*.

This work is copyright. Apart from any use as permitted under the *Copyright Act 1968*, no part may be reproduced, copied, scanned, stored in a retrieval system, recorded, or transmitted, in any form or by any means, without the prior written permission of the publisher. Without limiting the author's and publisher's exclusive rights, any unauthorised use of this publication to train generative artificial intelligence (AI) technologies is expressly prohibited.

A catalogue record for this book is available from the National Library of Australia

ISBN 978 1 4607 6156 4 (paperback)
ISBN 978 1 4607 1460 7 (ebook)
ISBN 978 1 4607 3932 7 (audiobook)

Cover design by Sandy Cull, gogo gingko
Cover image © Liz Dalziel / Trevillion Images
Typeset in Bembo Std by Kirby Jones
Printed and bound in Australia by McPherson's Printing Group

To all the blazing women
and all the blazing girls

Monday

'Wife beaters are hot.' That's what Cin said, right in front of you, as you walked a step behind her lairy little posse. Great. She glanced back as she headed off to her school camp, drunk on glee. Your heart twisted at the audacity, stupidity, innocence. The sheer wrongness of those words. Ah, the blazing Cin. Hormone cusped, on that vulnerable fulcrum between girlhood and womanhood, and of course you'd overhear. That was the point. As she looked over her shoulder like a tiny tinderbox Orpheus, daring you to come on this journey with her; to say something, respond, connect.

You did not. And they were the last words you heard from her. And it is very hard to write this. But set it down, set down this, in hardening concrete, you   must.

What you thought as she walked down the corridor: Nup, you'll not be giving that one the gift of attention. There's your job to think of, and your new job to think of; the delicious little nugget at the heart of everything now, the secret thrill pulling you through your crammed days. You are close, so close. But now this. A god-daughter's scuppering. Please no.

You are stalked by Cin's presence; in love with her, watchful and needy. You've never loved anyone with this voluptuousness or intensity. It is the love of an older woman for a young female of the future with an astonishing confidence and fearlessness you never had at that age. You're in love with the promise of her, the unknown arc arrowing into its future. Where will it land? Will it veer off course? Who knows.

Your relationship is lidded. Contained, ruthlessly, between Cin, her mother Mig and yourself. Mig who just happens to be your best friend. The three of you exist under a carapace of secrets; pick at the scab and you'd all bleed, unstoppably. So no-one does. But Lord, the cackly exuberance in that voice as it declared that wife beaters are so fucking hot. Oh yes, the F-word was tucked in there too. Of course. Cin learnt the swearing from you, before she came to this sandstone school, in her other life. Your other life. When you'd fondly use expressions like Cuntarella and its lesser-known sibling, Cuntalina. Alongside cunted and cuntalicious and that mother of all insults, 'shitty little cuntfucker'. As the Queen of Cuntspeak you found it all deeply satisfying, in an onomatopoeic, spitty, aggressive kind of way, cackling with Mig, until you realised the ten-year-old Cin was overhearing, and learning avidly from the connoisseur of expletives; and so you stopped.

Cin is Cinnamon. Your Cin-bin, Limou-cin, SinsiSin. Leader of the pack of the notorious, glorious Cins, the posse that owns this school corridor. They are the mangoes, peaches, strawberries in the fruitshop of this place. Membership: the brazenly short-haired Cinnamon, the glossily long-haired brunette Tamsin, reliably plaited Willa and – for some reason – Elle. Or is that Ella. Ellie. The bewildering, potato-y other of the group.

And as of 11.58 this morning, all lost.

In the land of the mountains that swallow people up. Vanished. No. Stop. Like a tic of wrong you must halt the words tempting fate, stem the panic getting ahead of itself. You are their principal and have control of this. Cin will be back, it's a temporary blip. But this is her doing, you suspect, it's got her fingerprints all over it. She has an excess of energy, like she's possessed. Flurries things up, steals attention, interrupts, disrupts. Triggers … situations. You can never relax with this one. Always need to be poised, in readiness.

And this would involve The Cins, of course. The double cream of the crop. Vivid with personality, Elle excluded, and a cult of wonder has built up around them. Not healthy. Oh, they know they're special within the school's collective, but your modus operandi for any child has always been: You Are Not Special. Yet Cin is. And by association her satellites. And now fucking this. Language, language. Stop. Deep breath.

You need to stay calm. In control. You are the principal of Koongala School for Girls and this situation with your students will be contained, resolved, and fast. The girls found, very soon, without a ripple on the surface of school life. They have to be.

Because you have a secret. The new job you've applied for that's the reason for your recent buoyancy, your silent glee. After decades at the schooling coalface, you're about to be handed a powerful and singular responsibility – heading up the advisory body that shapes the nation's curriculum. You'll be sculpting the learning of all high school students as the future roars at them. Lifting standards not just in one elite independent school that does very well for itself, but right across the country. Because a strong, deep curriculum is the most effective tool in reducing inequality, you know this, and something needs to be done to arrest the slide in standards. You've been told, discreetly, the job is in the bag, subject to referee reports. It feels like you've been working towards this position your entire life; it's the pinnacle, the crowning achievement. And now, now, you're almost there. So close. Except for. For—

Fuck this.

Only Mig knows of the want deep within you. The need to absolve yourself from selling out. You're the state school kid who worked in the state school system but then dazzled her way into the highest echelons of the independent sector. Koongala was the glittering prize in a glittering career but you were learning all the time; absorbing the lessons, in readiness. To make a difference. You were the first in your family to finish high school let alone university and education was the greatest gift in your life, catapulting you into an existence your parents never got. A world of shelves with books on them and pianos in houses and broadsheet newspapers and dinners that aren't at 5 pm and the national broadcaster on the radio and voices that don't sound like your family's; oh yes, you studied and elocuted and slipped your way out. You've been at Koongala for more than a decade, shaping a generation of clever, privileged, articulate girls. It's been a joy, but … you're over it now. Time to give something back. To help others, like yourself, get the golden ticket.

Who gets to enter the professional class? You know the loneliness of that path for the working class kid. Your own family didn't know a way into the Otherworld of the educated elite, didn't know the codes. You hauled yourself out with the help of great teachers and grit but are forever the observer, propelled by anger at the unfairness of the world. It's the furnace within you. This new job? The culmination of a watchful life.

The phone call came last night; the job is practically yours. But you know the panel will be panicking when they find out about the lost girls; *if* they find out. It's messy. Not a good look. They'll be getting cold feet. You need this nipped in the bud.

Cin found. But she's unpredictable. This situation could be anything. You bite your lip, draw blood.

At eight Cin wrote a book called 'The Girl Who Turned Into a Spider' because she wanted to be one. Declared she'd like to dig up bodies in the cemetery because she needed to look at them. Her mother always laughed it off as Cin's extraordinary imagination, her sparkling brilliance; 'She'll be a glorious storyteller one day.' You, hmmm, not so sure. Brilliant or in the gutter – it could go either way. You cautioned Mig about keeping her thoughts about her daughter's brazen shine to herself. Told her that no other parent wanted to hear of another child's prowess. They're just not interested in a student who's not their own, especially in that child's achievements. And you know from experience that the boasty mothers can be shunned. Mig got it, kept quiet and kept her distance, too careful for bragging and big-noting.

What is known: Year Ten left for its annual bush camp at 6.30 this morning. Sixty-seven girls, aged fifteen to sixteen. The Cins were separated from the rest, on a bush trail, at some point. None of the other girls said anything; it was almost as if they wanted them gone. Must not dwell. Helen Venty, the form mistress, carried out a roll call when the girls returned to base camp. Missing: Cin, Tamsin, Willa, Elle. Of fucking course. Parents must be informed. No, wait. Stop jumping ahead. Wait for clarity of some sort. Helen got one quick, panicky phone message to Pup, the school administrator, and that was it for the time being and you desperately need an update. Mobile phones and Apple watches were banned for the girls – this was to be a screen-free bonding exercise where bowed backs would be straightened and faces held strong to the sky. But maybe The Cins really need their phones, right now, desperately. Your heart dips at the thought.

The first you knew of this: Pup hurtling down the school corridor with wild in his eyes, calling out one of your office nicknames – 'Sarge!' – in actual public, bugger who heard. 'All of them. The Cins. Gone,' he babbled in great gulps of breath. 'Breensy too. He went back in after them. There's been no sign of any of them since.' Pup slammed his hand to his mouth as if quelling vomit and he's never like that. He's your confident beta, the best type of male; insecure alphas being the worst, of course, and thank Christ he's not that. Pup, otherwise known as Frank Delaware, is sturdy, even, unflappable. But his face, in the corridor. As if he knew that no good would come of four girls vanished – four! – and that your school could be irrevocably tarnished from this point and who knew The Cins' fate and this needed to be sorted, cleanly.

The public persona was instantly switched on. Ruthless control, ruthless calm, as you do when a parent goes rogue. What do we know, you enquired through thudding heart – oh God The Cins your Cin   no. You were efficient, enunciated, muted as you steered Pup firmly to where you could talk in private. Your old life stopped from this point, the life you could control, oh your runaway heart.

Because Cin is your best friend's only child. You call your goddaughter your Golden Flower, the name Sappho gave to her own little marvel of a girl so tenderly, so rapturously. And so it became the secret name used by you, and then Mig too, for the tiny bud of wonder in your midst. How you both marvelled at the stages of woman in that mighty little packet. And now Mig must be told. Can't. Until something is firm, known. It will kill her. Don't get ahead of yourself, girl. Mask of calm and bat wings, swathed around you, the protective shield for the bullets to come.

You should clarify: this is the child of your former best friend. Ex. Mess. Nothing hurts like a close friendship lost among women. She ghosted you a year ago and you haven't yet moved on. Sometimes, still, it pounds your heart. How to fell a successful woman's confidence, how to cut her off at the knees. For a girlfriend knows, by instinct, the Achilles heel of another woman, knows precisely what hurts, and Mig did. The shock of withdrawal was as vicious as a slap across the face. The roar of the silence. For this wasn't just any friendship, this was your best friend, your china plate, and you'd been more open with each other than with any partner or parent. You knew everything about Mig's life as she did yours. Her wants. Her needs. Her sex life. Her loves. But then you were dropped into a cold, cold place. Your mind was addled, poisoned by doubts. They come rushing in as you lie awake at night trying to work out where you've gone wrong and how to find a way back, because Mig has made you feel like the one thing a friend should never make another feel – a failure. Which has tipped the entire balance of your life.

Does anyone ever consider the loneliness of the childless godmother? The one who loves consumingly, with complication and flair and want. And that gobby, grubby flurry-upperer now gone is like your very own child, the closest you'll ever get, and you're feeling all the laceration of a parent's uncertainty here. It could topple you. But on you must plough, collected and calm, keeping panic at bay. Mig doesn't know. How can you tell her? A fairy godmother steps in in times of need, mollifies, rescues and instructs; yet you're the fixer who cannot fix this. Your phone is pinging notifications and on, on you must push.

12.28 pm. No word. You have to manage this crisis and head off any fallout; time to swing into action and alert those who need to know. To take a deep breath and call it. Fuck. Police yet? Parents? No, too soon for both – it will just lead to conflagration. A media scramble. So. An all-teacher alert. The bare bones of the situation. Not enough to elicit panic. Breensy's in charge and you've got every trust in that; his wife, Adela, doesn't need to be told yet. You press send on the staff email. *Rest assured, this will be over shortly, by bell time at the latest.* This can all be fixed, surely. Alisdair Callan, chair of the school council, is rung. You have a prickly respect for each other; he sees you as a highly effective champagne socialist and you see him as a toff. But you get on, in a gruff and jocular way, although give him any excuse and he'd lop you at the knees to have one of his own installed. You arrange a Zoom meeting with all board members for 2 pm. The tone is measured: you've got this, all bases are covered.

Except, er, where the girls actually are. But not going there, no way.

Furious note-taking between calls and texts; ballast for calm. How you operate. Meticulous notes across numbered journals spanning an entire career – you're up to notebook number ninety-eight. To understand, work things out, as well as the insurance against parents, board, lawyers and police. No. It'll not come to that. The girls will be out, pronto.

Waiting for updates, shallow breathed, palms flat on desk. But this is impossible. Obscene. On a school camp, no less. As the chosen fairy hoverer you've tried to spell Cin's existence with certainty her entire life, because as an educator you've seen the destructive effects of uncertainty again and again; the damage it does to a student. Children need certainty. Full stop. The quiet effectiveness of routine. Of regular meals and boundaries and attention. Yes, the latter most of all, the tonic of it. And now everything upended. You do not cope well with uncertainty.

Control is paramount. And how do you explain this to Cin's mother who you barely talk to now and it's freighted with wrong when you do; you feel uncomfortable when stuck alone with her. So you can't explain. Yet.

Must.

Six-year-old Cin used to snuggle in your sleepover bed and clutch the blankets and whisper, 'One upon a time,' in giggly anticipation, to signal the stories of the godmothers, Wicked and Fairy. You told her you were a bit of both but she always wanted the black over the pink. You gave her tales of pumpkins turned into carriages and ballgowns for formals and sleeps for a very long time, all year, perhaps, and pyjamas all day and princes – well, you'd always change that bit, your protagonist didn't need to end up with silly old doofus him. Cin got something much better instead. Freedom. Or let's say choice. The crown in a princess's life.

Then your little god-daughter would fall asleep, contented, her freshly washed hair smelling of strawberries and her cheeks flushed, and you'd gently extricate yourself from the bed and stand there, poised, in the room filled with the sleep of this trusting child and you'd just stay there, looking at her, breathing her in; and then this great warmth would flood through you, an enormous heart-swelling gratitude and you'd find yourself closing your eyes in unstoppable thanks. For her. The gift of her. Prayer is gratitude, oh yes.

Despite an icy fear for Cin and her girls, you must be strong. For everyone connected to this. Soon the media will be circling. The message must be controlled. You're only the sixth headmistress of the mighty, mysterious Koongala and you were told when you joined that the image must be carefully curated. But there was no way you were going down the tastefully highlighted, cashmere- and pearl-wearing path – that isn't you.

You had started out as a brilliant teacher in the state system, were quickly promoted to Head of English, then principal at several high-achieving selective schools. You were an educational innovator and it was noticed. But over the years the disenchantment set in. The demountables with the broken aircon. The quiz nights to pay for computers. The parents pulling their kids out for the playing fields of the private system. The pay discrepancy with the private principals – twice the work for half the income. When a headhunter approached you for the Koongala job you were told, given your track record, you could develop the school the way you wanted; cater to all abilities and develop the whole girl. You licked your lips. With the onsite accommodation, huge pay increase plus performance bonus you'd be set up for life. Security, prestige, status: this job gave you all that. But … this position is only the stepping stone to the real prize, almost within your grasp; a position that's well remunerated and respected within the inner-city latte set, because it's a chance to make a difference to every child in the country. And, well, the peer glory, there's that too, of course, perhaps most of all. To be admired among your own is the ultimate sweetness. But fuck, could Cin actually scupper everything? You've worked so hard for others, for so long, but now this. And behind the corporate anguish, Alisdair's gloat. Because this could be your undoing. The undoing of the uppity female at last.

Koongala didn't quite know what hit it when you arrived. The image: part art teacher, part designer maven. A blare of Marimekko, Dinosaur Designs and M.A.C Diva lipstick, all to combat the invisibility of the middle-aged woman; you will not be disappearing any time soon, thank you very much. Plus signature red bob. A wig, to be honest, your mask to the world that hides the wispy grey thinness underneath. A wig to firm you. And you do love a well-placed sequin. They always come out on International Women's Day, and if the girls want to add a sequinned hem to their uniform on that special day so be it. Dress-up You, with signature lip and bob, has made appearances on muck-up days and at formals and at reunions. You're iconic among a certain arty, intellectual alumnae set. Quite fabulously. You are the benign dictator in a universe of your own making. The Koongalettes are entranced as much as the parents. Well, most.

Today you'll be hearing from the small subset of problematic parents because you always do. They sniff blood early. They're often on the P&C or in close proximity to it. It gives them a sense of entitlement, a power to have a say, puffs them up. You told Mig, when she first became a Koongala parent, never to go near that sanctimonious little set. Why would I, she said with a laugh, too much fucking politics, urgh. You regretfully concurred. Told her the best parents are the ones you never hear from. Give me a girl at twelve and I'll make her a woman, you declared, and their oblivious parents never need to know how. You dislike politely. The P&C lot have no idea.

Cin has listened over the years. Absorbed so much of your working life, too much. Startles you with insights she's not meant to have. 'It's parent suicide,' she said to you once, of the P&C. 'No teacher will ever like your kid if you do it.' True, but a reminder to be extremely careful about what's said in front of her. She notices too much.

Cin is the girl who doesn't hide who she is and that's threatening to some; the strength in it. Who does she think she is, says the tone of the more conservative elements around her, and your response is always, well, someone who's living her life unconcerned about what you think of her. Sometimes Cin catches you looking at her, transfixed, and tilts her head like a bird that's just sighted a worm. She knows the weight and burden of your love as Godmother. Her secret protector bound by God, and in a church school at that. She picks at this knowledge like a wound that will not heal. Freshly plays with it like a cat with a hapless lizard. For example, that wife beater thing, the taunt of her words.

'God help God,' your mother laughed, when you told her Cin was coming to your school. Yet that child's unbound strength — the strength of the female of the future — is a tonic. World, just you wait.

But first we have to get through this little   hiccup.

Monday Afternoon

The media are starting to sniff something out. A newspaper contact is making discreet enquiries because you have finally called the police and they are leaking, of course. The contact is ignored. Nothing leads to nothing; no scrap bones for that lot. You're often invited to make media appearances as the thoughtful spokesperson of the independent school movement, and on teenage girls in particular. Your expertise: eating disorders, bullying, anxiety, academic pressure, youth suicide, screens, school refusal and the benefits generally of the private system. You are the media's go-to girl but no, you'll not be talking about this. The catastrophic fouling of your own nest.

Your fist punches the desk.

How could it be The Cins, of all girls? Not all students are Koongalettes, the chosen ones, but The Cins, well, they're top of the tree. You gaze at them in chuff as they go about their school days. They know you secretly admire them, especially Cin, but what has she done now? She has an instinct for wildness, insurrection, it's chaotic and anarchic. It's in the hot chocolate stains on her white Peter Pan collar, in the school skirt folded at the waist so it's a tad too short, in the never-ironed shirt and unruliness of the hair. Whatever she wears always look messy, like she couldn't care less; yet it always, somehow, appears as a strength. Cin has the courage of difference and gets away with it. Katherine Mansfield said the minds she loved the most have wild places in them; and Cin certainly has plenty in that head of hers. Your hands squeeze your temples. This feels like a monumental flipping of the bird, to you most of all.

Panic is now flexing its claws. Catching at your underbelly. You keen softly as the minutes of this ridiculous un-finding drag on, and on.

You had never been willing to take the professional hit of motherhood. As a young woman, you saw marriage as surrender and cooing over babies as weakness. At nineteen you declared that you never wanted children because your life would be too busy with everything else. But then, then, the moments of corrosive want in your late twenties when biology took over and demanded it of you; reminding you that we're all animals underneath and procreation is what our bodies expect. But the career trajectory always got in the way. You saw too many girlfriends' wages and status in life flatline after their babies came along – sorry, but you wanted to soar. And to have your happiness so entangled with someone else's, to have something so uncontrollable and risky as the barometer of your calm, no, not for you. Someone else can shoulder the stress. But now.

Pup hovers at the office door. A call you have to take. Elle's mother. Damn. Parents were next on the list to ring, of course, but you hadn't quite got there yet; Breensy's wife, Adela, will need to be contacted too. And now, immediately, you've got Elle's mum, whatsername, Beth to deal with. Pup writes it down in front of you, you underline the B; the pen digs through several layers, catches at the paper and rips. Can't recall ever really meeting, must have had an entry interview but it's lost in the mists of time. The school hasn't put out a notification; she must have a contact among staff. Annoying. This is all sprinting ahead too fast. Daughter a cricketer, that's right, outside of school, good bowler you think, perhaps. All you really know. Koongala doesn't do cricket. It takes too long and, well, sport, not your thing. If we must but not that. Elle has a body, unfortunately, like poor Warnie's. Chunky. Box on legs. Undisciplined. Normal. Who wants to be that. The only Cin obviously not a Cin.

Beth's voice sounds like she's not practised with thrusting herself into the world; like she prefers texting to speaking. You hear it in her tone: she is the mother whose child never wins an award on Presentation Day but slips through the cracks, and she takes it on the chin, stoically, year after year. You soothe Beth now, shut her tremulousness down, everything is alright. No she doesn't need to get to the campsite; you have her number, will call immediately with news. A teacher has gone in after the girls, a wonderful man, they'll be out any moment. Breensy *is* a wonderful man; an effective operator who gets things done and likes to win; he'll own this, sort this. Beth asks in a wavering cadence if anyone else could have been involved. Pardon? A stranger, a contact, on social media perhaps, a man we don't know about, who followed them in. I don't think so, you brisk, shutting down the panic. You hang up. Go online.

You are a meticulous trawler of the internet. None of your students know. Honestly, online too many of them are so careless. Ridiculously, stupidly. Cin, Willa and Tamsin all have more than a thousand public Instagram followers – on the accounts that you know of. Beth's dumpy little Elle, seventy-seven. And she's on private, damn. Elle, Ella, Elly, still not completely sure. All you know is that she's swept up in the Cult of Them, like she can't quite believe she's been enveloped by the group. Why her, with the rest. Something about the primary school Cin and Elle went to, perhaps, the well-worn grooves of old soccer teams and drama mates. Elle has always yearned for your girl; angled to be in her orbit. Other girls want to be invited to The Cins' parties and sleepovers, to star in their BeReals and TikToks. Everyone at Koongala talks about The Cins, including teachers, support staff and other mothers. It's a cult within the hierarchy of the school. The Cins know their power. Not sure why they allow Elle in but they're good at wrong-footing everyone with surprise; Cin's doing, again, you're sure. What's she up to?

Flurrying up the olds on purpose is her knowing, playful power. 'I like dick,' Cin declared, when you asked a while back if she might be gay. She was thirteen and it was the last proper conversation you both had, long after she was allowed in your bed for fairy tales, long after she was detached. She declared nah, she liked dick, as if testing you. She said dick regrettably, like she was disappointed at the heteronormative blandness of her sexual persuasion; she'd prefer to be something else.

You're afraid for this generation. For their brazenness, honesty. Because – as with domestic violence – the most dangerous time for a woman is when she's leaving the relationship. When she's found her power and is seizing the freedom; when she cannot be controlled. And these perceptive, stubborn, loud-voiced girls are shunning the entrapments of the patriarchy in a way no generation has before them. Because, well, why stay? They don't give a fuck. Which is dangerous. Because deep in men is the urge to dominate, colonise, erase.

A man's physical strength will always win out. And your girls have no idea of the brutal realities of the world, they're so innocent in this bubble of a place.

Feminism is seamed through this school. Subtly. After all, captains of industry, judges, generals and surgeons have always sent their daughters here, so one has to be careful. Don't want to frighten the horses. But you're not afraid of that far more important, gloriously powerful F-word, and of declaring in assembly that you are one. You're shaping your Koongalettes to take on the world, in the hope that they'll one day change it. They lap it up. Well, most. Some. The enraptured. Your mini-mes, your acolytes. Your lesson to them: don't be trapped in a prescribed life, girls, don't succumb. You want them to fly.

With Mig, biology took over eventually, despite her firebrand uni days. She said her body told her to have a baby and she had little control over the situation. It took her more than a decade to realise the dream but she got there in the end. Eight or nine gruelling IVF rounds. Her eggs, your eggs, then one last shot with her eggs again and suddenly, Cin. The forcefield of her, veering Mig's life. The child who crackles with intelligence and light.

You saw the form off this morning while standing among the wealthy, blonde Pilates mums with no books on the bookshelves in their houses, you just know. Yes, this is the post-book world. Women whose purpose in life, when young, is to marry well. Still. Which means a boat on the harbour and July in Santorini and January in Aspen after a vague influencer 'career'. You watch, with distance, marvelling at the confidence; the unthinking ease of the moneyed passage through life. Poverty stains everything. You know, because you came from it. Few of them know this about you.

Most of the school's parents have more money than the teachers will ever make. It is all in the Mercedes and Porsches in the turning circle compared with what's in the staff carpark. This restive, entitled, demanding parent body needs little lessons, now and then. For example, when you receive the lengthy email of icy fury from the legendary high court judge, demanding to know why his child did not get the cello solo in the music showcase; the email detailing how the school is biased against her because of 'her advantages in life'. Some notorious missives from aggrieved parents are 'accidentally' circulated among trusted teachers. For their delectation. But carefully. Needs must. Little spices in the grind of life.

You are courteous and charming to those you cannot bear. They will have no ammunition. Like Tamsin's parents, Hugo and Tink. There are other ways to punish. Tamsin is another who will never grace the Presentation Day stage and this will enrage and bewilder her parents year after year. All the little pricks you can inflict, without ever having anything pinned on you. Meanwhile there's your floating loveliness at form cocktail parties as you back away in your black velvet Marni platforms, back away and observe. In wonder. That these kind of fragile, egotistical, bullying people run the world, and always have.

Tamsin is one of those girls who a teacher looks at in Year Five and goes, thank God I won't be around for that one's teenage years. Too sensitive for her own good, too much drama. A girl who feels too much, who's endlessly storming off, whining and demanding and excluding. You wouldn't want to be anywhere near it. She stabbed another girl with a compass in primary school. The police were roped in, there were threats to sue, then it all mysteriously disappeared. Hugo settled. Substantially. Water off a duck's back. His surname peacocks into the room before he does and his money gets him off too much.

Mig said once, in the heat of an argument, that you think everyone is beneath your intellect and they can sense it. You've worked hard on this. To hide it, to like people when you generally do not. Mig laughed that you were too selfish to love, too watchful and careful and closed. She said you'd never learnt how to open yourself up to vulnerability.

1.14 pm and oh your heart, now, your pummelled heart. No-one knows you. Never has.

Mig said to you once that the most important question, at the end of our lives, should be how well have we loved. She said this as she asked you to be godmother all those years ago – Cin's *fairy* godmother, she laughed, not wicked, God no – the most important role in her baby's life. Apart from parent. You want to tell Mig now that you have loved well, both of them, and you will love her well again and will prove it by getting her girl back. Cin will return.

You have become a rigorous note-taker because parents are always threatening to sue over something. Thomasina must not be expelled for dealing vapes. Tiffany was not given a singing solo in the end-of-year concert. Tatiana is not in the firsts for soccer. Alba is being bullied by that Machiavellian little schemer, Nico; you have no idea what that child really gets up to. Quick, rally the lawyers, send the threatening letter, or let's make this a little more personal – storm the school in lunch hour and demand an audience. But your girl is a lying shit, sir – yet alas you can never say this. Smile, calm, fix. And take notes. A fresh notebook for today, in fact, because you need to get your head straight and in its storied history, Koongala has never done failure on this scale. It's never even had a suicide. That's the big one, that every principal dreads. You pride yourself on this unblemished record. We are a family, we will get through this.

The media are arking up, more and more are getting wind of 'an incident' on the mountains; texts are pinging. Pup says, 'Sarge, you need to be there.' It's two hours' drive away and traffic is building into its afternoon peak but yes, of course, you must get to the campsite. Before the media. Yet you cannot face anything right now but your notebook, to gather your thoughts. Plan. Prioritise. Face everyone you must. You press your palms flat to both cheeks to draw in calm, and … breathe. Deep. Phones are ringing, emails flying, typos, panic. So much to shut down. Not good when it comes to typos but can't catch them today. Your inner cheek is chewed until it bleeds; you turn to your nails, a strip of skin is torn off. Blood. Becoming sloppy, not you, must watch.

Always very careful in this job. With appearance. Demeanour. Voice. Meetings. Everything in its place, under control. Nothing ever goes awry, personally, and this will not. You pack your small ALPHA60 leather backpack but do not even consider taking an overnight bag, despite Pup's urging. No need. This situation will be tidied by nightfall. Yes. You do not tell Pup you're superstitious; that you still don't walk under ladders because it's Satan's territory or bring a knife as a housewarming gift. An overnight bag with however many clean underpants is only summoning the gods and you will not be inviting chaos, in any way, into this.

Your relationship with Cin feels like subversion within Koongala's high walls, an underhand grubbiness, yet of course it's not. No-one who matters knows of the connection between you. You have engineered for your god-daughter to be here; she jumped the queue to get in, which is no mean feat because you're meant to put down a child's name from birth or, better still, in utero. Yes, you pay her school fees via an anonymous trust, which Mig doesn't seem to want anymore, but you cannot give it up, you insist. Yes, this is love, your way, but no-one knows it.

You do not offer sneaky scholarships to the children of staff, unlike some other schools. It's too dangerous. Word would get out, among the kids most of all. But you do offer staff discounts.

What are they even wearing? Head aswirl. Are they warm for the night, if it comes to that – it won't – wearing, what? Summer sports uniform. Not right for the bush overnight, not warm enough. You designed it, should know. It's always about the aesthetics, of course. Idiot. Navy blue, double red stripe on the collar. Loose footy shorts of just the right length because the cruelty of the sports uniform for women is a particular bugbear of yours; how many teens have pulled out of sport because of white rugby shorts that show period blood and ridiculously short netball slips and school regulation swimming costumes that become see-through when wet, displaying the first flush of pubic hair; oh no, none of that horror in this school. And so you initiated an extremely practical yet aesthetically pleasing sports uniform overhaul for the girls. Sat on the design committee, in fact. It became a national conversation. You're good at that. Have a marketing team of six. This is a business, after all.

It was Cin's doing. She schooled you in primary school. Wouldn't go near netball, the nation's most popular female sport. Why? Because she hated the short dress. Loathed the girls' uniform at her public school, full stop. Hated that she had to sit cross-legged on the carpet, which showed her undies in front of the boys. Hated that it stopped her from climbing trees and swinging on ropes like the boys. Hated that it enabled them to look up her skirt as she climbed the stairs. Hated that they filmed up her legs when they got phones. So Cin started wearing soccer shorts under her dress until the school relented and let her wear the boys' uniform. Which she did, their very first girl, rejoicing in a newfound freedom. All the little ways that can be found to nibble away at us, and all the little ways to bestow confidence and strength in return. Cin's arrival at Koongala coincided with the introduction of trousers to the school uniform, if girls desired them. Funny that.

Hang on. Why are you even thinking about the uniform. The girls are in mufti. Of course, forgot. Reminded by the ever-capable Pup. Cin was wearing some vesty combat thing with a multitude of bulging pockets. You remember thinking she's probably got a Swiss Army knife in there alongside jelly snakes and a mini flask of vodka and a vape. But she won't have her school-monogrammed water bottle with her, she'll have left that behind on the kitchen bench; the third or possibly fourth one Mig's bought for her, and Cin will have forgotten to take it because she is that girl. And someone else will hand theirs over to her on the trip. Willingly, because the world always falls into her lap. Unlike Elle, who has to work hard for it.

Mind. Focus. Mountains. Immediately. And you just want to sleep. So tired, with the emotional toll of all this, with the many panicked people who need to be calmed down, with maintaining that façade of strength, competence, calm. You take a deep breath. Need to get moving. Get your head straight. But the parents of Tamsin, of all the missing, have to be formally advised; Adela still needs a call too. Your hand flies over a fresh

To Do list. You ring Pup. He can do this bit, inform them all. Even Mig, especially Mig, because you still can't face her. Pup can tell her, tell them all, you are heading to the mountains, you'll be waiting for them; you are their servant in this, at their beck and call. But Pup will be the liaison for the moment; you will be on the road and they have his number and can call at any point, he must stress this especially to Tamsin's father, Hugo, because you can't deal with his belligerence yet. You've had so much of it over the years.

You keep going back to the conversation from last night as you set up the Zoom to the school council you're wary of; the board so bound by convention. Your secret departmental source from yesterday was effusive and reassuring, and you know the conversation scraps off by heart because you jotted them down – *smashed it, the outstanding candidate, the only person for the job, can make a real difference.* But now you have fourteen Koongala council members to endure, over a situation that might overwhelm everything.

The emergency gathering is brief; you tell them you're about to head to the mountains to sort this situation out. Not everyone can make it to the screen. Busy lives. Good. The fewer the better. Alisdair is getting on a plane to Hong Kong; you tell him it'll be sorted by the time he lands. No time for questions, you need to jump in the car, nothing further to add. You'll keep them all informed. And   end call.

You can't help thinking of the delicious moment when you get to hand in your resignation to Alisdair. Of his crestfallen face when you tell him about the high-powered, high-status job you're moving on to. It'll make all this weasely bowing and scraping, all this endless, delicate managing and massaging of the board worthwhile. You cannot wait.

But the mountains, now, yes, with their whoosh of secret ravines and plunging cliffs and burbling creeks; so much immensity to be lost in. You jump in your Tesla, a perk of the job. Head to the campsite where the school buses will still be parked because the symbolic horror of driving off, without the four students and a teacher, is too much to bear for anyone right now; it signals abandonment. And what of the other students, what is their mental state right now? Pup holds the fort at school. 'Sarge, I got this,' and you know he does. He's a single dad, a widower who couldn't afford the fees when his financial advisor fleeced his business, and he was going to withdraw his girls but you offered him a lifeline; to be your right-hand man. He's never let you down.

A police liaison officer rings on the way to the campsite. Her voice is young, smart, working class, unafraid of authority and highly efficient. Her name is Robin and she'll be with you for the duration – a pause as you both mull over whatever that means. You can tell from her tone that she would have a very neat notepad with colour-coded Post-it notes along the side, and that not much will fall out of her head. Your kind of girl and needed right now, because you feel like you've got too much in your own head; stress is already a rock in your chest. Robin advises that a command post is being set up at the campsite. An initial search party is rallying to go in. Media are circling like sharks, making soft enquiries, tossing up whether to dig further or hold off. And don't they love a bad private school story, you say wryly to Robin as you accelerate the car; it always gets the clicks. They really hate those elite schools, especially journalists, who've tended not to go to them, you say.

Do you think, Robin hesitates, the students might have done this themselves? You're not discounting anything. You think of the skirts rolled at the waistband to make them shorter. Don't tell Robin this. Of course not, you snap.

'Go away. You are literally destroying my life. You are killing me. Now I die.' Mig has told you that Cin regularly speaks to her like this now and yep, that girl is drama. Which is why you don't quite buy any lost-girl theories circulating. Not yet. This feels a little too much like fun at the moment, a wagging, a bit of a lark.

When Cin thought her period was arriving for the first time she thrashed and wriggled and writhed on Mig's bed, flat on her back. If she was in Salem she would have been burnt as possessed. All that theatricality, agony, horror at impending womanhood and all a false alarm. Sigh. Yet when her period did finally arrive she was docile, lying on the bed in the foetal position, and needy and wondrous at her body taken over by this new force. Of womanhood. Cin was also briskly practical about tampon use. 'Leave!' Her palm was held flat in refusal to her mother. 'I know what to do. Don't need you. Away.' Despite Cin never having done this before. Or had she? Put something in there, you wondered. Wouldn't put it past her. Just to see, to know what it feels like, up there. That girl fizzes with a questioning curiosity. God help Breensy, out there, with her. With them. God help men like him, with this lot.

Tony Breen, your Head of English, is a man increasingly out of kilter with the direction of the world. He exists in parallel to young people, politely, as a gentleman, but in judgement; does not want a bar of their obsessions, oddities, passions. His manner, clothes, bearing and language reek of a certain kind of traditional upbringing and world view, of the like you find in the church or the armed forces, a world where men dominate and women serve. He's very used to this model, it's innate.

He is the Swiss Army knife of men. One of those blokes from a previous generation who can turn their hand to seemingly anything; the workings of a car, the building of a house, the setting up of a bivouac, maggots in a rubbish bin, a sick dog, a dead rat. People turn to him instinctively for help and his body reflects his engagement with the world; he's older than he looks.

Lean and toned, a cyclist when not helping others. His purpose in life is to assist the world around him. It is his raison d'être; he expects the world to turn to him.

Where does grace lie in a man? Generosity. You see it in the footy coach who looked after Cin's primary school soccer team and never raised his voice, never lost his patience, taking the good with the bad with admirable sangfroid. You see it in Pup, tirelessly organising cricket lessons for refugee children in the spare time he doesn't have. See it in the school dads manning the barbecue week after week at the rowing sheds. See it in these first responders heading to the campsite; men who have service in their bones. And you see it in Tony Breen, who lives for his family and your school with a generosity of spirit that hurts your heart with gratitude. It is a cloistering of care. The arc of his life, devotion. To family and to work, the smooth running of both. Yet Tony is one of those men raised to expect that the certainties within his role will continue, in perpetuity, and has little understanding of the future speeding towards him. Little understanding of the worlds within his world. Or perhaps he does, too much, and digs in his heels and holds tight. To what was.

There was such a hierarchical clarity to these men's existence once, of course. A firmness. They were so sure of their place in the order of things, yet all that is fracturing as it bloody well should. They lived with the knowledge that they were the chosen ones.

But now it's all being questioned, challenged, mocked, and by The Cins of the world most of all. Because, well, why not. You read on social media somewhere an oddness posed by a scientist: imagine aliens landing on Planet Earth. They're confronted by the alpha species, homo sapiens. They're trying to work them out. Half of these humans have a spellbinding ability to brew life, and the other half have a strange lump-like thing in their neck. So, which ones are running the joint? The great majority of the aliens would be getting that question wrong. And it's the bewildering conundrum at the heart of human life.

Is Tony lost. With The Cins or not. Is he nonplussed or furious. Does he want to punish or just get them back. Out there, on the mountains that swallow people up, away from us. What on earth is going on. Has he shouted at Cin yet. Is she making him laugh as they head out.

'From now on you keep out of my way and I'll keep out of yours,' Cin declared to her mother on the eve of her thirteenth birthday. That'll go well then, you thought. Her grandfather had chuckled from his watchful corner; this was the best child-imposed rule for the teen years he'd ever heard. Cin raised her thumb to him in triumph; she'd nailed it. He wasn't helping. You can just imagine his anguish over today. His only grandchild.

Stop your mind even going there. Right now. Stop the too much of everything in your head.

Need to get to the mountains faster. You overtake an infuriating truck driven by an idiot. Another. Why are these fuckwits in the overtaking lane. Weave among the traffic, bip your horn at a particularly odious tailgater, waggle a little finger high out the window in the universal sign for a small dick. Clotted with tension, shoulders like rock. Fucketty cunt fuck fuck. Koongala parents have no idea of this side of you. Not even Mig. Tight. God, yes.

There'll be Tamsin's parents to face soon. Christ and apologies to God. Your teachers call the lost group The Cins because of Cinnamon, of course, but also because of the other boss cocky in the mix. Tamsin. The kid whose fake pearls are real. 'She's very hard to love,' her mother, Tink, said once in jokey befuddlement. Perhaps because you're never fucking at home, you thought, because you're always jetting off to St Tropez and Courchevel, leaving your only daughter to the nanny. Correction, nannies. One of those mothers whose life seems an endless busy-ness of blowies and shellac pedicures and 3 pm margaritas before the Uber drops the child home. Whose children are relentlessly pristine with an absence of spots. And who are damaged, invisibly, and you just want to enfold them in your arms and hold them in stillness, until they break with the kindness of connection. But of course you do not.

Tamsin is the ice queen who rarely speaks. Flawless skin. Why are the class differences of the good diet so stark with these teenagers? She is cusped, at fifteen, with the kind of pre-womanly bloom that is intriguing because it could go either way. Souring any moment as the jawline hardens or the nose elongates, or blooming into the wonder of a female who'll never not be gazed at. Tamsin is beautiful, yes, but worryingly skinny. Her arms are heartbreaking sticks; as if she wouldn't be quite robust enough for the school ski trip. The teachers tell stories about her in the staffroom. From junior school, when she was told that the creatures in the brand-new worm farm needed water and she responded, 'Still or sparkling?' And from when she was learning her tens/hundreds/thousands in maths and piped up, 'My party cost in the hundred thousands.' She looks like a princess from a small European principality; there is something aloof and innately graceful about her as she watches the world, saying little. You can never work out if it's vacuity or high intelligence. She exudes what Philip Larkin called the strength and pain of being young. She unsettles you – because you cannot pin her down.

You always think of Cin and Tamsin as slightly jarring friends, not completely all in. Tamsin shaved Cin's legs, aged twelve, when it wasn't needed or asked for. Tamsin cut Cin's hair into a mullet of profound ugliness. Tamsin encourages Cin into talkativeness yet is selective with chitter chatter herself, at least among adults. There is something sly to her; why does she have to be like this? A child of immense privilege whose parents bought a flat near the school so she wouldn't have to get public transport home to the harbourside mansion on late concert nights. A nanny would be on hand to help. Cin has a wide-open heart whereas Tamsin's is guarded, shut off. A preservation instinct, perhaps.

So much projected sin with this lot. It's become a staffroom joke. They do sin but are not the devil. Drowning in Cin. It's a Cin. Some rise by Cin and some by virtue fall. Let those among them who are without Cin cast the first stone, etc.

These girls radiate an intense, ready sexuality; you remember those times from your own growing up. It's a squealy mix of boy bands and first kisses and exploring fingers and vivid imaginings as they fall into sleep and desperation to lose their virginity and kiss/marry/kill games where they take three of their friends of either gender and imagine which one they'd pash, wed or kill. They're so ready yet so innocent. Do they even know boys? Has it come to this? You don't know. Cin doesn't talk to you about any of that anymore. Nor her mother.

You wish you still spoke with Mig like you did in kindy, primary, high school and beyond. You grew up in the same block of flats, went to the same school. She was there on your first day of kindy and high school, there in the early hours after you lost your virginity and stumbled back to her college room, there at your twenty-first doing vodka shots and a speech, there at your father's funeral setting up the church hall for the wake. You shared everything, once. But now, the agony of rejection. After decades. Mig was your anchor through life, or so you thought. More constant and loyal than family, or so you thought. And now the winter of her silence. So immense, and so complete. But you need to call. Still can't.

Mig told you once, when you were still talking, that Cin saw right through your missing teacher. Tony Breen is Koongala's English doyen, yes, but he's also the school's disciplinarian. He has a doctorate and parents always love a doctor in their midst, even if they have no idea what it actually means. He told you in his job interview he'd happily be the Rottweiler to your pussy cat. You don't know me at all, you thought at the time. But he does the grubby jobs gladly. The awkward calls to parents, the suspensions, expulsions. Plus he's an experienced bushman. It's why he always volunteers for this annual excursion. Cin never liked him, you suspect. She told Mig once that he gave off a strange smell. You remember from your own youth the smell on some men, when you were a young woman, in all your potency, confronted by them. The older men you had no interest in. It was a carnal smell, like a chemical reaction they couldn't help. It made you back away.

Hugo calls from his chauffeured car on the way to the mountains. Of course he has your number, of course he rings knowing you're on the road. He wants a private search team for his Tamsin. No mention of the other girls. Doesn't trust that the cops are throwing everything into this, or the school. It's as if he senses you hate him already, that he always has to fight his corner through a general sneer at a perception of incompetence. He does something vague and unspecified within the walls of immense family wealth, no-one quite knows what. He has a pugilistic bald head and always seems up for a fight. But why? Hugo and Tink are scatty and reckless with others, always late, even with school fees even though they can absolutely afford it. Chaos is power to them. Tamsin lives her life in opposition to this. She is ruthlessly organised, neat and tight. Excels at school, as if it's the only realm she can have control of, as opposed to the precariousness of the rest of her life.

Hugo reminds you now of a tragedy from decades ago. Thanks, mate. Not the time but there you go. A boy lost from Koongala's brother school. Same kind of bushland. He had a fight with his girlfriend and stormed off in a huff. Got lost. Rang emergency services. Said his water and phone were running out but the operator didn't believe him; she thought it was a silly prank from some entitled private schoolboy and hung up. He died from dehydration before rescuers found him. Tragic, horrendous. You make all your soothing noises to Hugo now. This is Koongala, stories like this do not happen anymore, Dr Breen is with the girls.

That prick, Hugo says. You can feel the sour breath of legal action already. You accelerate.

'You expect me to be sad in life, don't you?' Tamsin said once, when you asked if she had any pets at home in an attempt to draw a softening from her. Her answer was no, because her mother only likes the smell of Diptyque candles in the house. She looked at you, strong. 'Maybe I know I'm going to be sad. But I'd rather be sad in a waterfront house than in some crappy bedsit in Kings Cross.' You both laughed; you liked her in that moment. Tamsin is self-aware, which is more than you can say for the parents. Tony has never liked her. Too rich, no hope. You hope he's being kind to her out there.

Then there's Willa. Her smile has secrets in it. Mixed race and gorgeous with it. Islander, Thai, Indian and Scottish, she has proudly told you. Or something like that. Gender questioning but frankly just working it out; pronouns she/her, for now. Your philosophy is to be open to anything with this wondrous generation, you're all for it, no judging. For a while there, Cin seemed to be on her way to gender reassignment surgery, and so be it, but then she went through puberty and came out the other side revelling in her muscular womanliness. Willa's still on the journey and brazen with it. She's a favourite although of course you don't have them, it's corrosive within a school environment. But Willa's the cool girl. Everything about her feels elegantly masculine, perhaps because she has four brothers. Others are attracted to her like moths to a flame. She's the school captain type who everyone, genuinely, likes. Sweetly interested in those around her, a listener. Rare. It's like a cool drink on a hot summer's day. You appreciate the care she takes with others, as if her edges have been softened by a complex life.

The girls of this generation own their singularity like they've made a decision to claim it, proudly, to instruct us all. They glory in their unshackled difference from that which has gone before them. What were your lot, in comparison? Pleasers. Meek and hesitant and pliant, as were your mothers and mothers' mothers. The servants to men and it worked very well for them; they made you feel wrong in your skin. But these new girls, of the new world, are bringing men up abrupt. It's exhilarating to see them shaking things up.

When Willa first came to Koongala, at the start of Year Eight, you asked if she was enjoying her new school. The uniform, she lamented, I look like a nun. She was newly arrived from a state school, which gave her a veneer of glamour. Her presence in this bubble was thanks to an inheritance from her grandmother; you quietly squeezed her in because fresh blood is always healthy in the mix. Diversity is a plus. Willa's poise with adults is intriguing. She talks to them like a fellow grownup. Someone who's not a parent has taught her. She slipped to you in those early days that she had to train herself to speak properly, because it was a new school and a new way of life and she'd forgotten how to do it. As in, she'd forgotten how to speak with kids her own age. If Tony is being comforted out there, it's by her.

Dream parents. Cara and Maude. Because they keep their distance. One is mama, the other mummy. They'd both been married and had their boys separately before they got together and had Willa. Not sure which is the birth mother, rude to ask. When Willa was caught vaping in the toilets alongside Tamsin the families were called in one after the other for The Talk. The first thing Cara said: What exactly did my daughter do and how do you want us to deal with it, as a family? You were stunned. This was the first time a parent had said anything like this to you; had admitted their child was a little shit and did not try to deflect, to blame someone else, wheedle and twist. It was refreshing. They're both Kia-driving public servants from working class backgrounds who were determined to get their daughter to this school because they know, like you, that education is the way out. The greatest gift. Tamsin's parents, on the other hand, just wanted the number one girls' school by reputation, you're sure. They're the parents who crave the social gloss that having a child from this enclave confers upon them.

Ah, that vaping incident. Hugo threatened to sue if you suspended his girl over 'such a bullshit thing'. His words. Tony Breen dealt with the situation masterfully, as he does. The girls were not suspended but they knew how disappointed you were. Hugo and Tink will still expect their Tamsin to be a prefect come Year Twelve. You'll get a new recording studio out of them, from the old sewing room, then gently let them down; it's just not possible, not fair. Willa is still on track for captain.

Hugo will hate her for it. Subtly put her down. You've seen it already on the sidelines of the touch footy pitch, because Willa, of course, is like a gazelle in action. Watch her run.

But then the fourth Cin in the mix. Elle. Why? Who? Every time you talk to her parents now you must make a mental note that their daughter is Elle not Ally, Elly, Amelia, Amelie or Ella. So many of them. Can't cope. Please can we get a ban on all permutations, you groaned to Pup at the start of the year as you scanned the class lists. Ditto all Mias, Mayas and Myas.

The Cins are not the most traditionally popular in the form. They're not the bikini and gatho set, always off with the private school boys down the road, they're much more interesting than that. You've always wished, for any girl you're particularly fond of, that they don't end up in the cool gang at school. Or aspire to it. Because the rules of cool are so confining and judgemental and rigid. Cool is tricky. It feeds on exclusion. Sneers at difference. It doesn't have the courage for singularity and, Lord, it feels so damned humourless. Being uncool allows you to be who you really want to be. Which is, magnificently, this lot.

Your car winds its way into the mountains. Zebra stripes of light flit across your path like a strobe of shadow and blare. Low clouds cluster on the horizon in a biblical billowing, as if they've been spewed forth from the earth's furnace by the gods of an affronted realm. There are the burnt black trunks, still, from a cataclysmic fire a few summers back, and a startle of fresh green clinging on. As you climb higher you enter a tunnel of trees. The air cools in welcome to this Other Place. All around you is an enormity of valleys and chasms and ridges as far as the eye can see. You feel alone here, so high up. Islanded by the impenetrable green.

The turn-off to the campsite. A hidden space unless you know of it. The road peters away into dirt. A world gone quiet. Looser, wilder. Branches reach out, something thuds on the roof, and again; seed pods perhaps, who knows. It's like inching slowly through a mob that wants you to turn back. Shadow flickers. Your eyes squint. It's hard to drive in this place, your shoulders tense over the steering wheel, you have to concentrate. It feels deeply private. Someone else's land; no need for you or want. Humans are the trespassers here and piss off. You want to drive helter-skelter from the place, in fact; do a startled nine-point turn and tear off. You press on.

The campsite. Unquiet energy. A clearing that doesn't want any of you. The ground is not tar but cleared dirt; tall trees ring the space as if shirtfronting any human intrusion. A band of dark, waiting for you all to move on. Trees as silent centurions, watching the humans who were not meant to get this far. A waypoint to heaven, or hell; an almost place, almost there. But to what? It feels like insurrection to be here. A portal opens up where the bushwalking path begins, a portal into another world.

Why did the school ever go here? Tony's choice, he pushed for this, and you were swept along by it.

The clearing is a hive of activity already. Police, marquees, school coaches, a waiting ambulance. You park the car. Put on your face. Inscrutable, authoritative, ready. Note all the girls on the buses craning, watching, stirring, note the frisson your arrival has caused. You stride to the huddle of Helen Venty, the form mistress, and the police. So, what's up. After The Cins were noted as missing Tony Breen volunteered to head back in, 'to round the little buggers up'; with no-one realising, at that point, the seriousness of the situation. After an hour of waiting for the five of them to emerge the decision was made to inform the school, so Helen called Pup. A constable says it started raining lightly at that point. Enough to erase any scent for the sniffer dogs.

First things first. Dismiss the student coaches from the camping ground. Rid yourself of distraction, get the rest of the girls home and safe. Soon the light will be dropping, they need to return to their families. To be held. No-one is to talk to the media. Pup will send out the email immediately, school-wide. He says on the phone, 'Sarge, no-one's panicking.' He's got this. There will be no alarm.

You address both coachloads of students. The girls will be heading home, their parents will be waiting for them, everything is under control, this will not take long to be sorted. You sense the palpable relief at your presence. Your hand is held up in a gentle stopping. No questions. A smile to all of them. It will be okay, we've got this. Your girls believe you, need to, want to. All your training has brought you to this point of authoritative calm.

Your   galloping   heart.

As the buses start to leave, laden with tents and sleeping bags that had never even been unpacked, you fall back in silence with a phalanx of first responders; there's a grim finality to this. A concession that yes, four girls are well and truly lost, and you now need to get down to business and get them out. Pronto. Oh, and a teacher is in the mix too, of course. His wife, Adela, has just arrived. She is Christian-mousey, beige. Always looks fragile. Faded, as if her entire existence is recessive, like she is watching from a closed window. You find it hard to accept a woman could be this anymore, that women like this still exist. So many of those Christian women slightly irritate you, for their choices. The willing surrender. Adela gets slowly out of her car as if exhausted already. You walk briskly to her. Hug her, demonstrably, and feel her harden in your arms, feel her resistance. She is not meeting you in this. You hold her arms and tell her that you'll find her Tony, that he was your friend. '*Is*. Is my friend.' Which she no doubt resents; a stiffening spine tells you this. Adela does not speak. She receives your emotion.

Ah yes, of course, she never quite approved of you, Tony told you that. She asks for the police, as if she trusts that world more.

Your clothes, next to Adela's, feel wrong. Today was not the day for the blare of a purple velvet suit and red silk shirt. Costume as armour, yet if you'd known that this morning was going to happen you would have dressed differently, of course. Muted, respectful. 'You're morphing into an art teacher,' Mig told you once, in chuff at the loosening into the kind of female you were long ago. A look aspired to, despite being the English teacher once.

The second bus departs. Now to work. A sky of grandeur assembles; clouds congregate as if listening in to all the earthly chattery panic, the barked commands from police. Everyone wants this shut down quick-smart because the light is running out.

It feels like the trees are leaning in, in some subtle sign of aggression from a watching, waiting pack. You shiver, and again. Can't stop but must; the campsite watches, the campsite waits.

Monday night

In softening light you stride to the void where the bushwalking path begins, to the loom of trees closing over the entrance into another realm. Spin, in wonder, in horror. You're on the roof of the world up here, with mountain upon mountain stretching out ahead of you. Air so crisp it hurts. Rocks as big as cars perching above sheer vertical cliffs. And humans are chastened in this place. Why on earth did we ever do this school excursion, why did we so rattle the gods? The campsite feels like a waiting place of some sort, a holding place, coiled and biding its time. Its energy is sad. It has the feel of a massacre site, once, long ago. You slap your head to try to expel the thought. Look across at Adela, on her knees praying at the edge of the clearing, by the trees' oppressive dark. The poor thing, lost in the unknowing, grasping at hope. You shut your eyes too. *Please let the girls be alive. Let them walk out of this.* The balm washes over you. *All of them, untouched.* Not sure why you add that.

Hugo arrives in his chauffeured Bentley; Tink is not far behind, driving her Porsche Cayenne. You're reminded yet again of the old truth of some couples, that when they set up house together she enhances his life and he compromises hers. Hugo gets his driver to park his car in the wrong spot, clocks the stares, doesn't care; his wife follows suit. Living proof of why people like that have the money they do. Because they're careless with other people, they don't properly see them. Tony told you that.

Mig said once that you didn't properly see people, perhaps, didn't give them a chance; that you were too blinded by the rages of class and shouldn't be in this job. Nonsense, you snapped. But please, there are too many families at Koongala with too much money. Where does it all come from and why is the gap so vast. Four or five cars, one just for the freeway. Nine-car garages. Car collections as a way to park money away from the tax man, because the luxury vintage car market will always increase. Houses with so many doors it's unclear which one is the entrance. Ski chalets in Chamonix. Apartments in Paris. Investment penthouses near Koongala, just for those pesky music concert nights that always run late.

Cin is acutely aware of the absence of money in her life. It's made her hungry. Focused. Angry. You recognise it. She wants it, and wants to triumph over these people, just as you did once. You had anger too for so long. At the unfairness of the easy lives, at the blithe disregard for others. You have always equated an empathetic awareness of unfairness with high intelligence; smart people notice. Care. Which is why Willa stands out.

Mig calls. You stare, flustered, at her name on your screen. A punch of emotion. Do you, don't you, but no. You haven't the strength to answer just yet. Need something concrete to impart. You're not as strong as anyone thinks, least of all her. Can't face her judgement, her accusatory fury right now. So to voicemail. But if anyone can survive this it's our Golden Flower and Mig knows this. Her daughter's early school years were spent in the bush. The restless racing sky was her roof and the sweet earth her floor. She's tough, possibly languishing on her back in the dirt, in glee, at this very moment. Cin always seems a little like she's marooned in a mistaken world, more wild than civilised. She'll be enjoying this basting in the bush, enjoying the soul-thrum under her feet. She's always been wedded to the wild places, filled up by sun and wind. The bush is her medicine. Her repairing place.

Cin lived in the city in her toddler years, but Mig dreamt of an insect-crammed girlhood for her child of nature. In the bush, in a little teapot of a cottage, far away from the city's star-bleaching light. The tipping point came when three-year-old Cin told Mig that stars only happen in videos, so Mig dived headfirst into a wilder life on the edge of a forest out west. It felt like she was protecting something ancient and precious within her child – the right to a nature-saturated life. The game of default with the bush kids around her was hide and seek; they endlessly played it, and Cin was always the last one caught. She loved this world, needed something more earthed. A broad canopy of stars, the delicate pick of a stick insect up an arm, a cicada shell's brittle curl, the stained-glass window of a Black Prince's wing. And so the bush became Cin's only church, until Mig realised her girl needed a solid education and didn't quite trust the public education system in comparison with what a slick school from the Big Smoke, with a road right through it, had to offer. By the end of Year Four the two of them had moved back to the city. Were living in a tiny, dingy flat in a shabby part of town; a suburb that most girls in the school would never have heard of and that most parents would struggle to pronounce. For the wild child in your midst you feared it might be like the suturing of an open mind; until you saw the Golden Flower watching it all from a distance, while immersed in it. Just as you did once. Cin had jumped ninety-eight places on Koongala's waiting list to secure a coveted spot, but she never brings any of her friends home.

There is talk. Online and onsite. That the girls deliberately separated from the pack. That there are boys involved. That The Cins slipped away for a lark, to vape or swig vodka or raise the temperature of the teachers a bit. That the whole thing is unsurprising because Cinnamon is a bit loose and came from a state school, no less, they're of a type. Fuck it.

Raising Cin is like trying to hang on to the tail of a kite as it soars into the air, into new worlds and new adventures, higher and higher. Mig said once that it felt like she expended all her energy on just keeping Cin alive. The little attention thief, from birth.

Bits and bobs of the media are arriving, setting up, the police are keeping them at bay. This is a developing story; you're advised to steer clear of microphones and cameras. With pleasure. More parents are starting to appear and some haven't even lost a child. Here for some kind of ghoulish support, you suspect. Great. Helen Venty has stayed onsite as back-up and school liaison; she can deal with this lot. The hanger-on parents are hovering like March flies, trying to catch your eye. Your time, your calm.

Pup is keeping you informed from the school end. The worst of the mothers — the regular lot, with all their gripes — are being vile, of course. Firing off emails, sounding out the media with 'concerns', having quiet words to teachers at the gates. WhatsApp groups are firing up. The most dangerous are the undermining, manipulative, passive aggressive mothers. When these women bully you, in their subtle ways, you can only imagine the depth charge that they are in their loved ones' lives. You see it playing out in their broken girls.

Mig has brewed Cin strong. You overheard Willa say, using the text-speak of the day, that her mother was a MILW — a Mum I'd Like to Laugh With. The highest accolade. You could never be the teacher they'd like to laugh with, to any of your girls, and to Cin especially as she became embedded in the school.

It wouldn't work. But Mig does parenthood well, instinctively. Parents are like a weather system in their child's life; the adult's sense of happiness and consistency is reflected in the child's sense of happiness and consistency. Stability begets stability. Mig works hard at that. To be the stable weather, always, in her daughter's life.

Her flat is modest. One bedroom. One sunroom, now her child's room. Mean proportions. Noisy neighbours. Cin's friends wouldn't understand the cram of strangers constantly all around them, wouldn't understand the endless policing of your voice for fear of disturbing others. Her friends are loud because they can be in their own detached homes; Cin longs for that. You know that ache for an actual house, a place unattached to anyone else's, because this yearning was corrosive during your own growing up. Cin no longer brought friends home after Hugo drove her back from a touch footy match one Saturday and exclaimed, exasperated, as he trawled her street, 'Which one is it? These bloody flats all look the same. So ugly.' Oh yes, Cin knows the bite of difference. Of social class embarrassment.

And anger, how to use it, to propel her forward.

You tell your Koongalettes that anger is a much-maligned word, especially when it comes to women. That historically we're not meant to question; to be explosive and loud and stroppy and furious. Yet many of us are. About so much. Anger is a force for change and when you see it in a female wronged or ignored or drowned out, well, it's magnificent. Because the sharp-shod hoof of fury strikes the soft underbelly of complacency and changes the world. Slowly, slowly. Anger is the bonfire that cleanses. It changes a world dictated to us by others, a world meant to keep us in our place. It usually begins with a story of profound unfairness that connects in wounded psyches. And we, as women, are always being told not to be angry. *Calm down, dear. Get back to your kitchen. Calm your farm. Ssshh.* Well, fuck that. Because how else are we to bring about change, if not through anger? Because women pay the price for male insecurity again and again, and we must never stop calling it out.

The chosen ones are in thrall. The others don't get it.

Gaden, the Tibetan school counsellor, arrives. Back-up to Miss Venty, a fresh liaison between parents and school. Deliberate. Everyone loves Gaden. They gravitate to his joy, his gentleness. And he's a man so they intuitively respect him more. The way of the world.

Gaden faced his own calls for dismissal from panicked parents after the John Whitt incident. The new geography teacher, who got an erection in front of his 8C girls. His first ever class. The girls all knew exactly what it was. Unfortunately Whitt's pale colouring meant his blush was extremely obvious as he stood there, in horror, in front of the giggling girls. He fled the class and resigned within the hour. When he could be coaxed from the bathroom. Appalled parent emails followed, calling for every young male to be dismissed. You stood your ground. Gaden was named, a lot, perhaps because he's so popular. He is a good man and his calm energy is with you now and you almost fall into his arms at the sight of him. She didn't do it, he says, first up; not knowing she's your god-daughter but anticipating where your mind will be going. I know, you whisper back.

But Adela. Her looking. Like builder's dust, all over you, inescapable now. You feel guilt at her anguish and want to scrub yourself clean of it. Where is my husband, says the set of her mouth.

Gaden told you once that Cin saw through him within ten minutes of him entering the classroom, on his first day, to introduce himself. He sees this as a good thing but not all teachers do. He's started asking her quietly how she thinks the school could be improved. You were uncomfortable with this at first, it feels too close, but Cin works at Macca's on weekends so is used to dealing with adults. She understands the workplace dynamics. Talks to adults easily, loves joshing with them and they're wrong-footed by it; they forget she's so young. She is different. Difference is dangerous. Gaden admires it and he's not the only one. She's a man's woman, he says, and Tony has remarked on it too. Trying to work her out.

The light is retreating. Your car is your office as you dictate notes and hotspot. Mig has called again, it goes to voicemail, you can't take it. No news to tell her. Not ready to engage with her just yet. Cowardly. You know.

Gaden passes on a rumour about a nearby boys' school. That this was pre-arranged. That there was some kind of meet-up planned, things happening, in the bush. He says it came from other girls in the form who've informed their mothers who've told the school. The Cins, sexually active? Surely not. You know many of the girls want to be rid of their virginity, pesky encumbrance that it is; they're desperate to have that veneer of maturity and one-upmanship over others. But this lot? Too smart, strong, selective – surely. You dismiss Gaden. Send him across to Adela. She mustn't be lost in this, and it's so easy to forget.

But   panic.

You ball your fist at your sternum – breathing is hard, tight, you cannot show it but cannot control this. You just want to scream at The Cins to come home immediately and stop this stupid game. Uncertainty is so stressful, the most stressful thing of all, and you're not coping here. Not that anyone knows. You're used to control, a relentlessly calm exterior, no leakage. And now the serenity thief has won and winning is *your* thing. It's why you never made the leap into having kids. Couldn't control their looseness, their failings in life, the endless disappointments.

The police officer, Robin, gently attempts to interview you. Your voice is trying to push its way out but it's not working. Properly. Anymore. Nothing untoward to add, Robin, but the fact that four teens are still missing. From far away comes Robin's quiet persistence; it feels like you're being held under by the weight of water. This is no time for a breakdown. Could they have run away on purpose? Is this a prank? Were they in trouble at school? You snap in response, just, fucking, find them. Please. Then apologise. Explain you're going insane with this. That you just want to get in there yourself, yelling like a banshee and ripping and slashing at the undergrowth until your girls are found and in your arms, held tight. Robin squeezes your wrist in sympathy. She's a good woman. You are not.

The media crane in their corners, trying to catch your eye. Your former collaborators. They pedestalled your school once but now they'll be looking for dirt. You turn your back.

Who would want this gig now? Only Mig knew the extent of your craving for this headmistress job once, back when you were nearing the pinnacle of your storied career. Plus there was the unspoken agreement that you were stepping into this job for her. Her child. Even though Mig was a socialist back then and once upon a time would never have considered a school like Koongala. But she softened as she deepened into motherhood. Saw unfairness in the school system and wanted a way into the hallowed world. Could never admit this to her family, and barely to you. We're all stained by our vulnerabilities.

Mig is the brave one. You didn't have the courage to risk the creative life. She's a ceramic artist only just finding success in middle age. It doesn't escape you now that she lives in a modest flat that the light never quite reaches enough, while you're in the Gate House, an historic house on campus provided by the school. It was built in Victorian times as a folly and is rich with wood-panelled walls and pressed tin ceilings and art nouveau detailing; a museum of high wooden beams and beauty and books. It has a dining room seating twenty and expansive harbour views. Four bedrooms, for you and the cat and dog. It's ragingly unfair. It is what it is.

Mig paints her own toenails. Who even does that anymore. Yet she always looks more glamorous and grounded than any of you in her workwear clothes, her men's shirts and blunnies, her uniform that never changes. It has to do with confidence. The confidence to be different, to be your own person, when the world is telling you as a woman to be something else. Mig's courage has flair and her daughter is learning from it.

As a fulltime artist, Mig walked bold into a precarious existence. She has risked exposure, honesty, poverty, failure, sneer. The working class kid who shocked her family that lived by the rule of hard yakka; none of that arty farty nonsense around us, thank you very much. The worry over money is ever present in Mig's existence but her choices are magnificent; the potter's wheel her meditation and nourishment. You envy the strength she draws from creativity. You both started art college but only she had the courage to follow it through. She took the risk while you left after a year to pursue an English teaching degree. And here you are now, in this camping ground too far from anywhere else, staring at the biggest failure of your professional life. And lacking the courage to ring Mig.

Mig is swallowed by her creative life. Her muscular focus veers her from the world. From a regular maternal existence of ladies who lunch and school gate politics and wine o'clock. Mig doesn't do reciprocal playdates, shared birthday parties, soccer runs. Does Cin know this, does she understand? That her mother does things differently but loves her no less; that she has to have a monumental selfishness to succeed, as a woman, in a man's creative space.

You have no partner, no one to offload to over the monstrosity of the missing. The last lover you had told you that you were wedded to your job, that it was hard to live with. He always ordered dessert in the restaurant when you were ready to go home. He was constantly late and you took it personally; it was a guerrilla campaign to unbalance your focus.

Yes, you thrive on certainty; not good with slippage. Sex is beyond you now. Haven't slept with anyone, male or female, for years. Never really liked it. Arranged yourself under a lover as if there was a camera on the roof, an invisible person art-directing the shot. And nakedness, ugh, and surrender, the letting go – always difficult. The only time conditions would be ideal to have sex now would be when you've lost fifteen kilos, have had a spray tan, your greys eliminated, nails done and a waxing all at once. Which is never. So yes, tight. And, of course, the traits of a perfectionist straitjacket your life. You have high expectations of yourself and everyone else. Every day needs to be productive. It's hard to loosen into relaxation. The fear of failure is all-pervading. Lists are constantly ticked off. Every hour is accounted for. And because of all this you wear a man's vintage Rolex, as time is always at the forefront of your mind. Cin loves the watch. Will have it one day but you'd never tell her that – she'd charm it out of you in advance then lose it in a week.

You are happily post-sexual. It's all beyond you now. Because increasingly as you aged, if ever your old partners went away on a business trip, there was the exhilaration of the freedom. You felt instantly lightened. Remembered the woman you once were. And then the joyful absence of them became addictive – until there was no-one left.

Why is a woman alone and man-free by choice so dangerous, such a threat. You feel Hugo's sneer, flavoured by fear. Over the years you've been called sterile, barren, evil incarnate, fugly, the witch; always by men, all fathers with a gripe. Fear of the hag is always strong, coiled beneath the surface, waiting to spring out.

This doesn't mean you don't love. Your heart is plumed, now, with a roaring love; your heart is a little wild bird, beating in terror, but you're trying not to show it in this place as you walk among them all, your face the mask of calm.

In a rush, suddenly, you text Mig. Easier this way. You tell her there's no news yet but she'll be the first to know. You say Cin is like a daughter and you have to be restrained from going in and hauling her out yourself. You say you feel like your hands are cupped around a tremulous candle flame here and that you completely understand the gravity of Mig's gift; to be the waypoint of light through Cin's growing up, and you always will be, always, and—

Nup, too long. Scrub that last bit out.

You do not say that you've never felt quite up to the task, with Cin. As if you were an imposter. Not practised quite enough with the responsibility of having someone this close.

When Cin was in Mig's womb she was sure she was having a boy. She was such a kicker. 'There's a lot of testosterone in there!' And you lost Mig from the moment Cin was born. You were praying – as you watched face to face in the birthing suite – that she would have her boy, so she would still be yours. Did not want her so obscenely blessed by a baby girl. You are not proud of this. But Mig had done the Google diet to change the acidity of her vaginal lining because she wanted her little girl so much. 'Dairy,' Google told her, so Mig crammed herself with ice cream and yoghurt and milk. 'Red fruits,' commanded an old Swedish wives' tale, so it was strawberries and raspberries and cranberries on top of the dairy. She was convinced none of it had worked until the cyclone arrived.

Mig was thanking God a lot the day Cin was born. At the centre of your existence, suddenly, was a little fawn with jet black hair, navy blue eyes and a knowing stare. Catching everything around her, slowly and methodically, and seeing right through her godmother as if discerning she could be Wicked masquerading as Fairy. Her eyebrows were light and you knew even then she'd be blonde, eventually. Her mother was transformed, firmed, with the radiance of motherhood. Yet pregnancy was a magnificent violence upon Mig. 'It's like a war zone down there,' she told you after birth, 'Iraq's got nothing on it.' She joked that her entire life was now dedicated to keeping her little princess alive – and now you've   failed   her.

I'm sorry, you conclude your short text.

Choppers now. The obscene thwump of them arcing over this massive terrain in a ballet of sweeping searching; you yearn for this to end. The lights of police cars as more arrive, and more. A new ambulance, why? Another. Are they specialised? You spin, hands at ears, can't think. A world gone mad. Collect yourself.

All parents have now arrived at the campsite, except Mig. Smooth words of comfort – everything is in hand, the girls will be found before nightfall, Tony Breen is extremely experienced. Questions trail in your wake. How do we know the teacher is with them? Do the girls have enough water? How could they have disappeared from the group? You pull away to take a call, pretend not to hear.

Yvonne Fenton, the deputy chair of the council. An old girl, one of three on the council and a staunch defender of the historical footprint of Koongala; of how it appears within the wider world. Nothing must tarnish the glow. She talks about reputational damage; do we need to hire a crisis communications expert. 'This is not a crisis, Yvonne.' She's not so sure. She's fielding calls – gossip, rumour, panic – from as far away as Boston, Shanghai, Glasgow. A text comes through as you speak, you say it's urgent and ring off. It's from your source on the job panel. They've gotten wind of something; what is going on. *All under control*, you text back.

But   but. Leakage. Needs to be shut down. How? Can't. Want to curl like a comma in the dirt and keen your anguish to the heavens; want to curl inward, into the ground, and forget. Because hope is veering wildly now and all you can hear is your booming, racing heart. Gather yourself, gather, mask of calm. You take a deep breath and go back and sit among the parents on a plastic chair in one of the marquees the police have set up.

These people need you. Hugo is still muttering about lawyers. We're doing our best, you murmur. Are you, are you really, he snaps. You say nothing more, dignified quiet is best. You cannot win with such belligerence; it refuses to see reason. Fuck this, Hugo strops, I'm out of here. Getting a room at a hotel. Come on, Tink.

But impressively, his trophy wife refuses to leave. Standoff. Tink stares at her husband. I will not leave, not dare to, my place is here. In case she, in case Tamsin … comes back. Which she *will*. And we have to be here for it. I have to be. Tink huddles deeper into her chair. A gulf between them, a turbulent silence. And so Hugo must stay too, amid the glare of the words. But you know this will play out down the track; that Tink will be punished for this insurrection and such a public one at that. You smile, secretly, at her in support. Woman to woman. She blinks like a cat in return, giving you nothing. Her world has been seen. And now she must retract.

Elle's mum, Beth, asks if you have one hundred percent trust in this Dr Breen. You look at her, sharp. She's as mousey as her daughter but one mustn't hold it against her. If anyone can find them Tony Breen can, you soothe. But you can see the rumours haunting the woman's face, stale old stories that have always trailed the man. Of course there will be scuttlebutt about a school's disciplinarian and Tony is a religious man, which makes him instantly suspicious to some. He's a former soldier, isn't he,

Beth's husband asks. Richard, an accountant. You've never met him before or maybe you have and he made no impression on you whatsoever, he is a dumpy middle-aged man with a pen in his pocket. A soldier, the man persists. Kind of, you answer him briskly. The SAS. An elite force. Re-trained as a teacher. He's a ruthless enforcer of rules, you do not say, good to have on staff. Throw anything at him and he can take it. He wanted the job because he has three daughters and needed them educated, with rigour, on a staff discount. They've now left the school but Tony remains a highly effective fixer in your institution. If anyone can find the girls he can. And you couldn't do this job without him.

Tony's biggest crisis was when a young art teacher sent out a confidential intra-school email to all her classes' parents, by mistake, which listed Koongala's major donors alongside their daughters' names, with an exhortation for staff to be 'kind' to them. It was a bomb going off. A mistake, of course, perhaps. Tony dealt with it admirably. Leave it to me, he said, you don't want your hands getting mucky. He was able to calm the parents while gently massaging the teacher out of her job. It took a month. Job done. No families lost.

Beth – dear, quiet, sparrow of a thing – persists. Hesitant, stumbling, her voice choked by the terror of what could be. Do the girls actually like Dr Breen? If he calls out for them, will they actually go with him? Of course, you assure her. She clears her throat. Do you think there might be other ... men? Bushwalkers, maybe, soldiers, kids. A pause. 'Boys.' You do not answer.

Willa's mama, Cara, tells you the girls remind her of penguins in Antarctica who haven't learnt to fear that thing known as Human. Haven't learnt to fear Man. They have no idea of the world because they live in such a protected bubble. You concur, adding that no-one else is out there, then realise you have no right to say this.

They're so ... ripe ... with their beauty. Long of limb, taut of skin, so moving and vulnerable with all that burgeoning life. Did some boys in their late teens enter the bush by the backroads, as soon as the lost call was put out. Is there a gathering of a cult. The cult in the bush thing is mentioned a lot. Meditation people, religious nutters, preppers. All out here, possibly, all close.

Willa's other mother, Maude, gives you a wink of support. As if she knows exactly what you're dealing with here in terms of parents and runaway internet talk. You love this woman. There's kindness in her weathered face, honesty in her grey hair. She said to you once, of motherhood, that it felt like she was pouring her life into an open wound. 'Does it ever even out?' She implored you for answers and you laughed, you had none. You've always liked her thoughtful take. Her willingness to let things go, to not sweat the small stuff.

Robin steps between Beth's wall of worry and yourself. Gives you a discreet smile of encouragement. God help the men with this generation of super-capable young women; they'll rule the world if humanity clears a path. Robin suggests you need a break. You smile in thanks and stay put; the parents need you, even if you're talked out.

Adela keeps looking across like you know something and are not saying it. You shake your head at her, helplessly, from a distance. She turns away. What can she possibly be imagining is happening? The unknowing feels icy. It's as if she suspects something you do not. You want to shake her and soothe her and admonish her; it's a mess of difference.

Cin, Willa and Tamsin do boxing in the school gym every Monday before bell time. They revel in their strong female bodies. Flex their biceps to see who has the biggest, marvel at their calves, egg the others on to give their hardened abs a punch. They're at the point of female development before the flesh softens and spreads, pillowing into readiness for motherhood. It happens to all the girls eventually. You see them fighting it, fighting biology, trying to thwart nature's insistence on procreation. Some stymie it more successfully than others. Cin was late with her first period because her fierce tomboy's body was waiting for more flesh to be collected on its bones; her body just wanted her to quieten and nest so it could thicken up, in readiness, for the next stage of a woman's life. She fought it. She's still toned, firm, strong. Her future is written on her body.

Body positivity is endlessly encouraged at Koongala. The Cins show off their ripped flesh in skimpy crop tops and cycle shorts but don't see their beautiful bodies, you suspect, as sexual; just something enchanting and wondrous to show off. To one another. Body as elixir. You cannot slut-shame, of course, must let them be no matter what they're wearing; Cin's pulled you up for this. But what of the males of the old world? How do they see them, judge them; try to contain and control and diminish. What of Dr Breen, with them now.

Dark is leaking into the day. No birdsong, yet you're in the bush, why is it so quiet. Everything feels hovering, poised, waiting. The media are trying to get to you for the 6 pm bulletins. Robin is fending them off. Those strong, fit bodies of the girls will serve them well, for one night they'll be fine. Please God. There's water from recent rains, good. But leeches. And God help Tamsin jumping at everything with her nerves; and Elle trying so hard but it never quite working out. Yet, yet. Normal is my superpower, ma'am, she said to you once, when explaining that she's never vaped after the vaping-in-toilets incident; explaining that she doesn't quite follow The Cins with everything. She snagged in your memory because of that. But where are the birds, where. What is going on with this place.

Mig finally arrives. You stride straight over. Let's do this. You do not touch, or hold, aware that no-one knows of the volcano lidded on your past. You just look at each other in anguish. Any news, she asks, taut. You shake your head. I can't bear this, she says, walking away, holding up her hand to stop you following. Other parents look, clocking history between you. Bad blood in the principal's office, perhaps, a suspension or a vape in a pencil case. Mig heads to the police commander's tent; Robin cuts in. In the dance of awkwardness between you both, you gently move Mig away like a nurse moves a patient on their first day at an asylum. She shrugs you off like a pandemic sneeze from someone else.

Mig loves Cin so much it scalds her heart and it's all on display now as she stands in the middle of you all, in the middle of this campsite, and openly weeps. It is love that thieves relaxing, that requires eternal vigilance, and you were meant to take over the watchfulness within the school. That was your role. But now uncertainty and accusation are vining their way through everything; are they injured, terrified or cackly with glee, the little buggers. Giggly and high with Cin's wiliness. The uncertainty is breaking each one of you, in its own particular way. Mig's weeping is just the most public.

This Year Ten expedition is a school tradition. To encourage team building. To teach bush skills. And to attempt to eliminate the strange and muting cult of perfectionism that is rife within

Koongala. Because the obsessive engine that drives your high achievers isn't enviable but tragic. You've recently launched exams in which it's impossible to achieve full marks, to try to stop the girls becoming obsessed with being the anxious Little Miss Perfects of life. The online maths test has questions that become progressively harder and even when the girl reaches the top of her ability she'll face problems she can't answer – teaching her that it's fine to not have everything, always, correct. The girls need to be encouraged to take risks, to not get upset when things don't go their way. Like now. You don't want young women whose lives are held hostage by fear of failure. Don't want the fearful, who won't risk.

Cin is the opposite of all this. Which worries you as the light drops.

The Welcome to Koongala talks for new parents are legendary. You tell the parents to get their teen to make their own lunches; it doesn't have to be perfect, they'll still eat it. And just before the start of high school clean up their bedroom, because this is the last time you'll ever be doing it. Take a photo of it, print it out and stick it on your teen's door. It's your reference point for what their bedroom can be – then never venture in there again. You tell new parents that their girls may shut them out in the years ahead, but they still need them. Those brains are under construction and won't be fully developed until their late teens. For boys, it's twenty-five. God help them if it's teen brains under construction all alone, without Tony, out there.

And yes, Cin is the opposite of perfectionist. Won't brush her teeth unless reminded. Won't wash her hair or put on deodorant without a nudge; when asked she used to swipe on a lick of it, outside her shirt, then stare straight at Mig and you in a challenge. The two of you could only laugh. She's so messy, scatty and laid-back she's almost horizontal, with a bombshell of a bedroom and a mucky uniform that's never quite right. Her wardrobe is a floor-robe, ditto her top bunk. She always gets to Koongala just after the starting bell but hasn't a trace of anxiety. Is the consistent lateness a power over everyone else, you wonder, a drawing attention to the self. There's a masculine nonchalance to it, a certainty that everything will turn out right – so why sweat the small stuff. She's a specimen to learn from but you could never be it. Not brazen enough.

Mig is sitting alone in her car, on her phone. Hugo watches from the parent marquee, watches your spider fingers weaving their web of words on the laptop, your tiny threshers recording all this as you transfer today's notebook jottings to the screen. You can barely read your handwriting, it's a wildness of agitation, thoughts pinging and question marks gauged deep into paper. Methodically setting this day down, in a new screen document, is the only thing now anchoring you to calm.

Messages of reassurance from the school community make you feel less alone. Pup is diligently forwarding them. *Sarge, read and weep.* No-one is blaming you. You are broken by kindness. You feel the prayers, the communal swell of them, shut your eyes in gratitude. Then hold out your hand to the scent-saturated, dusky mountain air. Want the lost girls to feel the love on their backs, wherever they are, stilling them into quiet. The world will get to them. You pray they know this.

It's getting colder as the day turns into evening. The girls will be ferociously teen hangry, like they always are when they walk in the door after school and flop their bags to the floor. Catering has been organised for the parents and first responders and how lucky you all are to have this. Unlike those empty adolescent stomachs out there, alone in the falling light. And Tony's, of course. No-one wants to leave the campsite because you all have to be here for the big return. Imagine if you weren't. No expense is being spared.

You turn waitress, offering parents wine, a goodwill gesture for any storms to come. Hugo cuts across Tink and smooths a glass from her hand, saying she doesn't need it, she's on the wagon, remember; some private war you melt away from. But then, drama. Tink snatches the glass from her husband and drinks it defiantly, too much at once; staring at him and daring him to stop her. A ripple in Hugo's cheek. Just this. It tells you that in private it would go much further. The status wife has turned, she has found her disobedience and in front of you all. Tink giggled at a school cocktail party once that her drink of choice wasn't tepid function wine, actually, but Mumm mixed with Coca-Cola, and you wonder what happened to that loose-limbed woman from long ago, the obvious drinker; perhaps her husband drove her to it. Hugo has the assurance of a private school boy who's never been told he's wrong, a man who's had his path eased through life by money and connections and the old boy network. He is not used to no, from anyone, least of all his wife; he barges through it. Mig catches the dynamic and raises her glass to Tink in solidarity. We don't want your grog we want our daughter back, Hugo shouts to you both. He's lost control of the situation, you all have, and he's not used to this; plus Mig represents everything his world hates. Single motherhood. IVF without a father's involvement beyond donation. Happy penury. Womanhood beyond the realm of men. Disobedience. Creative risk. Successful parenting.

You step in but Tink cuts across you, wearily placing her empty glass on a camping table and snapping back to the role of compliant wife. Containing herself, remembering her public place. She takes Hugo by the arm and pats it in defeated collusion, leading him from the cursed, uncontrollable women at the heart of this. He flicks his wife off but she continues to walk beside him; Mig and you share a glance at the vicious, exhausted warfare soaked through this.

You've seen it so often before, this type of woman. Who flirts with men, who is practised. And the man must be assuaged, humoured, because she needs him whereas Mig and you do not. It is a way of being that is alien to you, a throwback to another era when the female existed as the lamp to illuminate the male; to listen, nod, affirm. She is the woman who almost forgets you are there, in a man's presence, because she's so intent on her task. Of bolstering. How those men must have glowed, once, to be able to bask in this affirmation, to have been so continually assured their way was right. Once.

A text from Pup. *Sarge, brace yourself.* Rumours are strengthening that boys from the local school are out there, with them; some girls who've arrived back home have reported teens larking about. Unseen but voices, close. Possibly. Can't confirm. It all feels like stories building upon stories, a furnace of gossip now and please God no. Not this, they're not sluts, at least not that you know of. You stride across to Robin and ask if police are checking local schools. She says they're onto it. Could other men be out there? The parents catch it, look at you sharp. What, Hugo snaps. You ignore him.

Cin received her first dick pic in primary school. Year Five. She'd been there a term. Mig told you. Demanded from the school the boy's name because her child's innocence felt degraded and she wasn't having this swept under the carpet. Normalised. This is sexual harassment, assault, Mig said with the magnificence of a lioness. She said the boy needed to know this was not on. Needed to know for his future life.

The school principal, who was male, wouldn't give her the boy's name.

Cin told you who he was. She was good at talking to you once. Trusted you with secrets. You never told Mig; the loyalty was clocked. Your relationship, once, was all about snaring trust. About you being the godmother of wise counsel. About Naughty Days involving chocolate and girly talk beyond the realm of pesky parents. Beyond judgement.

Night is coming on fast. You can no longer bear to look at Mig, to witness her entire physiognomy changing, her body now hunched and recoiling. She's rocking and keening in her car with the windows shut tight. Drowning in her own private agony, fenced by mistrust. She glances across at you in the parent marquee and catches your eye. Doesn't move. Neither do you. Mutually afraid of each other, of the hurt you can both inflict. Yet bound, because you understand each other too much. The weaknesses, the vulnerabilities, how to catastrophically hurt. And so you circle, warily, like two battle-scarred cheetahs before attack.

You suddenly, achingly, want to joke with her like old times. Because you can imagine The Cins already sitting in a café booth in the closest mountain town while the oldsters crack apart in their camping ground. 'You talk too loud,' Cin threw across to Mig the last time you all walked through the city together. She then commanded her mother to walk five paces behind her. 'You walk too loud.' Then, 'You breathe too loud.' Before adding, 'It's so embarrassing,' for good measure. Mig finally retorted, 'What if I cease to exist? Will that do? Should I just die?' 'Oh my God, that would be the most embarrassing thing ever.' They're like a sitcom together. Mig and you were in stitches, silently, until you both burst into loudness like you were ten again. Cin turned and saw you arm in arm and joined in too and you all ended together, a joyous trio, walking together down the street. You want to remind Mig of this now, urgently; want to hold her, weep with her, like old times.

    Do   not.

Choppers, still, their lights shining down into the bush; arcing across ridges and into gullies. The obscenity of the noise, the affront of it. This feels like a war zone.

The missing sharpens its beak, scrapes at your underbelly, snagging softness. Robin tells you to get some rest because it's going to be a long night. Can't think of sleep. The lost are going to dig deep into everyone's restless dark. Parents have been offered hotel rooms but they all want to stay at the campsite. Hugo asks if the school is paying for the rooms. Without hesitation you smile, beatifically, of course.

Elle's afraid of the dark, her mother cries out suddenly. As if you can do something about it. All the parents chime in, the floodgates of fear have opened. Are the girls together? Split up? A – a – alive? You can no longer offer assurances despite being so good at plans and strategies and calm, to shut a situation down. But you can't, with kids, of course. You just want to break from all parents now and shout baited words to bring the girls back – scream threats of suspension, expulsion, the police – because you're a hostage to their absence, bound by need for them. And for Tony. A good man, a fair man, despite his tough exterior; there's an old-fashioned, Christian sense of morality to him. It is a life of service, and he's serving now. He volunteered to go in. To bring them back.

You approach Mig at the coffee table, fortifying herself for the long night ahead. You want a word in private. She nods. You move to the edge of the bush, awkwardly, can feel the power of the trees poised next to you as if listening in. You whisper that you heard Cin saying wife beaters are hot, it was the last thing you got from her and you're worried; is there a man in her life, something you don't know about; trying, somehow, for connection. Mig looks at you coldly. It's girl slang for singlets. Men's singlets, she adds slowly, like you don't quite understand English. Those ones that tradies wear. Mig looks at you like, really, you don't know that, really? It is one of those hot, shameful moments of mortification when you feel ancient and cloistered and out of touch; what planet do you live on, really? And why are you even pretending to be so embedded with the girls and their mothers, with all their world? You, of all people. You feel the weight of difference between Mig and you here; feel a hurting, inner wincing at your separateness.

Oh, you respond to her, of course. A loaded silence. Your life of connection, your entire history, vanished in that moment. Shrivelled to coldness, to nothing.

But yes, right, wife beaters. God knows why you'd never clocked it before. It is yet another description to tuck into the Dictionary of Subversion. These girls speak a language that is exhilarating and mysterious and wrong-footing and you can't help but admire it while simultaneously being shut out from it. Cin throws it all at you, deliberately, you're sure. She's so good at existing on the edge, to snag a noticing.

Night is leaking through the bush. The earth is relaxing into the relief of the dark, you can smell it now, the soil opening to receive its benediction of coolness and quiet. A fresh rescue team is readying itself to go in. Uniforms of yellow, with reflective tape, head torches and ropes, the best of the best. This is serious now. Your thudding heart. It has rained several times since the vanishing. Not good for the dogs.

Beth wonders aloud if any of the girls are menstruating right now, if they're in synch. No-one answers, something else to worry about, an awkward pause. She seems like she's on the edge of madness. Beth asks again about Dr Breen. You tell her his wife is in the tent opposite and why doesn't she talk to her herself. You don't tell her that Adela won't talk to you because she doesn't quite trust smooth metropolitan types like yourself. She thinks they're all degenerate, the thin edge of the wedge, and shouldn't be leading a supposedly Christian school. Tony chuckled when he told you this. As he spoke you saw an image of a woman in an apron, baking while twitching her kitchen's net curtains; a woman quietly seething, in stillness, as she watched her other life sail past.

It is rumoured Tony gives good marks to the prettiest girls. That he's asked some students if they're gay. He did contact every Year Nine parent last year whose child had signed up for a secret Gay Support Group known as The Click Club. His aberration, but you schooled him out of it. No-one quite knows why he has the job, except you. He does your dirty work, faithfully, never wavers. He leaps into confrontation; you need to keep your hands clean. And of course he'd jump in with going back for the girls – his life is poised in readiness. Tony would have volunteered to go back into the bush unthinkingly, yet he's been the cause of a few parents pulling their child from the school. His fallibility is that he is extremely rules-based. He lives by them. No favours for anyone. Good cop bad cop and it's always worked.

Tony and Cin, if they have found each other, will have had quite a few arguments by now. Led by Cin, her girls will be asking where in the Bible does it say that homosexuality is a sin and why are there no women in leadership positions in the Church and is God a bloke, really, who says? You lot? Because all we see, Cin will be saying, is Christianity as a patriarchal construct. Designed to keep the blokes in power and the women as their servants.

Tony, early on, wouldn't let the girls go to the toilet within class time because too many of them were doing it. He didn't get it. Was punishing them. Some parents accused him of wanting his charges weakened, reduced. You had to rein it in. Set him straight.

You walk away now, from everyone and everything. You wander down a small, overgrown offshoot of a track; by instinct you know you're not meant to trespass. You persist. It ends in a plunging cliff – a cliff! So close. This mysterious, confounding place. The edge is fenced off by a wilting mesh fence, too near the precipice. You step back, heart dipping. Look across the cliff, at the great cathedrals of rock face and the valleys stretching as far as the eye can see. All barely discernible in the dark. Mig comes up quietly beside you. You feel the frisson of her presence, her familiar scent. Breathe it in trembly and deep. Mig hasn't stood next to you like this in years, so intimately, so close. If Cin is dead then God help you, she whispers, because I will need to go too. It cuts into you like a knife slice. You pause. Breath held. What to do. You hug her lightly, silently. She does not shrug you off.

So. You're in this together. You tip back your head on tears. Of release.

What you'd both give to hear Cin's high whoop of a laugh butting the clouds, for your squealy Golden Flower to come bursting through the undergrowth, proclaiming, 'Away! No cuddles. Off. You are literally destroying my life. Killing me. Now I die.' To hear that, well, you would both give your lives. Kill me now dear God, for this, you close your eyes, you pray.

Can't write straight anymore, but must scribble down something, to even-keel, to stop the roar in your head from all the doom-thoughts swallowing you up. Praying to God fervently now, as the temperature drops. Be careful what you wish for springs to mind like a stain of ink as you look up to the high ridge. So much rock to fall off from, such a drop. What's out there. Who. The missing a secret code that cannot be unlocked.

A faint yearn of a yip slides into your heart. You feel watched. Something is perched out there in the dark bank of bush, observing, blinking, waiting. Again, the yip, more insistent. Of what. A flit of a thought again. That this is a joke, a prank. Fuck off Mum and a high cackle to the heavens as Cin throws back her head and laughs; you can just imagine them watching close and high-fiving at the fright they've given you all. Are they now bound by their silly ploy and it's gone too far, trapped in teen stupidity and can't get out. Is this a punishment to make you all really, absolutely, miss them. To have the grownups demonstrate their voluptuous love, without judgement and shout.

The wind picks up, canopies of the trees toss branches like wild ponies spooked. A hymn of branches whisper and chatter as if gossiping about the madness unfurling beneath them, all the minds zinging and pinging with rumour, gossip, terror. Of the unknown. A feral cat saunters past like a politician. Can't catch me, says its cool, slow gaze. If you had a gun you'd get it out because that's how you're feeling right now, you'd be aiming a blast and missing.

Cin would get the animal straight between the eyes. First shot. Never having done it before.

A cool breeze washes across your sweat, washes over you like a hand of God, stilling you down. *Please let the girls come out*, you pray, *I'll do anything to have this fixed.* Then you call Pup. He suggests closing the school until further notice, it's so distressing, but you hesitate because it would send a potentially catastrophic signal to the wider community. You'll keep it as an option down the track, you say, but your voice trails off, can't voice the next thought. No, you say to Pup, but you'll remain at the coalface, here, for the duration of this nightmare. The community needs to see you here. 'Sarge, we would expect nothing less,' Pup concurs.

You move away from the parents and medics and police and sit in your fold-up chair, huddling in a blanket against the chill. Cannot sleep. You're meant to retire to the nearby hotel for that but won't. If you have to rest, there's your car, but you will not leave this campsite in case your girls come out. Imagine the oddness of you not being there, for them, in that moment. You've given the parents your personal phone number – the shock of that – and told them to call any time if they want to leave. You're here for them, all hours; you love their girls, live for their girls, and want them to know this. None of the parents want to leave either, of course. Nor Adela Breen.

Mig carries her chair across and places it silently next to you. I need my baby back, she whispers. I know, you respond. 'What if someone's out there, Kick. Some bloke. A rando, as the girls say. Randos.' You've thought of that too but cannot respond because Mig has just used your old childhood nickname, the name you haven't heard for years, that your father used to call you, and she is the only one left who knows of it. You shut your eyes on the depth of history between you. Shut your eyes on tears, finally, but no, they must not come and they will not: you are the principal and you are watched. 'There's still so much to teach her, Kicki.' Mig chokes up. 'In that crazy powder keg life.' Oh, you know. Cin has told you in the past she can't wait for the full-body tatts, the sleeves of ink on each arm. Told you she's most creative between 2 and 3 am, that she's allergic to bed. Told you her life is all about getting 'that orgasm thing', in a spa bath if she must. Told you, 'I like dick,' regrettably, 'and not chick.' And all of it is said with a twinkle in her eye and you never know what to believe; it's just to get a rise out of you, of course.

And what is this missing, so   vast?

'I've failed her,' Mig says in the close dark. 'She told me there'd be boys and bongs, a secret gatho and no-one would ever find them and I laughed it off. A big fat joke, I thought, here we go again. And now this.' You say Cin was making it up to get a rise out of Mig, as she does. 'Yeah.' A rueful chuckle from you both. 'But what if—' She's our medicine, you rasp, can barely get it out. We'll get her back. It's all you can push out and so inadequate.

You want to tell your old friend so many, so many things. Secret godmotherly stuff. That you had to distance yourself from Cin at the end of Year Six. Yes, she'd always known you as the fabulous and feisty fairy godmother, but as she got older she became too bold with the relationship, pushed the boundaries. You were useful, so she used you. She was too forward, too familiar, her love voluminous and unbound. You were at her beck and call, and you know that's what a godmother is meant to be, but Cin went too far and you never explained this to Mig. 'Scooch your cooch,' Cin would command when you'd visit and accidentally sit in her TV chair; your face confused at her slangy words. Cooch? 'Shove. Over,' she'd say slowly, like you didn't speak English or were too old and decrepit for her. You've never told Mig that you had to pull away from Cin ever since she's been at your school. And that she hasn't understood, she's too young. Like a mangy cat, she just wanted to be aloof and abrupt but then would wend her way close, rubbing up against your legs, wanting in. Or tried to. But you had to distance yourself. You had a career to consider. And you know Cin feels the torment of abandonment, the sting of rejection, and you owe it to Mig to explain this. To her, and to her daughter. But you can't say any of it, within the immense penumbra of hurt.

You are aware, from all the damaged girls in your school, that what anyone wants from life is the gift of attention. And you are remiss. You thought Cin strong enough for the new you. She went into Koongala like a dirty mug into a dishwasher; it was like you were shaping this institution just for her. For all your thinking little wild-child feminists, a warrior army for future battles, future life. But the free-range, insouciant informality between Cin and you couldn't be sustained. You were soon to be her principal and something different had to come between you. Decorum. Distance. Discretion. Cin was bewildered at the retreat. And you deeply regret these last few years when you pushed her away, for the sake of your career. When she possibly needed you the most.

You want to fall to your knees in beseeching prayer; instead, you shut your eyes and wrap your arms around your shoulders, squeezing, hurting, tight. *Please God, bring her back. All of them. If you do I will shout your power and your joy to the heavens.* You are not particularly religious, of the kind prescribed by the Church, you see through it. But maybe you need to be, maybe this is a test. *I will do it, Lord. Do anything, to have them back. Have this job offer on solid ground. Please.*

There was hope at the start that this would all be over quickly. Tony would sort it out, the search would be called off with not a little embarrassment, the job done. Well, that's gone. You need a haven now, a harbour, to rest from the fractiousness of the world. You are rolled like flour in uncertainty; need pills, drink, something to push the world away, it's all too close. Robin chats with an ambo, the media still hover, fathers and mothers settle into silence. Adela mother-hens a group freshly arrived from her church and glances across at you, slightly aghast. What are they saying.

Mig sighs next to you. 'You know nothing about them,' she barbs into you, returning to the conversation about wife beaters. 'You don't understand them. You're not a mother.' Oh, you respond, winded, for this is like you're twelve again and fighting on that last afternoon of term in the regular three-monthly break-up that snapped tension and intensity while clearing the air. 'Get with it, Grandma.' Mig then chuckles as if in apology, and you snicker back, the relief washing through you in an unclenching rush. It's okay, it's okay between you. But of course   not.

Mig reaches for your hand. You hold it and squeeze in a secret language of yearning and bewilderment and, dare you say, love. You tremble your eyes shut and silently thank the heavens. It is enough, this, now, enough.

A cry of anguish from the peripheral dark, who knows who it is. Some parent who cannot cope. It feels like you're all immersed here in inky black water on a moonless night, unable to discern what is around you, under you. And some are flailing wildly, loudly, in panic; and others are going very still and quiet. To preserve themselves. Into the woods their girls have flown, to be swallowed up. What woodsman have they come across, what piper with bewitching pipe, wolf, goblin, crone. Order disintegrates and something darker and more unruly emerges, licking its lips. Somewhere – a speck in the black – is the light of a safe cottage for your girls; a light of civilisation and calm and pedestrian quiet. If they can find their way back to it. Cin most of all, leading the others out.

You had to call Mig after the Click Club incident. Had to. It was Cin's year and she had signed up the whole form, in response to Dr Breen contacting the parents of every single girl who'd signed up for the newly formed support group. Mig said her daughter's riposte to, quote, 'that cunt' was 'Spartacus-genius. She gets things done. Brilliantly.' You explained that yes, Dr Breen had perhaps gone a little rogue with this one, but Cin's actions were more about solidarity than protection and, more pertinently, undermining the authority of your teacher and, by rights, the school, and maybe her daughter wasn't quite the genius she thought. 'What? You're so friggin' … tight,' Mig exploded. 'No-one ever meets your impossible standards, do they? Well, have I got news for you. Motherhood, oh boy, it's the biggie, and you'll never understand it.' Cut, parry, thrust. 'It's about a loss of control, Kick. A letting go. Which is why you could never be a mother because you're too fucking tight. Physically. Mentally. Everything. And to be honest it's why I sometimes can't stand you in my life.' She hung up.

In its wake, a roar of silence.

It was your last proper conversation. That was it. Decades of friendship wiped. The failure, the huge failure in your life. And now this.

You are lonely. It is corrosive through you. You've somehow slid from having a lot of friends to too few and you're not sure how. You don't have enough to go to a movie as regularly as you'd like, an art gallery or a play, because you can't badger your handful of regulars too much. They have their own lives to live. Families, children, love. You have to space them and it's embarrassing to admit that it's come to this. You're surrounded by people yet the expansive alone yowls at night in your silent, accusing, too-big house.

You stand. A gulp of panic. You stand arrowed to the only things you care about now, your girls and your colleague; you stand arrowed and clenched but there's no target, no direction, in which to face.

Tuesday

4.26 am. There is a rip in the fabric of your life and you're not sure now you'll ever be able to repair it. You've slumbered, patchily, for a total of forty-six minutes. You fall back into thin sleep, in the driver's seat of your car that faces the press of the bush. In readiness.

Wake with a start. Dribble from the side of your mouth. Wake from a dream that you're a museum guard existing in stillness, surrounded by beauty – every day, beauty – it's the end point of the journey and a surrendering to wonder at last. But then where are you, as you surface from a blissful moment of normal. To cuntfucked this. A cursed campsite. A squabble and squawk of early morning birds that are usually the joy of your waking; all those chatterings of excitable industriousness that are listened to, with chuff, from your pillow at home. But not today. Two crimson rosellas wheel away from their towers of green, chasing each other and joyously screeching as they shoot across the sky; it is all so alive. Free. But then you. Staring, in stillness. At the waiting mountains that have swallowed four of your girls in the bloom of their life alongside a teacher you can't do without and nothing has changed here, nothing, and you're not coping and no-one knows it.

The morning light is a broken seam pouring out its gold. Already, a cram of notifications. A To Do list that's endless already and hello, it's only dawn. Your life is this relentless To Do list. You are weighted by an oppressive thumb of fear that this list will never, entirely, be cleared. 'On it' is the mantra, in the great Sisyphean rhythm of your life. But this vanishing cannot be crossed out. You ran on adrenaline yesterday and have woken exhausted and already wanting a nap and this could go on for days. Weeks. A lifetime. Fuck.

Mig is a little way off, concertinaed awkwardly in her camping chair, and how she can sleep in it is beyond you. She needs her slumber; this has been the worst night of her life. Side by side you gazed at the bush until the wan light of the new day, waiting for God knows what, and then you stumbled to your car. Mig would not leave the night, the waiting, the readiness.

You are no longer friends. Careful and silent but tethered by a shared past, and beyond admitting it.

When Cin exploded into Mig's life your best friend wanted for nothing, her world was complete. Inside it, her love was thick butter she basted Cin in. Mig was as calm as an eiderdown as she wrapped herself in her brave new life. But then you. All restless and rangy, the force wanting in. Wanting, well, a noticing of some sort.

Mig considered the Golden Flower a genius – undefined – and the years have gradually woken her from the delusion. As they do, with all new parents. You've seen it a thousand times over. When Cin strained on the potty after a false alarm and declared, 'My poo is waking up,' she was the new Sylvia Plath. When her painting was selected for the Young Archie Portrait Prize, aged six, she was the next Artemisia Gentileschi. When she won a public speaking prize in Year Five she was striding in the footsteps of Germaine Greer. The result? A child marinated in confidence. As certain as a male and expected to carry that presumption of success through life. It firmed the path. But girls are never so lucky, life chips away at them, cuts them down. Mig had to know this.

She didn't want to hear.

The camping ground is bleak in the wan dawn light. Robin approaches, freshly crisp with a bun firm in its net and smelling of shower. Any news? Shakes her head. You brisk her away, have heard enough. How is there nothing. Go to say sorry but she's already gone. You look around, stranded amid parents and first responders as they wait for direction, but you have none to give. Rub your hands on your trousers and head to breakfast, apologetic. For who knows what.

Adela is awake. Dressed and ready after a night in her own car. You smile in approval; she's organised, alert. She doesn't approach. As if you will be no use and she's already clocked it. Whenever you try to mollify her she turns away, doesn't want to engage; as if she sees through you, everything you try to be, everything you present to the world. Right.

8.10 am. Trees banter in the wind, birds are in raucous play. There's an unsettling restlessness to the day. This replenishing land usually blankets you in calm; you've always wanted to be slipped into it when you die, rested among the wondrous wild, but you're afraid of it now. It feels hostile, indifferent, cruel. And your girls within it? Hopefully just waking, readying for a big walk out. Hopefully Tony steady among them. Hopefully.

He was not pleased when The Cins planned to take the day off school to travel to the national Women's March in the capital. Oh, for God's sake, he rolled his eyes, please. Mig was going to drive them. Hugo wasn't thrilled about that detail either. Yep, he rang, unaware that parents aren't meant to entangle the principal in such things. 'I'm not sending my kid to your school to become a fucking feminist,' Hugo barked down the phone, like he was berating a Macau billionaire who'd just reneged on a casino deal. The venom of the man as he spat out the F-word. The revulsion. You hung up, something you rarely do. And so all of The Cins went to the march except Tamsin. She hated you for this, for a while, for being privy to the complicated knot of her parents. It was as if her messy life beyond school was seen, and she couldn't bear it.

You shouldn't have hung up on Hugo. A rare loss of control. There'll be none of that here.

But you wish to apologise. To all the people you've brusqued away on the phone recently. Hung up on. Snapped at. Dismissed. Wanted to stab. Not good. All the people who've been on the receiving end of irritation and a discombobulating temper that seems to rise from within you from nowhere now. Who is this woman. Not the person you've known your entire life. That community leader of commendable calm, that woman of warmth and restraint. But Lord, this, now. The mess of it. So to the many people you've come across – in the principal's office, staffroom, on the road or in the supermarket – you wish to apologise. To all those you've wanted to murder, you wish to apologise. The astonishing rage is as confusing to you as it must be to them. Because something unstoppable comes over you, an explosion of righteous fury even though something inside you is going whoa, what is this, please resume normal service.

Yet you can't.

It feels like your body has been going through a comprehensive hormonal reckoning as seismic as the onset of a girl's period, yet these changes feel worse. The process has been protracted and painful – over five years, six – and with a battering to your equilibrium the like of which you've never experienced. Buoyancy has been hijacked by an almost crippling vulnerability, coupled with a profound lack of confidence. Can't control the veering into what feels like calamity, can't tell anyone about this mystifying shift from the solid centre of yourself. Where have you gone? You want the old you back. That firm, positive one.

You remember Cin's horror in Year Seven at the thought of her periods coming on. Her revulsion at being so … womanly. It was related back to the staffroom by her Personal Development teacher and you all laughed at the wonder of her, of Cin moaning dramatically in the classroom one lazy Friday, not wanting periods or breasts or long hair or hips, anything so disgustingly 'lady'. As if they would impede her life. Yet look at the girl now. Revelling in the power of a blooming female body, conditioned into strength by a tomboy's free-range childhood. Alpha, on fire.

Menopause feels like the insidious corrective to all this. The Great Hidden in a woman's life. The only female milestone that you and your mother never really talked about. No-one did, publicly, for generations. It's a woman's great rupturing, physically and mentally, and you've never felt more endangered. Two days ago you barked at the self-service machine at the supermarket to piss off. Ditto the packet of washing tablets you could not open, and a parking sign that made your brain hurt to decipher. Last week you roamed the city with blood on the back of your dress and had no idea until you arrived home and took it off. Thought you'd stopped all that but the flood came upon you so suddenly and voluminously, with no warning. You felt broken. Unhinged.

There are sudden flushes of heat sprinting across your skin, a complete loss of libido coupled with what feels like a lifetime's accumulation of exhaustion, more frequent migraines and a bodily thickening that's deeply distressing, because this was never you. You were always the skinny one, effortlessly, and now there's a sludge of stubborn weight on your breasts, shoulders, arms and thighs and it will not shift. Yet this physical manifestation of menopause is nothing compared with the impact on your mental state. You're questioning every aspect of your life. Snappy, sensitive, low. You crave the time when you're out the other side, beyond all this. Yet keep going. As women do.

You want to alert girls and staff that the physical changes and rupturing moods are because of hormones, nothing else, but of course you do not. You gaze from the sidelines of your life in astonishment. Where have you gone to? Will the old, blazing you ever come back? You hope this new position will return you to a previous self; lighter, steadier, more positive.

Recently a new term of co-existence has sprung up in conversations with girlfriends: the short-term/long-term relationship, for those wanting a looser kind of coupledom. The workable bliss of a long-term commitment but in short-term blocks of actually seeing their other half. Because they're both so busy, and love their other lives. So they see each other in bursts of intensity then toddle off to separate worlds. It is convenience. Their own aesthetic. Own level of tidiness. It is living life how they really want to, unconventionally, and it's the only way you could possibly do a relationship now. Except there's none. No prospect. You are wedded to this job, this career path. Everyone knows it. It's your brand and you're locked into it.

What you're seeing all around you, quite deliciously: that the wifedom model of old is not what many females your age and above are subscribing to so much anymore. They're keen to embrace vivid living, not necessarily glued to a partner who may not want the existence that they do. All around you are old men clinging to their jobs, refusing to give way to younger generations, while the women are keen to dive into a fresh world, in all its permutations. These are the years for themselves, finally, after being there so exhaustingly for everyone else. You recently spoke of this phenomenon to Tim, your oldest member of staff, a maths teacher who could retire but is refusing to budge despite gentle suggestions. He's locking out not one but two generations of talent below him. 'If I retire, what would I do?' he lamented. 'I'd get so bored.' You do not know of one woman who has ever said this.

Women have things to do.

Pinned on the inspiration board near your desk is a quote from the painter John Olsen about how life is very beautiful and we must not waste our time on this earth; not deal with life as a mere warehouse, without the magic of trees and birds and rivers and love, especially love, for that would be a terrible mistake. Yet do you ever follow this wisdom of his words? No time.

You're always telling your Koongalettes there's courage in change. Liberation in saying no, actually; you need to normalise this word for your girls. Who wants to hold the world in aspic? Men more than women, you hazard a guess, because in the past it's worked so well for them. But women are waking up, you tell your girls, they are finding their voices, if they dare. To risk.

Mig stirs. You make her a cup of tea, lots of soya milk, just how she likes it. But then hesitate to take it across. Because the haunting of her lost friendship is as potent as the cruellest love affair, whispering under your skin for so long now. And it still cuts, and still. Tightens your chest. The sheer bafflement of the whole thing. The targeted silence felled you more effectively than anything had before this. The two of you had always revelled in knowing you'd have each other for good. That sure. 'Grapple them to thy soul with hoops of steel,' Shakespeare wrote of friends and you did, once, with her. Your career progressed as her finances stalled in the scramble to survive the creative slog; you lent her money for IVF. You were made godmother as reward, which you assumed cleaved you for life. But then the change, over many souring years, which culminated in that final phone call about the Click Club.

Yet even before that vicious little exchange, you'd email to catch up sometimes: Mig was busy. Soon, another time, next month. Then came a new snippiness about life choices, an accumulation of pricks until your heart began to flinch, in astonishment. Mig? She had never been this. Snippy, picky. It was like motherhood concentrated your friend's thinking in terms of the unfairnesses of the world, the unfairnesses of the haves and have nots. And you were at the centre of it, as a constant reminder, and she couldn't bear it; the difference in living standards that cast shade on her own life. It was as if she had to retreat, to save herself.

Scrabbling to connect, you secured Cin the place at Koongala. Paid the fees, no questions asked. Guaranteed supply until the end of Year Twelve in a trust only Mig and you are aware of. She knows you'd never jeopardise the arrangement yet why this, this nothing from her, now; leaving you lost in a lonely sea. Dropped into a cold, cold place.

Your breathing shallows. A sprint of sweat. The effect is physical. You take a deep breath and walk across to Mig with her tea. No news, she asks. You shake your head. She takes the paper cup that you've doubled without a word. No thank you, no anything. You turn and walk off.

The shock of Mig's withdrawal from your life could brew cancer, summon cataclysms, bring on early death; the potency of the withholding feels that strong. There's a vicious magnificence to it – oh, to have the power to inflict such destruction. You never get invited to catch-ups anymore, to a movie night or coffee or walks. And you were too busy with work, too broken with menopause, to notice you'd been cut loose. Until it was too late.

Until the clamour of the   loneliness.

Virginia Woolf once wrote that she had lost some friends by death and others through sheer inability to cross the street, which you jotted in a notebook as you dived deep into attempting to work this out. Was it about childhood competitiveness? Success? Your shortcomings? Your ridiculous workload? You'd see her with other women, other mums, and she'd barely say hello, as if she couldn't wait to get back to her brighter, sparkier, better friends. In panic and bewilderment you wrote, called, texted, but she wouldn't let you in. This was loss through spectacular retreat; a desolation of silence. The cunning of the retraction made you feel lonely like you had never felt in your life; no love affair had ever cut you like this. How to bring a woman down. Hobble her with insecurity in a way no man had ever managed.

As recompense you became friends with another woman, a colleague whose every conversation felt like a form of bristly competition. Helene was beautiful, in a fragile, rail-thin way, which speaks of other insecurities. She rattled your universe with every conversation you had. You'd get a knot in your stomach whenever she texted or called, felt sick when you saw her hovering in the staffroom to catch you. This was a mistake. Two lonely women do not always happiness make. You'd somehow allowed Helene into your life in the wake of Mig's ghosting, yet she was one of those women you'd never have befriended beyond the context of a shared workplace. It got to the point where she was vining your whole existence. Yet you could never fell her with silence; it felt too cruel. Because you knew its effect now. You did, in the end, gently distance yourself. 'Friendships begin with liking or gratitude – roots that can be pulled up,' George Eliot briskly wrote. Is that what Mig was doing with you? Yanking out the root.

What you've learnt: some friendships run their course and there's no shame in that. What can seem nourishing at a certain time may not be so beneficial a few years, or decades, down the track. As you get older you need the gentler, soldering kind. And often, you know now, it's not when times are bad you find out who your real friends are, but when times are good. You cannot remember Mig ever congratulating you for anything you've ever done or achieved. She was the schoolgirl who'd laugh when you tripped up; your clumsiness was amusing to her. She was the socialist who couldn't hide the sneer when you left the state school system for the private one; you'd sold out. The judgemental parent who made you feel wrong for your life choices; you spent your money on fripperies. Maybe you've been in competition all along and never realised it. Mig's turning away felt like disapproval at all your life decisions, a wily attempt to crack you into failure by forcing you to confront the way you lead your life.

How to measure success, as a woman? You don't know anymore.

The American neuropsychiatrist Louann Brizendine has a theory about the way women group together. She says it's programmed into them to connect intensely in the childbearing years, because they need the support and protection of other females around them when the male is often away (hunting in the old days, working in modern times). Yet the flip side of this urgent biological need is the way women control each other. If everyone acts and thinks the same way, Brizendine theorises, the group will stay intact and everyone will be protected. But if someone can't be controlled – if an individual acts differently, in a way not expected – then the other women turn. Viciously, brutally, insidiously. Trying to destroy the rebel's strength, trying to destroy *her*, in an attempt to have her change. Conform. So as not to show the rest of the women up. Because they need their choices in life affirmed.

You yearn for the mateship you once had. The two of you used to sit in the playground at Friday pick-ups, in Cin's last years of primary school, on one of your rare afternoons off when private school holidays had already begun. You'd sit in one long golden stare at all the big-boned, sun-smeared, rough and tumble state school kids running about, yacking away with your gossip then falling into silence. And it always felt very hard to get up from that seat. From that moment where you were both resting within the crazy busy-ness of your days, in a great exhalation of stillness. It was a moment where you could just be yourselves, sitting side by side in the unspoken richness of the great arc of your lives. Ah yes, with hoops of steel you held your best friend close. And now she has fallen back asleep on the roof of the world, your offering of tea going cold on the ground next to her, and you have never been further apart.

The morning light hardens with fresh rumours. A narrative is forming. The cops don't know what they're doing and neither does the posh city school at the centre of this clusterfuck. You lock in a crisis communications company to massage the new, disquieting whisperings. Reputation is everything and Koongala is one of the top. You can't afford to lose families.

An email from the department. Perfunctory, brief, chilly; an abrupt departure from the warmth of your source's missives. The job decision is 'on hold' until the situation in the mountains is resolved. Reading between the lines: the panel has gone cold on you.

You double over as if you're about to be sick.

Beth is talking all the time now, too much, it's a river of talking, she can't stop. You can feel the screws tightening. This is no longer a joke, a prank, it's been too long. Something more sinister is at play. Robin keeps going on, soothingly, about water. If they're near water, if they've got water, they'll be okay. Yes, let's hope. If not. Well. She doesn't elaborate.

'They'll have water,' you say. 'They're clever girls.'

Suddenly Cin's whoop of delight, far away. Yes? What? The hoot that feels like it's punching the roof of wherever she is indoors. You pivot to the bush, jog with intent. Stop as you realise everyone is looking. 'Sorry, I thought I … heard something.' Normality has stepped back to allow chaos centre stage. You are splintering here, publicly now, like an old wooden ship caught in Antarctic ice, splintering under unbearable pressure. Sinking doesn't feel far off. Robin leads you gently to your seat, rubbing your back and soothing. You shrug her away. You're not eighty-three yet, miss.

11 am. A chance to slip away to the hotel room Pup's arranged for you, for a freshen up. You change into the sober clothes that Gaden's brought from town. As you enter the small mountain village it feels like you're crossing into another space; passing through a membrane into a normal life, a world not your own. This tourist hub has no conception of the mass fracturing taking place just ten minutes away; it's obscene the way the villagers happily go about their business. You settle under the shower's enveloping heat, close your eyes, have to rouse yourself to leave its somnambulance. Imagine the horror of missing something

happening at the campsite, of not being there as the girls come out. The glaring absence.

If they do not emerge your career will be over. It's as simple as that. This job, and any future job, will be mired in scandal and shame. No-one will want you, no-one will forget. Ah yes, the principal who lost four students and a teacher. Careless. No coming back from that. The horrendous stain on the span of your life, and the possible legal action that would flow from it. A catastrophic failure in a career where you staked everything to stay on track; a partner and children sacrificed because the timing was never quite right. Yet what is this now – this shiny, slimy darkness deep within, like a troll crouched under a bridge, cackling away at the stupidity of the life choices. Was it all worth it, really. All the anger and tightness and envy and control, all the calculation and focus pushing you on, and on, ever deeper into the career that swallowed you up. You gave away so much. And you're so tired, now, of being strong for everyone else. Trapped within a loneliness that's endlessly crammed with people. That no-one else gets.

Are the girls strong enough? Part of the remit, for every Koongala girl, is to toughen up. 'Cope' is your curt mantra for this. You get what you get and you don't get upset. You don't have to be polite to the creepy man. It's not a post, it's a boast. Ah, all the little bluntnesses threaded through the school, all the little prods to firm. To stop the whining, crying, submitting and succumbing, to stop the big-noting and blaming others.

Because they'll get nowhere with any of that. Just get on with it. Life is unfair, so cope.

Cin will be telling the snakes what's what, stamping her feet to get them to rack off. There's a healthy dose of testosterone in that one. She used to delight in blindsiding people about her gender, which happened all the time during primary school. She had short hair, a bush-honed body and a masculine energy, and it was a win for her if a man treated her as a boy, in that tender, matey way they have of dealing with little boys they don't know. They don't treat girls as beautifully and Cin knew this. Exploited it. Wanted it. A man's woman.

3 pm. Do they want to be noticed, you wonder. Did Cin orchestrate it. The vanishing is now starting to trend on X and TikTok; this has the makings of a worldwide viral mystery. Oh God, no. In its wake will be notoriety, speculation, attention. You've been noting all the new activity on the girls' untouched social media accounts. Thousands of new followers, already, for all of them, except Elle.

A smoulder of secrets. A tinderbox of talk. What do you know of your school, really, in the subterranean depths of the interactions. Tony asked you once if that gobby Cinnamon girl talks, is she a talker, and you wondered what on earth he meant. You told him blank-faced you had no idea but it wouldn't let you go. Until life took over and you forgot. But now.

You long for the blandness of regular existence. Long for simplicity. To stop this over-thinking. About everything. To stop your brain.

Tony always called your girl Cinnamon as if he was afraid to say anything else. He was the only teacher who didn't refer to the group as The Cins. His name: That Gobby Lot. As if their voices really pissed him off. Their loud voices, their hard laughs, their untrammelled squeals and shrieks.

A briefing from Robin. Three strands of her hair are loose and you long to tuck them back. Don't. You're on notice. So, a fresh team has arrived, is going in, experts from interstate. Rumours are getting louder of young men entering the bush, to rescue the girls, to find them before anyone else. Police are concerned that vital evidence is being lost. Evidence? What is this tipping into? Social media is flaring up, there's an edge now, control is skittering. Males unloosed, contamination of the site, what's out there, who. Pup tells you with a glint of pride that CNN and the BBC are now reporting on it and old girls from all over the world are contacting the school. 'Sarge, we're famous.' 'For all the wrong reasons,' you snap back.

It's because of how the girls look. Crisp and innocent in their school uniform pictures that were released thanks to a police request. In case they were out there somewhere, Robin explained delicately, on the, er, loose. Not bloody likely, you snapped back, these are Koongala girls. But it's all a good story. The perils of the Australian bush, Little Girls Lost, stolen innocence. You'd be hooked. Tony is barely mentioned, like he's an afterthought. You wince – you're not the only one who's been consigning him to that status.

Mig is now bowed over, squatting on the ground with hands over head, shielding herself from the world. Cin is the hammock swinging your happiness and you might never have it back.

The vastness of the loneliness. Loneliness that tastes of failure. It's like a piece of ragged tin cutting into your confidence. The woman with her back to you now has felled a successful woman, triumphantly, in an utterly womanly way. And you couldn't help but admire it. The act was brutal. Stupendous. Magnificent.

And of course it would be someone from your old school group that brought you to your knees. You were profiled in the *Financial Review* as one of the most powerful women in corporate Australia – 'She Who Shapes the Female Leaders of the Future' – yet still get nervous about clothes choices around this lot, still feel the chill of teen-gang judgement all these years later. Like you're all fourteen again and noticing everything and you're the one who can never quite get it right. You stood out, sinfully, as a teen. And now, endlessly through life, can never quite get it right. With that lot. Why do you care so much?

What a thrill when you were named Godmother of the Golden Flower. It was a one-up on everyone else in the group. You, the chosen one, and by Queen Mignon, no less. There were all the lovely connotations of the title, not least a deepening of the relationship; just as marriage feels like a deepening between two people who really needn't bother with such an archaic ritual – yet do. You said yes to the gift of the position solemnly, thoughtfully, because you had an innate yearning for ritual, for the ceremonial pauses that charge a life journey with meaning like a lamp-lighter's glow along a darkened path. The request felt like a maturing, a stepping up to the mark, to provide a child with an anchor point of calm in an increasingly jittery, anxious and godless existence. Were you worthy of the title? Not sure. Had it made Cin a better person? No. But oh, the joy of the endless teasing about whether you were really Fairy or Wicked flavouring her growing up; she just couldn't decide; veered to the darker iteration more often than not, with a gappy, cheeky grin. All the laughs.

You fear for Tony out there, with them. Cin has a disdain for certain people. She can be thoughtlessly indifferent towards anyone she's not invested in. She blithely wanted to be rid of your Daisy once; the dog you thought she adored. She suddenly, ruthlessly, wanted a puppy instead. Declared you must get a new one as soon as Daisy died and for a while you were afraid she'd poison her. You marvelled at the muscular need when Cin really, really wanted something; it was a life force. A callousness. You had it too when young, before life softened you into noticing the world around you. Told you to be kind. Because you were a girl.

Cin is careless with her love and Mig falls for it every time, like a lovestruck teenage boy. Mig used to declare, with a sigh, she was her daughter's 'slavey' and Cin would laugh and squeal, 'Yes!' and reel in her mum even tighter. Her godmother, too. Tina Fey said having a teenage daughter is like being in the thick of an unrequited office crush and yes, oh yes. Have you both created a monster here, facilitated this, whatever it is. Like two mesmerised mothers with their first-born sons who they cannot get enough of and do everything for. Is this what women have always done, to unwittingly cement the patriarchy? Raised their sons as gods. Gods in waiting. Of our planet. Cin is a woman of the new world, yes, a Furiosa of the future and as a feminist you celebrate it; but, but. She frightens you.

Because of where this might end up.

Edith Wharton wrote of a curtain of niceness that befalls young women during adolescence, during that disorienting time when they're taught to mute themselves. When they shut off the wellspring of who they really are. Cin never has. Doesn't understand meekness, quietness, acquiescence. Scoffs at being silenced. Why would someone do that to her? She has to learn how to be in the world, as a girl. Hasn't yet. Maybe never will.

In the newly minted role of fairy godmother you wrote down little lamp-lights of observation for the journey ahead of that inky-haired bud of a baby and slipped them into a christening card with a tiny, silver Tiffany & Co crucifix. You wished Cin courage. Not to dim her light among men. Because so many women do. There's the pressure to soften so much. Appetites, wants, spark. Intelligence. Honesty. You wished Cin one true friend. Like you had in her own mother, because, you wrote, if you have the solace of that one person you can forgive all the rest. Irony, much. You wished her the courage to distance herself from people who wanted to flatten her. Because they'd try, throughout her life, they'd see her spark and want it snuffed. You hoped, all those years ago, that Cin would cultivate friends for what's in their heart and not for how they look or what they do. Or what they could do for her.

She succeeded with The Cins. They're a good bunch. Will end up good people and isn't that all you want as parents. You tell Cara and Maude now, and Hugo and Tink, and Beth and Richard as they come and go from your marquee during this suspended day. You give them as much time as they need. Tell them their girls are good eggs and they'll be looking after one another and they should be proud of that. Hugo looks at you like, really, as if everything you say is a lie.

You wished Cin freedom from fear. From what other people thought of her. You wished her a wariness of that reducing little word 'dependent', for it means letting ourselves be controlled by another person and there's a whiny unhealthiness in it. You encourage all senior Koongalettes to stride into an independent life, financially, mentally and socially. Whispers from the top end of town: that Koongala is one of those girl-power type schools, breeding fierce little chicks who like to peck. Excellent. You wished Cin the valour at some point to throw away the map, as you do all your girls; to walk away from the life prescribed for them. You never tell their parents this. You wish them an appreciation of failure because seeing others strive and fail, and strive again, spurs us all on, for we're witnessing the indomitable human spirit in action. You wished Cin strength to respond to her inner voice, because it was always seeking goodness, happiness and peace for her. You wished her that beautifully quiet word, grace, and the courage in kindness. A nourishing sense of empathy. Curiosity in abundance. And creativity. To exhilarate her, still her down, nurture her.

Her mother is the pole star for all that, you told Cin once. Mig's muscular ceramic urns, vases and bowls look like they've emerged from the depths of the sea, all tentacles, barnacles and anemones, all undulating seaweedy loveliness. Yet they have razor-sharp edges. You've drawn blood on them. 'At last, my wicked stepmother pricks her thumb!' Cin yelled in triumph and promptly put your digit in her mouth to stem the bleeding. Mig is now collected all over the world for her witty commentaries on nature, domesticity and the feminine mystique. She's had the courage to expose herself creatively throughout her adult life, to risk, and to pick herself up and keep going when the male gatekeepers and critics ignored her. She's only now coming into her own financially, in her fifties, as her work is finally noticed. Did you ever ask her to take over payment of Cin's school fees? No, not even as your relationship disintegrated. You'd never do that. You love Cin too much.

In conclusion you wished your god-daughter bravery. To be honest. To go against the grain. To stand up for herself and others. Because you know there are only two ways to live: as a victim or a fighter, and you wished her the courageous latter. And most fervently of all you wished her requited love. A vivid heart. That it may never be crushed. At Cin's christening you shut your eyes in prayer as you held her in your arms, for you feared even then that love would be her Achilles heel, the only thing that would break her in life. As it has you now. You feared that she might have a heart flung wide, to her detriment. As you do.

Your last, fated, wish for your god-daughter was the solace of the land. Close, always. You wished for the replenishing potency of it like liquid gold through her veins. Which is why you feel she'll be alright now, you think, hope. That they'll all be okay. Oh God, please, yet hope is wobbling as the day lengthens, as night falls yet again. You walk to the edge of the clearing, into the bush, just. Wrap your arms around the smooth coolness of a ghost gum. And pray. *Please God, make them come back. I've not been religious enough, have been the pretender, hiding in cowardice. This will change. Please.*

Of course they will come back.

Wednesday

Beth is babbling low like a creek, trying to weave a soothing through all the parents now as well as herself, but shut the fuck up you just want to scream. Deep breath. Close eyes, and pray, a plea in the clean light of the clearing, away from all of them but especially the babbling brook.

You hold your forehead to the cool of your mighty gumtree, with your hands clasped under your chin, and pray again. Do not hide it. You've never done it so publicly before but it's good for the parents to see; Koongala is a religious school, after all. Two bishops sit on its board and the girls attend chapel. The oak lining in your small church was famously extracted from a bombed church in Kent. As for religion and you, well, what happened, decades ago? A veneration of ... what? Mystery. A veering towards it like an ocean liner subtly altering course for a new destination in the great ocean of life. Yet the destination? Unknown.

Once Mig and you pierced your ears with safety pins and wore black polo necks and ripped opaque tights, God completely absent from your world; once you were fierce and unbending pitbull atheists, sneerers in the mould of Richard Dawkins. Yet occasionally you would stumble across a church service and just … sit … the nerdiness of the action usually in some foreign place where none of this aberrant behaviour would be observed and reported back. Mig was never alongside you. You never told her of these secret assignations. You were too self-conscious. To her, Christianity was the religion that thrived on exclusion. The bully over other religions, sexualities, women.

Yet, yet, there was something all-calming about these illicit experiences, a leak through the veneer of aspirant coolness, a gentle drip, drip, through your restless, anxious, often bleakly alone twenties. You felt righted by these occasions, balmed. Lit. Still do. To the extent you were able to convince the school board of a religious seriousness when it came to this job, despite not being a regular churchgoer. And despite Mig's scoff.

In your thirties, as a young teacher on the rise, you sensed a need for something else. An anchor of some sort. One day of glittering loneliness you walked up the road to a tiny sandstone building that had been a coracle of solace for generations of fringe dwellers. Sat alone and anonymous, and let the music wash over you. Found yourself regularly slipping into Sunday Evensong, brought down into stillness by the spiritual enveloping of a service mostly sung. You felt calmed, bright; those evenings were clean, the shining hours. And highly secret, an embarrassment tucked into your life. You told no-one.

You don't do church as a ritual that's craved on a regular, instinctive basis; you only do it when you have to, to keep up appearances. The bishops on the school council don't know this. Do not know that Christianity to you is a patriarchal construction, created to keep females in submissive servitude. You secretly work against this ethos within the school; your Koongalettes will not surrender. Most times, in fact, you say no, it's ridiculous, you're with the gentle atheists on this one; tipping a hat to the graces within organised religion but not sucked in by them. But as you age you have more respect for the mysterious in life, can't quite turn your back on wonder. And sometimes – oh! – a little heart-tug. A noticing, an affirmation; a tiny, soldering grace note. Like at night, when you used to babysit Cin, and you would stand in her room filled with her sleeping and a great warmth and gratitude would flood through you, and again, in the wild places, where the silence hums. Antarctica's ice desert, central Australia's sand desert, or under a full butter moon; there it was again, oh yes. And yet again, right now, as you open your heart to God and feel a great calm wash through you on this mountain top; it will be alright, it will be alright, it will be alright. It is your tuning fork back into   stillness.

You walk strong to the parents. Who would like a cup of tea, a biscuit perhaps. Who wants a hold. Beth does. Then Richard.

Then Cara and Maude. Trembling, you touch. Amid tenderness and tears, which you all try to stop.

You have no idea where this ocean liner sailing on its unknown path will take you. It feels like it's veering towards the most shining qualities of religious practice – generosity, compassion, quietude – which have nothing to do with the strictures of the organised religion. Yours is a wilder, more instinctive thing, deep in your bones. Those who declare their faith now seem so brazen, fearless, bold; you admire them. Wish you had their clarity yet do not. You walk in doubt. Once thought believers were stupid. Deluded. What you do know, the only thing you know, is that religion is a miracle of survival. And there must be a reason beyond our knowing for its endurance.

You look across these mountain ranges. Know that places of potent spirituality do not belong entirely to this earth and there's wonder in that. Like this site now. The clearing feels like one of those ancient places that concentrate your being, if you're still and quiet within them, that soften your presence into something ceremonial and inclusive, where some echo of a long-lost ritual embraces you. It rings with a strange power. Was it a burial ground once? The site of a massacre? A ceremonial gathering place? Its energy feels poised and present.

Meanwhile the faint whisper of a tugging ... *it will be alright, it will be alright* ... as your heart flings wide, into balm.

Yet the older Koongala teachers, with their calcified Christian rigour, have no idea of the insurrection building around them. These teachers are like frogs in boiling water as the world trains a gimlet eye on their cult of subservience. Your students give the fervent young Christian Development teachers hell, in the coldly logical way of children; Cin a gleeful ringleader. 'Sir, what do I do if a minister touches me, like, how they do?' 'Sir, where does all the money go?' 'Sir, why is the Church so intolerant of homosexuality when Jesus says love thy neighbour?' As flies to wanton girls are The Cins; they kill deeply Christian men for their sport.

Pup rings. 'The school's in mutiny, Sarge.' Parents do not want to send their daughters in, actually, perhaps forever; the situation's too messy. Social media is going off about the immense privilege of the place and the type of dipshit parents who send their children to it. What to do. Should you shut Koongala down for a day or two, perhaps, to regroup? But then you'll have some parents demanding you stay open because they've paid for this right, and fair enough. You can never please everyone all the time. You instruct Pup to send out a mass email – the school will continue for those who need it. Those who want to can stay at home, no questions asked. This is no time for panic.

You are panicking. Day three, and no progress. You attempt to spread the wings of calm over you, to breathe deep.

But. Howl. All the wrong in your head is jabbering and yabbering too much as you face food from the catering tent yet can't stomach it. Haven't eaten all day today, are existing on coffee from a too-colourful catering van. It feels like an affront. Your girls got swept down a river. Fell off a cliff. They're starving and dehydrated with no way out. A pack of men got them, vagrants, schoolboys. Tony raped them, killed them, who knows what he had in his backpack. 'Dr Breen doesn't, I don't know,' Beth hesitates, 'have kindness in his voice.' Oh Lord, the two of you are synched. But she's losing the plot. Just ahead of you yet you're almost caught up.

The difference is that she's showing it.

You had always warned Cin against men like Tony without really realising you had one in your midst, because he was so useful. Warned her against the controlling man. The one type Cin must never fall under the spell of. Tony has to be told, still, on occasion, to tone things down. There'll come a time in fact when he'll have to be gone and perhaps it's soon. After this. He's responsible for one too many families leaving Koongala, no matter how infuriating their little princesses may be. But he's old school. From the time when men's voices would drown women out; reduce them and they didn't even know it; put them in a lesser, colder place.

Adela watches you. Of course. You nod and turn away. Feel seen. You have to get on with your day, needs must. Pup needs a promotion, yes, sooner rather than later. The confident beta finally eclipsing the insecure alpha. The world is coming for that lot, they've had their moment. It's like Adela can smell your thinking. I will not give up on Tony, you want to say to her but don't. More trouble than it's worth.

Adela's husband is from an age when girls were called Sharon, Nicole and Fiona and had affairs with PE teachers and disappeared. Now it's Isla, Arabella and Clio and they're aware. They have good skin from good diets and from being pushed into fitness twice a week after school plus Saturday mornings. Your social class – Tony's, Mig's, yours – never had skin or bodies like that. As a teenager you hated that other world for the ease of living, the way their lives seemed so effortless, creamy, blessed. Yes, the anger fuelled you. When you told Mig of your new job as Koongala's headmistress you saw the flicker of the sneer and knew exactly what she was thinking – why couldn't your talents be kept for the state sector? Why sell out? The money, babes, the money, and the newspaper profiles. The thrill of it all. The power. But you could never admit to that.

The endless day of nothing softens into afternoon light. 'Was this … you?' Mig whispers furiously at one point. 'Are you punishing me?' Her knuckles are white in a new clench. You do not engage. Her wild love is on full view now. Has a little baby ever been kissed so much, she said in the months after Cin's birth, drunk on euphoria. No wonder that girl is what she is. The self-assurance, the ruthlessness, as she gallops into the future expecting the world to bow to her. You would facilitate that, it was your unspoken promise, the ruse to veer Mig back. Which didn't work.

Yet Mig was careless with Cin too, as if she already recognised the female resilience in her; that we cope because we always have. Once she folded her baby in a stroller amid its pile of winter blankets and threw her distractedly into the boot of the car, before hearing the squeak of affront, of the child squashed. Mig's head was too full of a new commission; Cin was bent double like a folded compass. There was also the time when Cin fell off her bed, at three months, surprising her mother with a joyful roll. But the interloper always bounced back. You remember the fierce strength coming off her at her seventh birthday party, off all the cluey little females with their glary power. The hard edges, the sharp energy. All the drama and flurrying off, all the huffs and puffs of offence taken. Who's being ignored, who's excluding, who's showing off. The boys at that age seemed so much more vulnerable, clingy, needy. Open and practical, all surface. How complicated and wondrous nature is in its wily corrective. Why does the female not ultimately ascend? Biology, you suspect. The pull to motherhood with its need to soften, compromise, nest. All animals underneath.

And now this lot.

The Cins are very aware. In Year Seven, after school, they used to pile into a nearby café. One day they noticed a man at a corner table taking photos of the mangoes and peaches in that place; they noticed he was there every day, taking photos of the young ladies in their uniforms. So The Cins took photos of him. As a group they presented the pictures to you. The police were called. The pervert was caught. End of. You can't pull the wool over the eyes of this lot. Or can you?

The dread the increasing dread.

They tell you things now. You had something happen, when you were their age, and you told no-one. Only Mig knew, but you never discussed it because you didn't discuss those things, in those days. You were a latch-key kid, raised by a single mum. One day your photo was in the local paper for winning a public speaking competition. Your name, of course, your full name, alongside your suburb; and so your phone number and address could easily be found in the Yellow Pages phone book. Then he started ringing. The Man. He caught you most afternoons, after school, when you were alone at home. He called you by your name, as if he knew you. Told you what he was going to do to you. How he would remove your clothes. Where he would insert his fingers. You had never heard talk like this, had no access to porn, you were a good girl. And because you were a good girl you listened, in politeness, fascinated and horrified, curious and appalled. Why did you not hang up immediately? *Why?* It was rude, he was a grownup, you had never hung up on anyone before. That only happened in movies. You were terrified, you were intrigued, you were good, you hated it, you didn't know what to do. So you listened. And you still can't explain why.

One afternoon you were at school, late, at an art club. Your mother happened to be home that day. She picked up the phone. The Man said he had you tied up. In a secret place. He told your mother what he had done to you and what he was going to do to you. The police were called. The principal retrieved you from the club. Mig's mother drove you home to your mother. You remember how no-one made a big deal of it, how everyone was very muted, like they didn't want to panic you. The police told you they were putting a listening device on your telephone. A tracker, so they could find out where the man lived. But the thing was, to make the situation work, you had to keep him talking the next time he called. Had to egg him on, so he would stay on the phone long enough for the police to work out where he was calling from. You had to listen all over again, and he was empowered now, because he had spoken to your mother too. And she had also listened. The good girl. The good woman. Polite.

You did it. The Man was caught. A nice suburb, a professional type, middle-aged. The police had their recordings. He was arrested. You remember your mother's relief. Remember the shame of the whole thing, how he made you feel so grubby you never wanted to talk about it, ever, with anyone. And no-one ever did talk about it again. Not the principal, not Mig's mother, not your mother. It was brushed under the carpet like it had never happened. You remember there was a part of you feeling sorry for him too. A professional man, of good standing, from his lovely suburb. And his life ruined.

You were conditioned to feel sorry for him. Conditioned to feel that you had done something wrong. Conditioned to feel shame, your shame, not his. You were conditioned. And now, looking back at all that from the other side, you know how wrong and twisted this was. How bound you all were, as females. Flattened, muted, ignorant. This will not be your girls.

The Cins don't do muted. They are not flattened. Their language is regulatory, like the slap of a palm on your cheek. 'Not cool.' 'Get out of my room.' 'Get out of my life.' 'Don't slut-shame.' 'Let me be who I want to be.' 'My wave of feminism is different to yours, you're second wave, old hat, you know nothing about *my* feminism.' Like we've never been through this before. Never loved. Never fought the battles we continue to fight.

Clouds are closing in. A new, hard wind. Wild petrichor on the air and you've always loved that smell but now you do not. Nature is roaring, shouting its triumph over the puny humans on its earth. Everything from before now feels antique. The sky cracks. You hadn't noticed the gathering steel in the clouds. Rain comes, too quick, as the gods of the sky rage in a sudden southerly buster. The rocks are the girls' shelter, you hope. Can picture it. Elle crying. Willa shushing, with her arms a roof over the whiny shivering. Tamsin annoyed at everything, wanting out and blaming everyone else. Cin twirling under the shower in ecstasy, but then a realisation, a dawning. Of a possible fate. Of the ridiculousness now of being lost. Her clenched fists but no, she will make this work; her indignation at the stupidity of the world while Tamsin is laughing at her getting wet. She's always the one who laughs, of course, when someone trips up, because she is her father's daughter.

But Tony, where is he in this? Can't picture him. He's got knowledge of the bush, of this area, he's been here many times. He'd be equipped, with his water and whatnot. Why isn't he leading the girls out? It's taking too long. *He's* taking too long.

The rain subsides, the world is chastened. Police walkie talkies jabber as the rest of you wait under ponchos of plastic. You imagine Cin now annoyed at Willa but not saying it. She doesn't do explosion. Has never had a need to – everything falls her way. But Tony would be the type to press her buttons. Can imagine the fracturing around this point. Are they even together.

Liam, Willa's eldest brother, delivers her dog but the police won't let the animal loose in the bush. 'She'll track her scent,' Liam remonstrates but they say it's too late, the rain has already thwarted that work. Reluctantly he drives the dog home.

Everyone is trying anything now. Splintering as a group. Hiving off, not trusting officialdom, trying their own ways to sort this. Hugo is talking of a parent-organised search, of lawyers and private detectives. Why is this a crime scene, mate? What does he know that we don't?

Adela, in her separate marquee, is joined by her church family filtering in after work. It's good to see her with her people. It feels strong, enveloping. She needs this. Tony is deeply embedded in his suburban evangelical church and used to power in it, comfortable with dominion in all spheres. Sometimes you have to keep a tight leash on him. At meet-the-teacher gatherings at the start of the year, for instance, when he used to command the stage and go on and on about his family and career when he should have been talking about the school. This was Tony's moment to shine with ownership, of course; but you told him privately, in the end, to keep it brisk. He accepted it, with a mock salute – you saluted with a chuckle in return. He's good-looking in that slightly antiquated, suburban-neat, alpha-pumped way. A source of fascination and fear. You find him attractive. Have no idea if the girls do. Can imagine Cin's horrified 'ewwwww' at that. Every school needs a Tony to keep things shipshape.

The parents now stay in their marquee. Not talking as much. What is there to say. They laughed early on that their girls would be fine because Cin was with them; she'd be ripping off snakes' heads with her teeth and sucking away leeches and felling trees for bush huts. Now they're quiet. Spent. Fear is cemented in every face. You all dread Robin coming over to you with 'news', whatever that means anymore. Hugo is constantly scrolling social media. Beth quietly keens.

The temperature is falling, you can feel the bite in the air. None of you want coats, in some strange solidarity with whatever your girls are going through; you will do it too.

Marquees, caravans, media tents and waiting ambulances are separated, for the various groups, like closed fists against the world and one another. You're all poised as another lot of searchers go in. Will this be the lot to crack it. You pick at sparse food, because you've all lost your appetite. The bush cannot be this cruel. You're twisting a strand of hair, almost pulling it out without realising. Adela watches through narrowed eyes. Her suspicion is infecting her cohort. All the eyes, on you. You want to scream to them that you did not do this. It's not your fault. You have to bite down on your lip to stop.

No-one to talk to. No partner or friends are trusted enough. Except for Mig, once. The loneliness yowls increasingly as you age. Every night after work you walk across the silent school grounds to Daisy and your cat, Dot, who just want food endless food. Dot is new. She loves with the aloofness of a teenage girl. You crave the moments she wends close, all milky mercury;

need that medicine of melting belly warmth on your lap. It never lasts long enough but makes you feel, for a moment, that you're actually okay, loveable, normal. You remember touch from long ago, as potent as voice. Your father stroking an earlobe as he drove the family car, a kiss on a closed eyelid from Mig, Cin's bedtime cuddles; a locking in, a docking, a plume of warmth pushing everything else away. That makes you forget. But you're long past that now. Still want it though. Tenderness, somewhere in your life.

The police are trying to keep the media away. No-one wants them. The cameras in your faces, the reporters hungry for fresh angles. They're getting restive. Starting to shout things across to you whenever they catch you looking at them. 'Do you take responsibility for this?' 'What do you say to the parents of the missing girls?' 'Were there any concerns about the teacher?' You do not like this new tone. This is now a disaster for Koongala. Every private school dreads appearing on *A Current Affair* or, worse, *60 Minutes*, dreads being painted in the wrong light.

Yvonne, the deputy chair, rings again. We need to do more to corral the media, she crisps; perhaps have another word with that crisis comms lot. It's all on you, she says, and is this wise. Then the killer line: the school has been brought into disrepute and your management is being questioned, I'm sorry, but it's the truth, and we need to get control of this narrative before

Alisdair gets back into the country and he's on a plane right now, cutting his business trip short. You tell Yvonne, very quietly and very calmly, that you are onto it. You hang up as she queries whether you're media-savvy enough under all this stress and strain. Thank God she doesn't hear your reply, and thank God her position is up for renewal at the next AGM. You'll start agitating, silkily, for a replacement as soon as this situation is done.

Sky congregating. Darkening trees, restless in the breeze. Too much out there. Snakes. Thirst. Spiders. Rockfall. Others. All the falling. Failing as night closes in, again. Night Three, the obscenity of that. The girls, your anchor to life. You look across to Mig, gnawing a finger. Not the only one.

Broken by impatience you run into the bush, yelling for the girls as if they're hiding and close and your sternest principal's voice will bring them back, yes, surely. Police sprint in after you; Robin leads you gently out. Parents watch, in shock, with hands over mouths and bitten lips. You look at them apologetically, humiliated, scarcely knowing what you've just done. 'We're all under a lot of strain,' Robin says softly, speaking in the gentle collective as she holds up a hand to the parents and the health professionals, mother-clucking; everything's alright, back off. She soothes you down. Her superior, Police Commander Ian Jonty, says with frustration that your actions might have disturbed forensics. What? Why *forensics*?

The crickets are coming on, night is pressing in. There is mist on the distant water and in the hollows of the hills. It's like you've all entered another realm. The day softens into black, too quick. You move a little way away, to the pale twisted branches of trees like hands writhing in wrath at indifferent gods. Bark is draped like saddles over branches. The world is stilled, waiting, silence a presence. No closer to anything, except astonishment.

Hugo is furious. Unspecified now. He bashes a stick against a log as if beating a subject's back. Beth's keening has become sharper, directed at the sky. No-one stops her or goes near her; it's as if she's now beyond repair, stained by a fatal wounding and to be avoided at all cost. Everyone is afraid of contagion. Not even Richard, her very quiet husband, approaches now.

The sky is playing up. The wind too. Clouds glide across each other in a towering, theatrical shunting. There's mischief in the air; it's as if a mighty soul has just passed. You shiver like a horse flicking off a fly. Antennae ears, as you strain to listen to the encroaching black. A cloud slides across the comfort of the moon. Once you were the shiny Christmas beetle with its tough carapace armouring every bit, but now, now, you're all underbelly; all wildly beating, terrified heart.

Tink is quietly sobbing in a corner. Stuffing her mouth with the bottom of her shirt as if afraid of this unseemly intrusion upon anyone else, afraid of us knowing of her frailty, yet can't help it. Tamsin is an only child, like Cin.

Oh God, a third night. Fog nestles across the ranges, settling in for the evening ahead. The fog colludes, the clouds lower, the heavens reclaim the earth. It all seems to be saying humans must retreat, it is time; this world of naked dark is not for them. But you cannot.

How can you all bear the pressure. A wild beating terror yowls in the silence. You strain for the rasp of a voice, a sniffer dog's bark. Nothing, of course. The aim has always been to toughen up the Koongalettes for whatever the world throws at them. Will this do? Is it enough? All you know is that it isn't a game anymore. And if it began as that they'll now be too scared to come out.

Your body feels lit. Strike a match and boom, you'll combust.

10 pm. You wait, husked, for what you don't know in a star-abundant sky. The wind is up and mean with it, as if wanting you all gone from this place. You've always loved falling to sleep with the earth and air close, wrapped in fresh sheets that have the dancing sun trapped in them, but not now, no; and it feels like never again. A watching dog inside you waits.

But then, then. The calm washes through. As you remember and hold faith in the fist of your heart. It will be alright, they will come back. Your body unclenches with the balm of surrender. God is with you. With them. Prayer as gratitude, gratitude as prayer, yes.

Search parties now work in increasingly despairing shifts. It's obscene that this bush could defeat your wild fledgling child yet it could, so easily, of course. It's almost like she belongs to the other side. The wilder side. Her bedroom smells feral, musty, not quite of the civilised world but she doesn't seem to care or notice. She's a child of the earth, of clingy damp leaves and two-trunked trees and wrapping spiders' webs and racing moons and moist loamy depths.

The police dialogue is hardening. So much has been searched, so much expertise expended, bush trackers and canyoners and choppers, the best of the best. Yet nothing. Nothing. Nothing. Under the hum of a generator's light Police Commander Jonty pings questions at you. Ah, the big boys now. Bring 'em on. Do you think the group might be deliberately hiding? Nonsense, you retort, thinking of Cin, that it wouldn't be beyond her. A grand scheme, a complicated noticing, an extravagance.

Robin adds: there weren't boys involved, from another school, perhaps? Not that you know of. Wild theories now, everyone grasping at straws. Maybe they're not even in the bush but in an abandoned, windowless house, in some nearby town, a shed. You snap at the suits that your girls are lost full stop and need finding; parents take note. Good. They need to see it. Then you apologise to Robin because she's been nothing but stoic and compassionate through this. She is the better person, and you are unravelling.

Get some sleep, she says.

They'll be starving now. All the secret M&M's and Sour Straps will have gone. You know the favourites. Dark chocolate Lindt for Cin. Expensive taste, like she wants to belong. You also know that Mig will have bought a bar for her for this trip and grimaced at the cost; would have grabbed the chocolate in her lunch hour, the day before; would have written the word Lindt on the palm of her hand as a reminder. Routine and rules and certainty are how Mig has done motherhood because she had a chaotic girlhood herself and has learnt. It's evolution. She lives by the solace of certainty, as a mother, and it's worked.

Will the girls be sharing, behaving, squabbling? Cin and Willa don't commune quite like they used to, which was all TikTok dances and silliness and squealy giggles, boy bands and bikinis. There's the stillness of a gathering maturity to them now. As school progresses they're becoming weighted down by adult pressures, adult things; life is getting serious. You suspect their bond is softening but have no idea why. You told Cin once that all she needed was one true friend to get her through, just one, and you always thought it would be Willa. But now … you're not so sure. Tamsin is a bit too tricky and competitive, too hard to love. Yeah, Cin had laughed with you once, too much drama with that one. Elle is … what … the little follower, and maybe that gets annoying to be around. How predictably has the group dynamic played out in the bush? You ache for all their exuberance and energy and cattiness, all the tea, to be back.

The internet is now flinging wild conspiracy theories. Hugo is lost down the rabbit hole, anger vicious in his fingertips. Police incompetence. Schoolboys. Bearded bush walkers. Vagrants. The local rapist. Dracula at the blood bank. National Parks staff who've not maintained overgrown paths, not locked away danger spots. Swollen creeks. Sinkholes. Old railway tunnels and mine shafts. Landslides. School incompetence, oh God, because no, Tony did not carry a personal EPIRB locator device when he rushed back to round up the girls. Why the fuck not, Hugo jabs at you. Eh, eh? Yes, yes, his bad, yes.

Adela's eyes are on you, into you, late. *Just fucking fix this*, she texts wildly at midnight. Gosh, sassy girl. And, ah, that little word 'just', your personal bugbear that you've warned your girls about in assembly talks. The kind of instructive assembly your dear Adela would never have been privy to growing up. It's in her stance. Because the use of 'just' is a pesky little womanly tic, a subtle linguistic reduction. You've told your girls that the excision of this one simple word can feel like a transformation in a woman's life. Makes them feel bolder, taller, and less … well … female. You give examples: 'Just need to check …' 'I'm just going to think about it ...' 'Just want to know ...' Irritating, yes? Because it makes the teller seem less certain, needy, deferential; makes them seem like they're more than happy to bow and scrape to a greater authority. Removing it renders the discourse, dare you say it, more male. Your girls duly nod and take notes every time you wheel the words out. As should Adela, but you'd never bother trying with that one. There's also the endless apologising, which has to stop, all the sorrys and could we trys and hope you don't minds. It's about the desire to make ourselves smaller, quieter, less disruptive; more compliant and attuned to what the world wants us to be. We are socialised into self-doubt.

Fucking fix this? you text back to Adela, removing the 'Just' at the start, *ym doing my best*. Press send with a jab. Then read the 'ym' and groan. Because you have also told your girls to always check their spelling before they send texts, to convey professionalism. You've told your Year Twelves to get rid of the first and last sentences of their job application practice emails, then read them back. The tone is so often more direct, bold – and male. Yes? You leave them thinking. About how they want to present themselves to the world. Goddesses or doormats, in the immortal words of Picasso, a problematic alpha male himself. Goddesses, please, yes.

Deep in the night in the land that swallows people. You crave the fatness of normality again because what you have now is thinness. Of peace. Serenity. Quiet. Up here, in this lonely eyrie, where a huddle of broken people shelter from the rifle butt of the world. You stand in a rush and hold your face to a star-swept sky. What's up there? Who? Anyone? Feel so alone in this world. Unwatched, abandoned.

Help me, Mig texts. *I've lost my pole star.* You text back: *Trying my best.* And her reply pings back: *What have we done to them?* No idea what that means. Ignore it. Do not go across to Mig just as she does not come across to you; two women, alone in this wide dark, two women who were best friends once. What is there left to do. Say. You text a broken love heart.

Thursday

5.58 am. Jerk awake in your reclined car seat. Heart pounding over unspecified terror. The dream you were immersed in has instantly vanished. Can't catch it. Where are you. Ah yes, that, of course. No change. You feel like you'll never break now from the glare of this time. The spotlight of intensity. It like there's concrete in your torso, slowly spreading, hardening, pushing out breath. Making it difficult to remember what normal was like.

The air hums with silence as if alive with some malevolent force. Unseen, waiting, crouched. Daylight rips open the dark. So. Day four. Are they even alive now. Stop it„ stop. Knuckles are balled into temples to squeeze away thoughts.

You glance across at the parent tent, the epicentre of anguish. Are not the only one awake. Hugo and Beth look across at you, unsmiling, like they've entered another plane of existence that is beyond most humans. A twilight life of mere endurance.

A cold that thieves rest. You're curled awkwardly again, shivery in the unfriendly mountain air. The Cins will be exhausted. Tamsin will be fussing. Cin will be hugging her into strength. Willa running her fingers through her hair and forming a tidy plait with her cool, inscrutable almost-smile. Elle will be hating all the attention accumulating at the feet of Tamsin the beautiful, whose needs take up so much energy. Cin will sense this. Tony will have no idea of any of it.

Willa's never been good at the smiling thing. Males don't get it. She's meant to be something else, for them, the piece of meat she categorically refuses to be. Meant to be giggly and girly, reduced, easy, diminished. 'Give us a smile, love,' they throw to girls like her; want to control them, have them obey. Willa has always resisted. Doesn't get the attempt at dilution of her strength – eh, smile for you, what? She knows her worth.

Her parents just leave her alone to get on with school life and thank the Lord for that. Parents are the worst aspect of the job. The child usually obsessed over the most? The eldest, first, only child. Because that first baby is the experiment; the parents are still working it out. The second child is wily because they can't compete with the eldest physically – they're the cunning one. The third benefits from the parent loosening through exhaustion. Willa is the fourth, with grown-up siblings and it shows; she's the most self-sufficient, resilient and easy-going of the lot. It's benign neglect with consistent love and it works.

Elle is bordering on an eating disorder. Correction, eating disorders, according to Beth. They usually seem to spring up in the families of high-achieving parents, who breed in the child the crippling desire for perfection. Those girls who are always trying to control something in their life – weight, popularity, looks – but can never control the expectations of their parents. Can't they see what they're doing, you often wonder. Those alpha parents with their alpha jobs who have to win, never fail; and that ruthless quest encompasses the child. But Elle's family isn't anything like that, and you don't know where the child's smudge of darkness comes from. Your heart goes out to her as you think of her out bush, with the others; your heart goes out to all the Elles of the world. The ones always a beat or two behind the cool girls, who never quite belong among anyone. And shame about this one's face; she'll never be a looker. There's the knowing of what's ahead in the hunch of her shoulders, poor love, and in the self consciousness over her shape. Meanwhile Cin intrigues right next to her with her fierce prettiness. Does Elle resent her for it? Resent them all?

Cin's vest has multiple pockets and zips and secret compartments for secret things. You've spoken to them about the importance of pockets. They free a woman's hands. Make her stronger and more nimble as she navigates the world. You've told your girls that a lack of pockets is a patriarchal construct that distracts women from existing as firmly as males in the world, because having to hold a handbag makes you feel burdened and distracted. Perhaps, yes, you went a bit far with this one – you've always wanted a Birkin. But the senior girls lapped up the message. You're careful with targets. Mustn't ruffle feathers. You're preparing your chosen ones to think, objectively. To speak out on unfairness. 'Because we can and we must.'

The Hugos of the world never know of such things. Tamsin would never tell him, you're sure. She is a Koongalette, after all.

The aim is to not breed the crumbmaidens – those pliant petals in thrall to the misogynist, who willingly do their bidding while hoping for some scraps in return. Little sayings are sprinkled throughout Koongala's world:

A man is not a financial plan.

I want doesn't get.

We do not wish women to have power over men, but over themselves.

I don't need your sass – I have my own, thank you very much.

Lord, may we carry ourselves with the confidence of the mediocre man.

Well-behaved women do not make history.

A woman's place is, of course, everywhere.

I'm afraid I cannot be trusted around fragile masculinity.

Females, we get things done.

No is a complete sentence.

And from the goddess Ms Woolf: Dare to overwhelm the limits assigned to us.

Koongala girls are taught that women stand on the shoulders of women who've gone before them, the first-wave feminists who chained themselves to railings and threw themselves under horses. The girls understand that they've benefited from those sacrifices, just as they've benefited from the second-wave grandmothers and mothers and godmothers and aunts who've campaigned for changes to legal and political systems. The girls are here at this school, being readied to seize the day, because of those who've gone ahead of them and cleared the path. It goes over the heads of most, but not all. In some the flame is lit, to be carried into the future; to be cocooned in the daughters to come.

You have plans for a freshening up of the curriculum in your new job. Subtle but necessary tweaks. To put more female writers on the English syllabus. More female composers into music. More female painters into the story of art and more female scientists into biology and physics. Championing the neglected and brushed aside, the stolen from and forgotten. For the nation's boys as much as its girls. In terms of the boys: to show them that women can be leaders and gatekeepers in creativity and innovation; to accept and expect this. And for the girls: well, it's that old trope. You cannot be what you cannot see.

With the Presentation Day speech on the last day of school you always make one request – that the girls spend one whole day in pyjamas, in bed, over the holidays. Because they deserve it. Alumnae repeat many of your famous little mantras back to you but this one is the winner by far, especially at reunions. You can tell the women who continue to stay in bed all day, in pyjamas, into adulthood. Smile at them. Enigmatically. Oh, you know.

Morning light is soft like a cat's paw from behind a curtain. You stretch into it. Onward. I want doesn't get I want doesn't get. Is it some cosmic joke. You look at the parents around you stumbling into the day. You're still trapped with one another and it feels like your whole lives, now, will forever be entwined. Hugo and you, eternally bound like drug dealers chained together and thrown off a boat. Great. Adela. Mig.

Robin asks if you'll give the media a quick briefing. No is a complete sentence, you tell her. Robin cocks her head, smiles, raises a thumb.

No thank you, not today and not ever. It's the word of the peri-menopausal woman who's finally found her voice. You tell select Koongalettes it's taken you decades to be free from the shackles of that obedient female Yes. That it's exhilarating to be rid of all the restrictive societal bindings – and one day, perhaps, they will be too.

A terrifying want is curled within, a need when it comes to the new job. The life plan, which kept you awake most of last night, was to retrieve the new job however you can. Because this is your only life, and this new job is your last chance to make a difference. You've been existing for too long within Koongala as if a great thumb of pressure is pushing down on you and never letting up, and you've just about had enough. But you worry that this new position is slipping through your fingers like sand the longer those girls are not found. 'On hold.' Fuck that.

Yet, yet. So many women around you are breaking free from the expected trajectory. Quitting jobs. Divorcing. Enrolling in a course. Opening a shop. Realising the dream, at last, in the little time they have left. To be trapped in a life, unable to simplify it – what greater torment? But a woman single by choice and exhilarated by it is a dangerous thing. They know it. Don't care. You're not quite ready for the great release into that next stage of living, the third trimester of existence; but the next leg of your career, oh yes. Bring it on. If you can.

Adela is shaking her head like there's no hope left. Beth is openly weeping. Your brain feels like a diver in the darkest depths, crushed under the weight of speculation. You want to break from your spinning thoughts and shout defensive words to everyone, this isn't my fault. You shut your eyes, scrambling for a God, an anchor, anything; promising you'll do whatever is wanted to get them all back. Have this stopped. A hostage now to absence.

Are there boys out there? Men? The girls don't know the power of their bodies, the gazes that follow them, eyes and licked lips, the intrigue of who they are to everyone else. Especially in a pack. They walk around with their bikini slivers and itty-bitty shorts and crop tops but you cannot judge, no-one can, you can't say anything in concern or admonishment. This is their choice. But they don't know their power. Their susceptibility.

It has rained again overnight. Clothes will be wet. Of course there'll be leeches out there. Cin hates them too, it's the one thing she's afraid of, she's told you. Alongside dentists. And thick ankles. And being shorter than her mother – and turning into her.

9.04 am. Tink walks across to you in hardening morning light, arms crossed in defensiveness around her shoulders. Tells you that 'Fuck off, Mum' were her daughter's last words on the day they left; that Tamsin batted her away, laughing in something like disdain at the posse of women all jostling for their show-off Facebook shots. Tink wanted a picture of her daughter with the girlies because they were all catapulting into adulthood too fast. Removing themselves, determinedly, from their parents' hover. Tink's glittery smile. 'I couldn't catch it. My last shot. They were gone too quick.'

And then there was your Golden Flower, running off with her gang without a thank you to Mig for dropping her to school. You saw it from a distance and your heart twisted at the thoughtlessness. Yet her mother never minded that behaviour because there was the awe and the bliss that she was the creator of this, the wonder at so much dazzling life. Plus the two of them could always talk in the capsule of their car on the way to school, where Mig had Cin trapped and safe. Alive. That was the endless challenge, to keep her out of harm's way. There was no rest. Because high jinks, taking chances and risk seemed hardwired into Cin.

Past tense. Must stop that.

10.23 am. Mig still asleep, in the front seat of her little Mazda with her forehead resting against the window. You feel such tenderness for her. She looks beatific over there. Her face has been beautiful since she was a child but it's softened and rounded over the years, with a feathery, vulnerable grey at her temples. She looks so much like her mother now, so much like the woman you knew during your growing up. Mig is radiant with age but thickening like you and you're pleased there's this in common. That peri-menopause stole both your waists. That from the side you're both starting to look like Lego bricks. Safety in numbers.

You resist the urge to open Mig's door, to put a blanket over her, to straighten her into comfort. She's barely slept these past few days and needs to gulp this moment of rest. Should hate her yet can't. She left you stranded in the rubble of loneliness. No-one else knows of the explosive fight over the Click Club, over her girl. Mig didn't want you in her life and you were so busy, for so long, you barely noticed. Until you did. Consumingly. Still feel the trauma, the breathlessness, the panic and shame; the social failure around feeling too much. You were made to think you were wrong. Mig broke your confidence and perhaps she'd been waiting her whole life to do that. To have you crushed. But now, just tenderness. For your old friend curved so inadequately in her car seat, just like she used to on road trips once, when you'd find a car blanket covered in dog hair and put it over her.

Cin was – *is* – always more honest with her brutality. She told her mother she wanted Mig to get married then divorced so she could have two bedrooms and two Christmases with two lots of presents; 'I'm not greedy. Well … yeah.' There's a chip of ice in them both. Gaden calls Cin, affectionately, The Bin Chicken, because she leans over tables and steals food from everyone else. She calls him Little Mouse in return. Gets away with it and you had laughed when she told you, laughed as Cin punched the air in cheeky triumph. 'That's me. Bin Chicken!' It is the magnificence of the new woman, and you and her mother are both putty in the face of it.

What do teenage boys make of these girls, so bright with their brazenness? The lost boys following the Jordan Petersons and Andrew Tates of the world; boys who might be out there now with your girls. It's getting tougher for young women, if at all possible; you can feel the world hardening around them because they're so obvious with their disdain and contempt. Why bother with the men of the old ways, that dinosaur lot? Yet the dinosaurs still roar. Trample and destroy with indignation and affront. At being caught out.

You saw the film *My Brilliant Career* with Mig when you were both thirteen. Left the cinema wailing, 'She didn't marry Harry' – it became your mantra during the high school years. A periodic wail of despair over a heroine who didn't run off with the hot bloke. How very dare she. Sybylla left Harry for her brilliant career, to live freely with an exhilarating mind – and as teenagers you did not approve. Yet when Mig took Cin, Willa and Tamsin to the play of *My Brilliant Career*, a generation later, the girls left the theatre debating whether Sybylla was pan, bi or lesbian – and the question of marrying Harry never entered the equation. Because, well, why would she? When a gloriously wide world awaited her, of satisfying work and freedom, in a brilliant life.

Cin posted about seeing that play with her besties, minus Elle, on opening night. Mixing with the stars of the latest teen streaming hit. Your intake of breath when you saw the post – *why* do so many of these girls never make their accounts private? Among the *u r sexy!* and *so pretty* and *eeeek so cute* and *u r a lol* and *fckn miss u so much* there was snark; the clag of envy in the jealousy factory that is Instagram. *Thnx for the invite* and *ewwwww* and the like. Elle, God love that brave little outlier, posted a solitary sad face emoji, which said everything about her exclusion from the coveted set. You felt her pain. Social media would have crushed you as a teen.

The morning lengthens. Enters the time of no shadows. Mig is still asleep, no-one wakes her. You check her breathing, the rising and falling of her chest, through the car window. She used to like her pills once, pre-motherhood, just checking.

A stirring. Left-hand edge of the clearing, an area no-one is concentrating on. A kerfuffle. Shouts. People run from all corners of the camping ground like cats to an injured bird. You rouse Mig before sprinting over yourself.

A squeal of a whoop, abruptly halted. Maude stops at the sound like a whipcrack in the air. Screams at the sudden knowing. A clot of activity, police holding you back. It is, oh God, Willa, Willa, that glorious girl. Cara runs from a portaloo yelling what, what. You fall to your knees in flooding thanks.

The teen stumbles into the clearing like she's been expelled violently from the bush; she trips and falls as if coming to the finishing line at last of a gruelling race she has won. A paramedic reaches out to catch her but her mothers angle in, moving with ferocious intent. Mine! Away! Mine! The rest of you are silent, standing back at the reverence of this moment; at the private tenderness of a holding that feels like it will never stop.

So. One returned, and who, who is next. There must be a next. Of course. Must. Searchers run into the bush, other parents. You want to also, desperately, but your priority is being here with your student, your alive student, your beautiful miracle girl.

Half an hour later, Tamsin. Carried in the arms of a fireman. She is unconscious – no – 'It's okay, she's asleep,' says her rescuer in astonishment. 'Fucking fabulous sleeping. I found her leaning against a tree. In a bed of ferns. It was like she'd been placed there. As soon as I lifted her she fell asleep, just like my toddler does.' He is crying now, a grown man crumbled. The crowd swarms.

Oh God. Oh God. Thank you. Hugo stabs the air in triumph, Tink holds her hands to the sky in worshipful thanks. Tamsin wakes. Is helped into a standing, a walking. Guarded, as if hello, oops, sorry, what's the fuss. Holding herself in, not giving away much. But then she catches sight of her parents and strangers and flashing lights and police and it is like she is suddenly unspelled, in that moment; she stands there and screams as she enters civilisation, in joy or terror or release. Her cry is unearthly, like nothing heard from a child before. From a human. What's gone on out there? Something feels jagged, off. Then Willa's maniacal laughter joins the hubbub as an ambulance is clocked alongside a bristle of police. As if it's the last thing she wants. Jagged, off, yes.

And only two? Your heart tightens. Just two. No. Surely. God could not be this cruel. Willa and Tamsin are engulfed by a great swelling of relief, from all of you, like a wave breaking upon the sand. Chuff exploding in your chests. Two back and of course there'll be more. Surely. Hugo pushes through the cram of first responders to get to his daughter, 'Make way, she's mine, get off.' Tink sobs. Willa's Cara won't let go of her girl and two medics move in to gently, so very gently, prise her off.

You stand a little apart, watching the clustering of euphoria, the heady swirl of this rescue, the foil blankets and raised mobile phones and astonished laughter and applause. Close eyes, in gratitude. Sky slips through you like the sun's blade.

But. But. Then. Minutes lengthening into the yawning absence of anyone else. Willa and Tamsin not talking, bewildered and shaking their heads, no they don't know where the others are, what, what are you talking about, and then a lapse into the enormity of rest, relief, silence. Minutes threaten to slip into hours. The huge hole at the centre of this. You glance across at Mig, arrowed to the bush where Tamsin and Willa came out. Her mouth is tense, lips gone. She's white as if emerging from an extended bout of migrainous vomiting. She catches your eye. A shield of no, go away, stop this hell. Beth claws at her hair in rhythmical strokes, in impatience, despair, frustration, all of it you presume; seemingly unaware of her audience. So close, all of you, yet not.

Then. Then. Too long behind the first lot, oh God, oh beautiful generous glorious God, your girl. Your Cin, your SinsiSin, Sinbalin. Carrying Elle into the clearing in a piggyback. From a section of the bush that's nowhere near a track. They stumble into the clearing as if the bush has vomited them out, expelled them from the gates of a very singular hell. Cin slips her charge gently to the ground then takes her by the hand, not letting her go, as if dragging her back into the centre of civilisation because she must. The two stagger into the clearing, half human half animal, and collapse to the earth and do not get up. Blanketed by silence, or is there a whimpering lost in it. Elle's left leg has a filthy piece of cloth around it. Dried blood. Paramedics fight their way through, whisk her off. 'We weren't – didn't – want but – no,' Cin mumbles, incoherently, batting the men away and looking from you to her mother like you're the only people in this. She's talking from a deep slumber that she's not quite clear of. Mig wallops her girl with a hug that engulfs her, shutting out everyone else, and Cin relaxes into the security of the holding and falls into a deep unshakeable sleep, which the paramedics can barely rouse her from yet need to, must; to keep her in this world, keep her conscious. It's a sleep of the dead yet Cin's very much alive; she's had enough.

So. Here they are. Your Cins. All four of them. You reach out a palm and hold it, poised, basking in the themness of them. It's like a halo of radiance around them but it is merely, miraculously, life. It's all happening everywhere around you, in a daze of so much.

Cin is in Mig's arms, then she's staggering to the ground, she's woken by an ambo; all glary with exhaustion, with a dazzling energy of brittleness and brokenness. She suddenly shakes her head and thrashes her arms, fighting the world off like a toddler jerky with tired who's caught in the thick of a tantrum and can't find their way clear of it. The terrible twos, the terrible teens. Another ambo looms, firm and sure and soothing. A calming needle slips in. Robin tells you that Elle's leg has a cut but it's fine; she'll live, she laughs.

Now Cin is sitting on the ground, earthed. Breathing deep with palms flat to the soil but then, then, she begins. Something else, beyond this. She starts beating her fists in a rhythm as if conducting her breaths. It reminds you of a drama technique she's somehow absorbed, to steady herself, before she bursts onstage. The other girls look across from the hubbub of their various rescue clusters, caught in the headlights of the act, stilled. Cin stops her tattoo, frozen; she is as suddenly silent as the rest. Like she is directing this.

Noted: the concentrated stillness of them all. Plus the deafening silence amid the rubble of elated relief, the voices sucked from each. The moment feels triumphant, tribal, removed; something instinctive and dark and of the earth. This is about them, not you, a warning and a challenge, to the other girls, to the bush, to the wild; that they are all as one and the rest of you are not.

Mig rushes in, as if to drag her daughter back.

You do the rounds, murmuring your thanks to the first responders, squeezing shoulders and slapping backs; smiling at your rescued girls, blowing kisses and raising thumbs, teary and jubilant. Mig is holding Cin like she is a quilt thrown over her, shutting out everyone else. You attempt to step in, do not get close. But, but. The crowd warmly parts to let you through; come on, ma'am, you're part of this. A laugh of shaky wonder as you crouch by your girl. A hover of touch, you can't help yourself. A croak of a barely there, 'Hey, Bin Chicken.' Cin looks at you and a crooked smile bubbles up from somewhere inside her, the old rogue buried deep. Your finger touches a bruised cheek. A slow ballet of hello. A fingertip dance. A tremulous tenderness. Mig allows it all, just. She tries to mouth something but her mouth won't work, won't let it out. You nod, abrupt. All so unused to how to be, over these long gruelling days. The human buried deep.

Your face since the vanishing has crevassed into Get Fucking Lost and now it is released. 'You alright?' you rasp at your Cin but she doesn't reply, as if she can't, because she's not; she shuts her eyes, trapping tears, yet only a single one leaks, just. So. They've all been through epic, wringing things you know nothing of; they've grown up.

You survey the wreckage of this. Something catastrophic has happened to these girls; they are changed. Mig and you both feel it together and try to herd them away, to veer them far from the scrutiny of hovery police. That can wait. This is women's business now, no time for talk, for anything but a deep clean sleep. A giant of an ambo moves in, a clot of wilful black hair on head and forearms. Cin scowls, shrinks. You've never seen her forehead scrunched up like this, it's etched by new wrinkles of worry. A grown-up face.

Something low and dark is prowling her thoughts, circling and not letting up. It feels like a slow-burning fuse deep inside, with all of them, in fact. Cin keeps glancing back to the bush as if something malignant is watching them from a distance. Mig steps between the trees and her daughter, shutting the bush out.

You look at each girl, from one to the other. Mud in great streaks is across their cheeks, up their arms and on thighs and in their inner legs; it's almost as if they've streaked it upon themselves. They're marinated in earth and normally you'd celebrate that but this looks deliberate, like some kind of ritual of rewilding. There's a strange, dank smell coming off them, as if they've crossed over to the other side, a wilder side. Clothes are half off but commando style, shirts are in turbans or knotted around waists, there are brazen bras and midriffs and shorts rolled on the waistband and ripped; revealing a flash of underpants, a butt cheek, a tear into places usually hidden. *Tuesday* blares the band of Willa's underpants, *Saturday* says Cin's, *Monday* says Elle's, as if they've shared them or swapped. And no sign of Cin's commando vest. 'That's not Elle's shirt,' Beth states, realising too that something is off. 'She's wearing the wrong underpants. They're not hers.' It's as if the girls have been on some secret guerrilla course involving strange bonding activities, joined a nudist cult, been weaponised against you all or gone mad. Who knows.

They do not speak. Apart from that first jumbled statement from Cin before she clammed shut like the rest. Too exhausted for proper talk, or words have been spooked from them, or they've moved into some mysterious trauma state. All you know is that something, some malevolent force, has sucked the sound from them. The mothers move in close, ringing their babies, keeping other eyes out.

And someone is still missing, of course. You realise alongside one other person, amid all the joy of the children returned. Adela stands there, ashen, statued, amid the flurry of busy-ness. None of the girls look at her except Willa, with a dawning realisation of something amiss. She cocks her head, stares, narrows her eyes then swiftly turns her back. Adela looks across at you, to do something, to save her. You nod, bite your lip.

You cross firmly and hold her. She does not shrug you off. You tighten your grip. Do not let go as the world bustles around you, will not let go, and suddenly realise you are holding Adela up.

A shout across to Robin to get the TV cameras away from their faces, get the media out from this. This is trauma porn now. It's a job to keep the reporters at bay, the police can't do it briskly enough. You haul out your principal's handbrake of a voice. 'Thank you. It's time for the girls to recover in peace. Move away.' That does it.

But, but. Something is off and you can't put your finger on it. The first girls came out one by one. Then Cin, who dropped the piggybacked Elle in a stumble and without pausing for breath fiercely clutched her friend's hand, almost as if she had to drag her back. Is Elle a close mate, really? Why is she with The Cins, why is she ever with The Cins. First impression: Elle does not want to be here. You straighten your clothes. Back to business, work to be done. Because these girls look broken and older, by years, filthy and bruised like they've been through immensities. It will be a long road back.

Willa won't look at you now. She's the no-filtered chitter-chat of the group. You'll need all Koongala counsellors on board for this. Elle has just slipped back to Cin. Has gripped her arm so tightly she has to be prised off by a male paramedic because a female can't manage it. You would have karate chopped it off, quick smart, but there you go. Cin rubs the marks of Elle then keeps her hand over them like she doesn't want anyone to know. Too late.

But the school is saved, thank the Lord. And your new job, your new life, you hope. You got the girls back, you righted this; and Tony will return soon. You make a show of hugging all the parents; Koongala is a family, a community. TV cameras watch from afar. Cin looks at you coolly as if she knows your thinking, ah yes, this is a business, of course; Tamsin too. Onto you. Right.

1.02 pm. The Cins are now siloed in separate ambulance hubs. Everyone extraneous is stilling in wonder, surrendering to gape. The vehicles have been poised, in readiness for this moment, for days. You survey the scene, the mother of them all, their queen, and tip back your face to the repairing sun. Shut your eyes to the beat of the beautiful red in your lids. Your chest opens out and it feels like two lovely wings are unfolding inside it, in peace. At beautiful, wondrous life.

The media are still trying it on. Of course. Robin moves in to establish a phalanx of industriousness around the ambulances, cutting off the view. You smile benignly at the reporters. Do not show them your contempt, might need them in future. Know not to give them ammunition.

Careless commercial television stations once reported Koongala, falsely, as the sister school of St Swithin's, the problematic boys' school too often in the media. The poster boys for a single-sex orthodoxy that's dying out. Rugger and razzle; the impenetrable wall of testosterone. The media trumpeted before checking whether Koongala was aligned with the boys' school whose students had disgraced themselves with a charming little ditty filmed on a train. The clip went viral. Straw boaters and striped ties. 'Chicks are made of tits and holes, grab 'em, stick 'em with your load.' It took a mighty effort to extricate Koongala from that grubby little soiling. And God help you now if some Swithin's lads had decided on their own, private, rescue party. The media would throw you to the wolves.

A quiet update from the chief paramedic. The girls are fine as far as he can see. Exhausted and dehydrated and starving and scratched, yes, but there are no broken bones and no stitches required. All that's needed are rehydration drips, a deep clean and sleep. You're drunk on joy. You stand tall amid the crowd, reaping the communal warmth; stitch you into it right now, to forever remember this glorious lightness of relief.

But Tony, says Adela's face. She stands alone. Right at the spot where Willa came out, staring into the abyss. Straining for sound, the snap of a twig, a footfall, a voice. Her assessing look returns again and again to the last ambulance station, still, poised, silent. Because of course there are five of them. The fifth ambulance waits for God knows what now. You turn from Adela so you don't have to see her eyes on the hustle and bustle around the four teens vivid with miraculous life, and on the silent ambulance station next to them.

Right. Not over yet. So not.

And you can smell it, the perplexing change in the girls. It's like they've walked out of childhood forever. Have stepped into being something else. What happened out there? They feel like they've been tipped into adulthood. Into silence, containment, watchfulness, rage. Tipped into adulthood, by what? They're tight among themselves. Something fresh binds them. It's in the sneak of glances, hands trailing like a secret signal, a flit of a finger, an impenetrable wall of silence. Where is Tony? Why hasn't he come out? As Cin gripped Elle, after they emerged from the bush, her knuckles were bone white and it was more than a hand held – it was a belt.

Your god-daughter smelt of the earth when you briefly touched her cheek; of wet blackened soil and dripping leaves, of weevils and wasps and burrowing worms and the stinking fur of animals and high screeches and forbidden night. You were addled in that moment of touching, caught in the sanctuary of her. As for Mig, well, you had delivered for your friend like you never had before, you had kept your nerve and seen this through; the nightmare was dissolved and you just want to bask in her joy now, brushing off the strangeness. For the bliss came and it was good; it was like God had breathed warmth into the bellows of Mig's existence and everything had been warmed up, with light.

But focus, focus. Fingers run through hair. It's time to move this world on. Get the girls to hospital for a proper check-up. Sort the parents. Speak to Pup, Alisdair, Yvonne. Get the media cleared out. The police move in, ordering lookers-on to step away; you can now shower and sleep properly at last. Because you feel found. Your pluming heart amid this. In a world scorched by wonder. God answered: your girls were returned.

Cin is placed on a stretcher. You dare a whispery tickle under her chin as she's wheeled into the mouth of her ambulance, dare a revealing of too much. But she lets you, in the moment, her guard momentarily down. Just like old times when she was a tiny wondrous thing. She shuts her eyes to you in an immense receiving. You hug her suddenly, enormously, ferociously, lost in a vast relief. The thud of your chests pressed close, for a moment; it is obscene, intimate, theft. You can feel the wham of her heart like a wild, terrified bird and you sense for some reason that this is the last time Cin will ever let you touch her, but do not quite understand it yet.

Back to your notes. So much, so much to set down. The girls all look like they've been attacked; by the bush or something else, branches, rocks, creek. The ambulances will soon spirit them away. You're not allowed in any of the vehicles despite enquiring – parents are, of course. You know your place. Let me know if you hear anything, you say hopefully to various people. Hugo turns his back, you are dismissed. Right. To return to your silent, waiting house.

Robin whispers, gently, that all girls will be 'checked'. A blank look. Internally. Robin picks her way through her words. Oh. To determine whether they're all, er, untouched, she adds. We don't know how they found their way back. What happened or with who. Eh? If they had help. Getting out. What? You bristle at the implication that your Koongalettes couldn't have survived this by themselves. Of course they could. They are The Cins. The best.

But please God, yes, untouched. You imagine the lawsuits. Hugo's bullying, determined face.

Tamsin grabs her mother's phone and takes a selfie with the media scrum behind her, then another with police and paramedics. Her mother asks to be in it; Tamsin shakes her head. The torment of the parent is writ large in the moment, the torment of the parent rendered powerless. She's a survivor, Tamsin, and seems the most unscathed of the lot. With her new silence like a coat that's almost a jauntiness. At being out the other side, of whatever this is. It is a thick, determined silence, layered over the reticence she usually has.

Cin shrugs away your assessing eyes, directed at her too much. But it's like she's changed overnight from being your cheeky, taunting, gobby girl into something quite different and it breaks your heart. Please God, no, not her spirit broken at last, that fragile fierceness you've spent your life preserving. She is knowing, watchful, withheld; her wide-open heart has flinched shut. You glance across at Mig, she feels it too. But won't engage with you, at all, just lifts up her palms as if in some gesture of future protectiveness.

The girls have stepped across a border into another country, another life; it's as if they've all gleaned a future they're now lost in. Are you okay, is the mantra from everyone, is everything alright. All the adult attempts to extract them from their muteness, yet nothing works. Where's Dr Breen. How did you get back. But all anyone gets in return is a silent leave me alone, rack off, go away, I know nothing; it's all in the sullen shakes of their heads. Yet knowing nothing is not the truth, perhaps. They hold you at bay with their secrets as they're readied to be transported together, apart.

Before the ambulances finally move off the police instruct you all not to confer. Dr Breen remains missing. This is now a police investigation, of a subtly different kind. The girls will be interviewed separately. The seriousness of the situation is deepening. Several of the parents pipe up; Hugo asks about legal representation but Police Commander Jonty's raised open hand silences him. Not the time, mate. The police want four individual accounts. You ask the commander if you can be there too. Representing the school. No, say a chorus of parents. They've tipped into a stance of protection. They'll be questioned too.

    Everyone   apart.

The girls wear their knowing like a helmet now. It shuts them away from the rest of you. At moments in the return they had gazed back to the sheltering bush, as if something in there would follow them out. They had looked across at one another from their separate rescue stations but did not smile, did not acknowledge each other. There is a pact of defensiveness in the set of their faces now, like they they have practised this. Something has sucked the openness from them, they're armoured up, readied. And quite brilliantly for leaky teens, because none are slipping up with it.

The ambulances depart with lights flashing but no sirens. The crowd falls back and watches silently in a huge army of exhaustion and hope; the battalion of a battle won. Inside the last ambulance is your wonder-find, Cin, like a depth charge of willpower as she lies inside her tube of steel within her walls of silence. If anyone is going to crack this she will be key, you're sure. Listen to my stare, her eyes seemed to say, as she was wheeled into the ambulance's depths.

Noted: The Cins all move now with careful in their limbs. Like they've been skinned.

And Elle doesn't trust herself with what she knows, it's deep in her body. Can't quite face you, can't meet your eyes. You stiffen your spine for the battle ahead.

Robin walks across as you're packing up your laptop and notebook. Mig has refused permission for Cin's physical examination, the internal one, at the hospital. It's a shock. The only parent not consenting. You think of the Italian Koongala mother who doesn't allow her girl to use a tampon, as if it will somehow sully her child; introduce her to a grown-up world not wanted too soon. She complained when you introduced free tampons and pads into Koongala's bathrooms. But why Mig, now. This isn't her. Has Cin told her to refuse permission. Does she know something or suspect it. Mig won't budge on her stance. 'She's fine,' she had snapped, according to Robin. 'Nothing like that happened. For God's sake.'

As the day shuts down a fresh search team goes in. They're focused on finding Cin's vest. On clues. About Tony. Adela's daughters, newly arrived from work, fall to their knees with their mother in a line of prayer. The sun sets over the mountains and a sudden chill comes over you. Your mate is now alone. With a plunging coolness in the air. Perhaps he was always alone, perhaps not. You look out to the endless wild closing over him for yet another long night, wherever he is. Have you failed as a principal. A colleague, a friend. Have you all failed, by not caring enough for the vulnerable lone male among you. Assuming he'd be fine. Assuming too much.

You look back at the cathedral of bush with its light streaming through the trees like tent ropes from God. They are found, your blaze of girls, and this world is seamed rich because of it.

But, but. You again hold your forehead and palms to a tree's smooth coldness and pray for Tony's safe return. Adela looks across. You nod in sympathy and hold up your hands in prayer and she sobs a thank you then claps a palm to her mouth. Between you both, a softening into grace. An older woman steers her away. Tony and Adela's church is a community that has fenced itself around her. There's been a constant melling of congregants over the last couple of days. Hot meals and blankets alongside a fierce, accusatory warmth. They turn the huddle of their backs upon you now; a wall.

But the girls. You can't scrape the oddness from your head. Little moments, little slips. Willa saw Cin and you embrace when she came out of the bush, her eyes a blade of open. Before Cin was wheeled into the ambulance she looked across at Willa and smiled with secrets in it. And Elle. Something so odd before she, too, was swallowed up by the paramedics – she ran across and hugged ice queen Tamsin, literally clung to her, something she'd never dare in real life. But this isn't their regular world anymore. Tamsin's not a hugger, and especially of someone as uncool as Elle; it was like a wombat trying to grip a swan. Tamsin remained frozen and unbending until Tink peeled the encumbrance of the lesser being away and steered the child back to its mother. No love there. Beth accepted poor Elle without a word and with a certain stiff-backed coldness. At the public humiliation, perhaps, at the cringe-fest on display involving her galoot of a daughter. Who knows. Who ever knows the dynamic of murky history between mothers. Sometimes not even themselves.

Paperwork, police dispatches, sign-offs. Frequent checks for a departmental email saying the job is back on – but not yet, too soon, of course. Yes, you are leaving the campsite and now you cannot meet Adela's eyes. You can feel the weight of dark glances, though, whisperings and admonishments from all the church people; feel their indignant sense of abandonment. But there is work to be done, so much, crowding in. Officialdom is pulling you back to the school yet you are torn, of course, this is hard. Just before you head to your car you stride over to Adela and grip her reluctant hands and rasp, 'I'm sorry, I'll be back,' before fleeing. She is very still in response. Gives you nothing.

Finally you fall into your Tesla's cold blandness. Sit very still, for a moment, in the cloistering of alone at last. Do not engage with the assault of local eyes directed at the hoity-toity redhead from that posh inner-city place; the curious have been gathering and are cordoned off. These are mountain people, doing their mountain thing; that insular lot from the place that swallows old plane wrecks, abandoned mines, ancient pines, bushwalkers. You inch the car through the curiosity-glut; it parts like two waves retracting. Eyes from other worlds check out the car and its blond interior, so rare in these parts, yet a dime a dozen in yours. You straighten your scarf in business-like defence, one hand still on the wheel. Not good in crowds like this. It could turn at any moment; you've lost a man, a good bloke, and you're a chick-boss fleeing the scene and you can feel they don't trust you and want you punished, want you staying, broken. You feel the fractiousness of gender politics coming into this.

But Tony, your Tony. How you laugh together, in your office, after a gruelling week, gin and tonics in hand and his feet up on your desk as you chuckle away at the most ridiculous absurdities of the school; he'd love to write a book about it all one day. Wanted to be a writer once, headline literary festivals, win awards, but life took over. You sit there laughing like two naughty schoolkids at the back of the class at the criminal barrister who stormed into your office in his lunch hour to demand his princess be taken off detention. At the two mothers who got into a fist fight at the athletics carnival over the affair both of them were having with the token hot, single, school dad. At the media proprietor barking the instruction down the phone, 'No comment, Allegra, no comment until Daddy arrives,' to his weed-languid daughter sitting chastened in front of your desk. At the rose gold Porsche 911 delivered to a girl at the school gates, with an enormous '18th Birthday' bow on its bonnet. At the heiress enquiring, without a hint of irony, whether she could supply a new theatre so that her daughter would not get expelled, actually, for spraypainting a giant penis overnight on the central quadrangle; 'You don't have to name the damned building after us. A new swimming pool, squash court, do you need one of those?' How Tony and you would cackle away at the best of the emails, pleading and wheedling and abusing and threatening or honeying you up, so obviously. It was all about control. Of you. Which you saw straight through. Tony is your release valve when the school hits peak madness; your punching bag, sounding board, professional confidant, china plate. Dear, dear mate.

And now he is gone. What happened out there? It isn't looking good after several long days; his chances of survival, utterly alone. Does your driving away look like acceptance ... that he will never come back ... and you know it in your bones? No God no   please.

He'll return. Raising his thumb at you, grinning and whistling like nothing has happened. And meanwhile a waiting desk at Koongala calls you back to its mountain of admin. Your home calls you back to a long, hot shower and the relief of a very itchy scalp, lovely fresh clothes and a proper sleep at last. Daisy and Dot call you back, as well as your students, the four Cins most of all. Yes, all of this calls you home and Tony would be the first to understand. And so you leave the campsite area at last, accelerating away from its access road with purpose.

Your lost girls fill your thoughts. Islanded by whatever went on out there, all they've got now is one another. They have you too, of course, the fairy godmother to them all. But you need binocular eyes to see into their future. As the media watches, and the police; as you all bullet into new post-vanishing lives. Trauma-free, you hope.

Your hands are fretful on the steering wheel. You suddenly notice the speedo, you're driving way too fast, you need to calm down. You pull over, alone, away from everyone at last. From the moment The Cins vanished the missing became the bully in your life; you were like an animal stopped in the headlights of the world. And now you can breathe out, finally, as you lean back in your seat, in silence at last, breathing out all the attempted stops on your life.

The phone rings on the way down the mountain. Pup, with an update. Five families have pulled their daughters from Koongala, they don't quite trust it anymore, and others are considering. The steering wheel is thumped. Five lost sets of school fees, possibly more. The board will not like it, Alisdair will know who to call to sound out. You tell Pup these very annoying families will have to pay any extra terms' fees because they've not given the required term-long notice, as per contract. Pup's hesitation. 'In these circumstances, Sarge, really?' You bark, bloody well yes. Rub your eyes, speed up. The complicated clot of never-ending, messy life. There's always a curveball from somewhere and just when you need it the least.

Have to get back to the office, to work. Restore normality, chisel the girls out. No, too soon, let them rest. Must temper the impulses, slow down, breathe. Mig used to tell you that all the time. So. You'll give them a few days of recovery, then when they're back at school you'll wheedle your way in. If they come back, but they will, they're The Cins, after all. Strategy: return them to regular life asap, for mental health reasons. A line that always works on parents – because they dread some kind of mental catastrophe the most. The shame, the helplessness, the having to explain, the dead weight of it in their lives.

Koongala has three psychologists on staff plus there's a backup of counsellors from the Department of Education; they are on hand for The Cins as well as anyone else during this, for anyone who needs them in the wider school family. You must reiterate this to everyone.

You drop in to Mig's on your way home. Checking in. She's back already from the hospital, not exactly welcoming but lets you in. Cin is home, surprisingly. Curled in a voluminous hoodie on the couch, safe at last. Robin told you all the girls were being kept overnight for observation. Mig explains, with iron in her voice, that Cin is home at her insistence and resting finally after her ordeal, which none of you know the extent of. Her voice tells you that's all she's going to say. A banker's screen of thick glass has slid up.

Cin, meanwhile, is like a wild trembling thing swamped by the couch. What trauma has seeped deep. Mig won't let you touch or speak to her. You look back at her daughter as you leave. To be so alone in the world, so young; you sense something new and unknown on her and are maddened by it. Between wetted fingers something has snuffed out her flame.

You head home, finally, to the silence of your house. Aldo, the school caretaker, has looked after the pets. Dot has pooed sloppily in the bath, as she sometimes does, in indignant protest at your absence. Daisy greets you like you're a long-lost ghost risen from the dead. The house smells old, as your grandmother's did long ago. It's a madeleine scent from childhood, a smell you can never stave off now. The musty cling of life's third trimester, an old person's stillness collecting in the corners, in the very fibre of the place. You're not ready.

You fling the French doors wide in your study. Need to flush your world clean with fresh air. Aldo takes Daisy for a walk; you want to but there's no time, too much to do, a crush of paperwork to clear. You sit at your desk and crack on with a barrage of emails, a torment of demands from parents, staff, board. Suddenly, a whirr of a swoop through the French doors. A bird, a juvenile magpie, slim with frailty, chased in by two other maggies who veer away at the last minute. The young bird flits in a flap of panic through to your living room and bashes against its French doors and windows, fighting for light and sky, craving the high blue and shitting itself in panic.

You run forward, horrified, throwing open the doors, but the bird won't go near them, because of you, perhaps; it careers around the room in terror, flapping and flitting into the ceiling, furniture, walls. You cry go, go, get out, trying to direct it with flustered hands, but it's as petrified of you as it is of the room. What to do, what to do? It is trapped, you can't save it, can't deal with this. With a scrabbling frustration the bird bashes itself against the glass of a window in a corner, and thuds again, and furiously again, then tumbles to the ground.

Silence. Stillness. Oh God, oh God.

You creep over with fluttering breath, hands at your mouth in horror. One wing is askew; the bird is trying to move it, to stand. Can't. Its wing dangles, useless. The creature holds itself in stillness as you approach. A world on tenterhooks. It stares up at you, wary, terrified, its wild eye the colour of dark honey. Eye to eye, creature to creature, and what next, what to do, you're too tired, too wrung out for this. It's okay, you tremble a whisper; stay put, you command, ridiculously.

You run outside to the garden shed, grab a shovel and gloves then run back and gently scoop the bird onto the iron lip. It's so small, young, helpless. Its colour is a soft, mottled brown – it hasn't hardened yet into the crisp and efficient black and white. The damaged wing – you bite your lip at the sickening wrongness of the angle. It's no use calling a rescue service, there's nothing they could do; you need to get this little one to the trees, to the earth, back where it belongs. It has gone very still, trusting. No choice. Tenderly you carry your wild creature to a tree you know that magpies nest in. Hey there, hey, you murmur continually. Tenderly you nudge the creature's brokenness onto the ground by the trunk, tenderly you tuck the wing next to the body; its bones are so small, fragile.

And hesitate.

Should you decapitate the magpie right now with the shovel; put it out of its misery quick? But no, maybe its wing is only stunned and it will flap back into usefulness at some point; maybe there's a mother somewhere, a family, who need to be here for it. Are you doing the right thing? No idea. Can't think straight. Head scrambled with too much.

It's only as you walk away, trailing the shovel, that you realise you're crying. Everything is too hard. You stand still in the cool air and weep to the sky.

10.03 pm. Just before exhausted sleep, Robin calls. The police force's top psychologists, masquerading as medical staff, are conducting advance sorties. None of the girls will divulge what happened. They shake their heads with the same line, with whispers of talk that won't quite come out. They know nothing. Never saw their teacher. He never found them. They speak as one, Robin says, even though they're separated. All muted, all shut down. 'They just need sleep,' you murmur yet hang up frowning. It's like everything outward and sunny and glowing in The Cins has been stymied, they are … anemoned. But by what.

A late email from Hugo with a whiff of drinking to it. He's bringing in the lawyers as promised. His daughter has changed, it's the school's fault. Ah, so even he's noticed it and is unnerved by it. Beth reports Elle is fast asleep. She's next to her on a hospital cot, worried but coping, just; Maude and Cara are with their girl and they're good, no bother. You don't hear from Mig.

The girls' silence is wrapped in a quilt of protectiveness. Their only protectiveness, and it feels like it's masking a great fragility. That they are driven by fear and adrenaline here – and that, quite possibly, the last thing they said to each other was, 'Don't breathe a word.' But you can feel the fluttery terror under the steely resolve. You just want to hold your little girl tonight, like old times, to tuck her up in bed and hear 'One upon a time' as you lean in to smell her strawberry-scented hair. She used to call you G, for Godmother, and Glammy, but all those exuberances have long gone; it's ma'am now, like all the other Koongalettes. Yet it's a universal human desire to be needed. Wanted. Like you hope to be, in Cin's life and Mig's once again. But your friend feels the teen revulsion too. Mig told you deep in that first night of them gone that Cin puts down the passenger seat when she gets in her car, so it's almost horizontal; she settles her

Beats over her ears and switches off, into her own world, so that not even their faces are at the same level. And that Cin's most frequently used words to her now are, 'Leave.' 'Stop.' 'No.' 'Go.' 'Unfair.' 'Close my door.' 'Get out of my room.' 'Away.' 'I'm coming' (but not). Followed by an occasional wail of longing, 'Muuu-uuuuuuum. You can cuddle me now. But quick. *Quick!*' Then the child would snuffle up for the fierce holding but in an instant it was done and gone. Mig feared on that harrowing night that she'd never hear those words again in her life, those meagre scraps, but now they'll be back. Lucky her. You have that need too, yet no-one who wants you enough.

The fairy godmother, of course, does not have children. She is – those awful labels – barren, sterile, difficult, selfish. You are none of these although the world will assume otherwise and tell you. Everyone is connected. None of us is alone. Or should be.

10.37 pm. A text from Robin. Adela has requested DNA be taken from all the girls. Right. This is veering into something else. You have to respect it; you've been so exhausted by the enormity of the missing students that you've kept on forgetting there is someone else, huge, in all of this. So. Should there be further investigations? You suspect they'll reveal nothing except the ravages of four days out bush. Robin says all the girls have been in water at some point. Tell me what happened, you want to scream at them, trust me; but you know all you'll get is a wall of blank. It's like they've been on an intensive drama immersion camp and have devised a uniform response and it's fiercely maintained and quite, quite magnificent. Ah, The Cins, too clever by half.

11.02 pm. Robin rings. The girls have been thoroughly cleaned up so no DNA was taken. A muddle of wrong, Adela's request came too late and she's furious. Should we have, Robin enquires. What? Taken DNA samples, from the girls, she muses. God no, you hasten, laughing too quick. Robin pauses. You can feel the crammed thinking. Tell her, gently, to get some sleep, she needs it and this is not over yet. Hang up, head hurting. Of course this rescue is good, optimal, yes. Of course you all need to celebrate.

But Tony. And the band of four cloistered in their ring of silence. In something like a trance, which feels like an umbrella over them all, shutting the world out. You'd be taking DNA from them, quick smart, you'd be insisting, alright. Don't trust The Cins as much as the police. You're not telling the bloodhounds that.

As you fall into sleep you think of a pinned butterfly, still alive.

Friday

A deep, deep sleep, the first in days. The oblivion of the jetlagged. You're exhausted because your life with your girls is constant vigilance, a readiness to spring into action at a moment's notice. Sometimes you even filch an afternoon nap in recompense. For there's always some fire to put out but it's usually a spot one, not this conflagration that now threatens to consume your institution. Career. Life. Your existence has been cloven in two by this: pre-disappearance and post. There's no past now, only a raging present. Future unknown.

Messages checked. You would've been called if, if, but nothing, of course. He's still out there.

You burrow further into the cocoon of your blankets. There's an arresting density to The Cins now. Their silence feels thick, heavy, contained. But your girls — more pertinently your girl, your glorious girl — are safe. Is that all that matters, really? It's been an exhaustive quest to keep Cin alive over fifteen years of her careless, flippant fearlessness. Oh, for the cautious child. It keeps them alive. But with Cin, no rest, no reprieve.

5.32 am. You jump out of bed. Today is procedural. Sherlocks and shrinks will be circling in a pincer formation, trying to get to the bottom of this. What is gleaned so far:

– The girls were well and truly lost.

– Tony Breen was never sighted, by any of them. He must be in a different place.

– The girls were 'near some river thing. Or creek.' That was the narrative circulating among first responders during the time of return and you have no idea where it originated from and there was nothing more concrete than that. And there are a lot of creeks out there.

– The wispy scraps of story that have been gleaned from the four of them are not deviating.

So today the dive deep.

But first, the garden, amid a cram of raucous morning birdsong that usually sings your heart. Yet not today. Your little magpie is gone. Probably a fox. You feel a prickle of powerlessness, of tears, washing over you like a menopausal hot flush. Hope the bird's family found it, that it wasn't braving the night alone in terrified abandonment.

Police are concerned about possible contamination of accounts. The Cins will still be kept separate, and interviewed again. An email reminding your enclave of parents is sent, then a text just in case. It's anal but there has to be no leakage, no collusion. You've dealt with stay-at-home mums over too many years to know how slack some of them are, bewilderingly, at getting stuck into emails; hello, what do they do with their lives. If you want something done ask a working mum, it's a mantra you can't spread among the student body, but it's a common refrain in the staffroom. Excuse me, but what exactly do you actually do, you've wanted to politely enquire of so many 'busy' mothers. And, er, Pilates and hair appointments, dog walks and lunches do not count. The Cins' parents are told to remove all devices from their girls and rest them up. So they can all return to normal life as swiftly as possible. For the best.

But of course the teens will find a way to do their Snapchats and Instas. They always do. They've been off their phones for days but they'll be rushing back no matter how much the parentals try to thwart it. When Cin used to be trapped in the car with you she was constantly taking pictures of herself, hand high over head, angling her face and thrusting out her chest. No idea why. Phones are banned in school. They remain in lockers during class time. Burner phones and smart watches fill the gaps, it's a constant battle of wits.

You miss Cin being in the car. Her dominating playlist, her incessant chat. Where have you been, she'd say. It all stopped when she joined Koongala.

You think she's a virgin. Not sure, but she's too strong to be controlled, by anyone. Except for a boyfriend one day who she'll fall head over heels for and then it will be bets off; she'll be lost. But she doesn't have that edge of sexual knowing about her yet, the hard veneer that removes a girl from the pack. It's a sheen of triumph and knowledge, of no going back.

There was one particular moment when you knew yet again you had to distance yourself from your Golden Flower. Cin, Mig and you were walking down a street on a summer holiday weekend down the coast, near the beachside cottage you inherited from your father. Cin was in an itty-bitty striped bikini, one of, oh, two hundred. She said she'd gone from a No Cup to a D Cup in no time, nonchalantly cupping her new breasts. You hadn't noticed, because they were always hidden under hoodies and vintage Adidas jackets. 'Look at my titties,' she declared, brazen and celebratory. Of course you didn't look, didn't encourage it, but what had happened? The full-on tomboy had become suddenly this and was revelling in it. It was intriguing to witness what puberty could do to a mindset, a way of being, a gender confusion as hormones roared. Mig and you had just let her be whatever she wanted to be. Yet you felt a sudden prickle of alarm at Cin's new body-familiarity and language around you; none of it sat comfortably, as headmistress.

'Got some tea to spill,' Cin used to say in her early Koongala days. Gossip, about other girls. You realised fairly soon that your

Golden Flower had reached a point where she had to stop spilling the tea, no matter how much you loved it. It was dangerous. You had to stop a lot of things. Friendship, companionship, love. But she'd started to separate anyway, to the point where she was like that kite soaring into the air, declaring she wanted to buy a van to live in, asap, and move in across the road from her mother. When she got her period for the first time, at your cottage, it was like she firmed overnight; stepped into a waiting room for adulthood. There was an arresting calmness washing through Cin at last, a knowing. Which is when you again pulled back. After all, who wants to be seen. She needed space to be free, to grow into herself.

New rumours this morning of boys following The Cins into the bush; boys with prior knowledge of the expedition. Rumours of gathos. Chroming and vodka and boner garages. Other form parents are sending in emails and screenshots, passing on titbits. Their child has heard this and that from an unnamed source; did you know the shocking history of this girl, that boy. These Mothers of Others are carefully, calculatingly, digging in the boot. Accusations of boner garages are a new low and nothing can be verified, of course. You toy with turning everything over to the police but no, this is a school matter. Better you know about this than the blue heelers.

'Boner Garage' is what teenage girls are writing on bare tummies. Adding, most helpfully, an arrow pointing downwards. The scrawls on bare flesh are then artfully photographed in bedrooms of fairy lights and boy band posters and lava lamps in celebratory birthday selfies. Happy thirteenth birthday, little one, and God fucking help you.

Your heart breaks for them. That these females define turning thirteen by those two bleak words. *Boner Garage.* It's an age marinated in symbolism, a fulcrum into growing up, when the world deepens around them – yet you just want to protect those precious, deluded young things in your midst. Boys won't admire the girls for writing 'Boner Garage' on their bellies and it won't stop them using them for sexual gratification. The experience will be desolate and the females will not feel empowered afterwards, they'll feel viciously lonely. And at the end of that reducing little event they'll ask themselves, oh, is that it? How I'm meant to feel? You know. Because you've been there yourself through all the glittery, bewildering one-night stands of your youth. Oh, is that it.

Yeah, precious one. Yeah, that's it.

Koongala girls are continually schooled on the danger of the electronic footprint. Friends of friends see their public accounts, as well as, ahem, teachers who trawl and all the dubious adults beyond their world. And out there, somewhere, someone might have got wind of an excursion they shouldn't know about. According to the latest WhatsApp gossip. Mind. Stop. It will not. And it suddenly occurs to you that your lost and found girls have other Insta accounts you know nothing about. You'll have to check every single comment for fresh clues to all this; fresh paths into new people and accounts.

Can't imagine any of your Cins writing 'Boner Garage' on their bellies. Elle, perhaps, for likes, but can't imagine the rest. Not the type. Too strong for it. The Urban Dictionary definition of the term is 'a vagina that has been pounded so much by erect penises that it has become a resting place for said penises'. Surely not Cin, especially, she's too secure in herself. And your girls are taught to wait, if at all possible, for a sexual experience that's about reverence, transcendence and generosity, because as Iris Murdoch once said, 'There is nothing like early promiscuous sex for dispelling life's bright mysterious expectations.' You wish them courage, whoever these boner garage girls are. Not to dim their light among men.

But what exactly have The Cins been through? On this fresh morning of return each child is huddled separately, shutting off the rest of you. Their hovery, anxious parents most of all. Text updates are received from four hubs. The girls aren't talking to their parents; and who knows what they've communicated among themselves. Their faces are blank. Their old selves have disappeared. Have they been drugged, brainwashed, can anyone say what's going on or have they been schooled into this.

Your take. Unspoken. There's a discipline to it; a strength of will perhaps controlled by a charismatic leader. The choice, for every child in this school, is to belong. It's a corrosive want. Is a craving for inclusion nestling deep within this, whatever this is. You rush from your house, need to get out. The quiet of this enormous building on the edge of the school grounds now feels like a barrier, an affront, a rebuke. A bird flipped at the life choices of a woman. You brisk off to work ridiculously early, before the hordes, because there's now too many questioning eyes to avoid.

Hands thrust deep into pockets. Make a note: must seed the idea of a Pocket Appreciation Society. The Cins will be in on it and it might draw them out. They seem bound by some secret knowledge but what, and why. You recall the French term *folie à plusieurs*, meaning an obsessive, delusional disorder shared by a group, often teenagers; an irrational belief transferred from one individual to others that catches fire and runs rampant. Yet the concerns of the tight posse are invisible to everyone else.

You ring Robin. Ask to be present in all interviews. A firm no, it's a police matter now.

Cin's the only child they've allowed home overnight. Mig's not afraid to be difficult. Couldn't care less what others think and because of that lives a liberated life. She has the fierceness of a lioness when it comes to her girl. You always note the single mothers of only daughters in the parent lists; they'll be the undaunted, tricky ones who'll bluntly call things out. Shut down. Block. What did Mig, perhaps, not want the hospital finding out? What does she know?

But they go too far, that type. There was the mother who insisted her daughter be given a meaty role in the school play, despite her daughter being too anxious to actually audition. Your reasoning in response: why give a student a role if she's too scared to actually try out in the first place; what message is this imparting if she wants to be a professional actress? Apart from how to be a diva. *You get what you get and you don't get upset. You are not special.* Yet the drama teacher agitated on behalf of the mother. Threats were made to withdraw the child. The mother won. Of course. Well, that precious petal would never be showcased again, because you do not forget these things. Why is it not understood: the best type of parent is the one the school never hears from. They will not learn. And the upshot of the whole audition drama was that every *Wizard of Oz* now had to have three Dorothys, on alternate nights, every *Wicked* an A cast and a B cast, to keep the pushy parents at bay. Sigh.

Parents are so anxious now, plus entitled. A lethal combination. They want to control. Have a say over how things are done. Phones don't help. Daddy is texted instantly if something doesn't go the child's way. Teachers are recorded. Recordings are weaponised. It's wearing you down. You've loved this job, but now you can't wait to get away from it.

9.09 am. All girls, besides Cin, are asleep in hospital beds, hooked up to drips. No phones, police outside each private suite. You never know who might get to them or what each girl might attempt. They remain untouched, thank God. Tony remains vanished. It's hard to think of him still out there. Alone, cold, weakened by thirst. Now cursing you, no doubt, for sending him on this blasted trip. No more whistling, no more grinning, he's over it. Must ring Adela. Poor, dear Adela. Soon.

You visit the families in hospital. Not wanted. They're umbrellaed around their precious returnees, shutting the school off from their nightmare. Which feels like inexplicable failure. So yes, still a nightmare. Each girl changed, and their families wanting them back.

Willa's mothers tell you she had a knife, which has been lost somewhere, and it's the only thing Willa seems devastated about, to the point they can't mention it anymore. It was an antique folding knife with a carved bone handle that lived on Cara's work bench. She makes linocuts and uses it often; Willa pocketed it for the trip. 'So unlike her.' You hold up a hand and tell Cara you will not be mentioning it, the knife is gone, full stop.

Willa will be asked about it when she gets back to school. You don't tell the mamas this.

Back in the office, fielding calls. You suspect the WhatsApping is continuing madly between parents. Your head is padding like a tiger among them into places it shouldn't. The girls' story is straightforward, isn't it? But you must call Adela. Later, yes.

Mig lets you visit, reluctantly. 'Make it brief,' she says, curt, over the phone. Your car nudges its way through the media scrum waiting at Koongala's iconic, black-painted iron centenary gates, which regularly appear in newspaper hatchet jobs on the nation's schooling elite. Stories of the funding unfairnesses of the private system, of the obscenity of the tax breaks. You do not want your Tesla appearing in photos. You will be judged. Trolled. You grip the steering wheel. Must accept, toughen up, brush off.

Mig's flat. A nondescript, rectangular, red-brick block. You park in the visitors' cramped parking zone. Thuds from the garage. Cin is inside, boxing with a punching bag; Mig uses this room for storage, and parks on the street. You watch your Golden Flower in silence, from its open door, marvelling at the muscular arms in their boxing gloves and the strength in the braced thighs. Yet so much anger in the jabs. Adult anger. She flicks you a glance, barely acknowledging you. You don't move, arms crossed. Cin doesn't stop, doesn't say anything, just flexes a bicep at you in a cartoon strongman pose. Seeking love, challenge, praise, perhaps. You applaud, silently. Say you're so happy she's back but your voice slips, chokes up, stops. Cin cocks her head. Turns her back. A concentrated stillness as if she's gathering herself. Truth feels rock hard and stubborn between you, an unwanted guest.

You ask Cin, casually, what happened out there. Get nothing back. Beg her to tell you something. Nothing. Say come on, please. Finally, through muted, rusted voice, 'Nothing.' Come on, Cin. I wasn't born yesterday. 'We got lost.' You tell Cin you hate uncertainty. Find it hard to live with because it fucks up your life. 'Really? You really want to be in this job, doing this?' Another jab, vicious. 'Fuck off, Sarge,' Cin suddenly laughs, 'this is not your place.' You bristle. You say her language is unacceptable; you are her principal. A volley of jabs. She's still laughing but it's veering into something else. 'Yeah? Not here.' Cin stops, breathing heavily, and moves towards you and shadow boxes so you are stepping back, and back, and back. She's nudging you now with her whole body, too close; challenging, punishing, pushing in, she's damaged and you're indulging her but want this to stop. Get off! you snap, why does everything have to be a fight suddenly, a competition, about what? Cin lets out a concentrated cry of frustration, anger, rebuke. At your presence. 'Fuck off, Sarge, just fuck off.' You step back into the wall, hands splayed against the rough surface as if you've been blasted into it by the affronted force before you, the force of a beloved god-daughter, blaring hurt.

Your eyes shut in a vast stopping. You say gently, tenderly, that you just want some certainty, that's all. Through closed eyes you can sense a crazed energy radiating from her, like everything is wrong in Cin's head but she can't articulate it, get it out. More pretend punches, more play but gentler now. You hold up your hands in front of your face, in protection, blinking. Cin suddenly stops. The glove centimetres from you. 'You're dangerous, ma'am,' she hisses, then pig snorts abruptly in your face.

You are?

Carefully you step away, using all your willpower not to shout in her face. This child had always existed high on a hill, in bellowing light, her arms wide to the world – but now. Balled in on herself. Diminished. Broken. Stuck. She'd always been so joyously, exuberantly … much. During the toddler years her scribbles were exultant through her mum's sketchpads, the cutlery was secreted off 'to Africa', Mig's jewellery scattered. More recently it's been her shoes disappearing; tweezers and shampoo and sunglasses and books. It's like Cin's raison d'être is to possess; attention, energy, sanity, treasures. But Mig and you agreed early on that this flurry of a wild spirit, this living force in your midst, must never be crushed. Yet how you wanted to at times. 'Cinnamon!' was the familiar cry of frustration. 'Get over here. Right now.' She creates disturbance, as art should, as women should; to upend the status quo and progress. But, but. 'Cinnamon! What have you done now?' Yet the child's sunny side was always so replenishing and consistent. Medicinal, as a fascinating new female of the future. So you'd forgive and forget and move on; recognising that she lives heroically, and be secretly chuffed. But now. What is   this.   What.

Speak to me, you say, talk to me like old times. But Cin is spent. She asks in a cracked voice if Doc D'mean – sorry,

Dr Breen – has been found. Sorry. D'mean, did she just say, what, you misheard, what's going on. Yet she speaks like she genuinely cares. What do you know, she asks. You look at your god-daughter, tilt your head. It's all rumours, you respond, everything, you have no idea. Cin glances at you like come on, are you serious. She *knows*. Something.

Cin pushes into you again, hustling with her new, charged energy. 'What are they saying, Sarge, come on, give us the tea.' She says that Tony – calls him Tony now – is a former navy captain. No, you say. Oh yes, she snaps. Why are you here, she jabs. Because I care about you. No you fucking don't, she jabs, ever since I've been at your fucking school. She says she knows Tony shot a cat once. Used a slingshot. That in the old days he'd bring former colleagues to his office during lunch hour, a band of navy blokes. 'Bullshit.' 'I *know*.' That he's an insecure alpha and they're the worst sort, aren't they, because you told her that once. Remember? No, you do not. Cin says she knows Tony beats his wife, knows. How can you tell? I've looked her up, she says. I'm good at online snooping and it's in her face. She's a victim, just look. Facebook. The face. You know nothing, you snap. Cin tells you that Tony has hit his nephew. How do you know, Cin? Because his nephew said so. He goes to St Swithin's, she says, my year. You lean forward. Swithin's. The school all the rumours are about. What rumours? The ones about boys in the bush. 'Scooch your cooch,' Cin commands. She's had enough.

This new way is astonishing, even for Cin; there's an unsettling edge to it like the flickering of a faulty fluorescent light. She's treating you as not quite the principal anymore. As if she no longer cares about consequences. As if some threshold has been crossed, into adulthood, and you're on the way out.

You both head back to her flat in a tight silence. Cin's energy now feels too electric for this small space, dark and shut off, jittery with sparks. You draw the lounge room curtains for privacy; to cage in the warmth, perhaps, or keep the media out. Cin smiles as if she knows what you're up to or senses a new weakness; it whips a lash into your heart. You don't know your girl anymore. Her brow is deeply furrowed. This is new. It's too soon for a teen and she'll cement wrinkles if she keeps on doing this; it makes you want to smooth the groove out. You do not dare, do not touch. Your heart is pounding. Mustn't show it.

Mig doesn't want talk. Perhaps feels shut out, too, or is afraid of what might leak. You suggest that they both come down to your cottage, maybe, soon, to rest, in a healing place. Yes? As a recovery place for all of you, you falter, a sanctuary. But no, just silence, blocking you at every step. Finally Mig smiles, just. She says she's never seen you calmer or more at peace in your little coastal place, but now is not the time for it. Or wilder, Cin interjects from the kitchen, or crazier. But crazy is good in her book. Honest. 'You should get down there quick smart, girlfriend,' Cin yells across to you, 'you really need it.'

You leave. Tell Mig on the doorstep that Cin has this strange new hardness to her, yes, perhaps, and you're worried. Mig snaps that it's all a front and you don't know her daughter at all. That she has a huge, soft heart, which will one day be her downfall; she loves too consumingly, too much. And as she talks you feel the abyss between you widening, calcifying into the dynamic of principal v. parent. Mig is saying something again about love and you respond mechanically, yes, of course, you know. Mig suddenly hooks into you that you have no idea what love means. Pardon? When have you ever loved, she cries, when have you ever risked it? You step back. Leave without saying goodbye. Heart smashing with confusion. Can barely start the car. Have no idea where you're driving, or how, until you pull up in a side street two suburbs away having sailed through a red light. You don't know where you are. How did this happen. Can't drive anymore. Must. Suddenly accelerate too fast from all of it, everything, the mess of this fucking week. Cin's manic jabs in your face. Her raw hurt. The consuming nature of Mig's love. Her fierce protectiveness of Cin. Her abrupt brokenness shutting you out. Yes, your friend is aching and jagged and spent and it feels like you're all falling apart here when you should be loosened, released, into lightness. The lightness of relief, over four girls found. But no.

2.35 pm. A call. Robin. A man has just walked out of the bush. You flop back in your chair in exquisite relief. Oh God, oh God thank you, Tony at last. Robin tells you he's not talking. Like the girls, you exclaim; what *is* this? A beat. A silence. Then Robin continuing, it's not Tony, not him, you misunderstand; it's a hobo who looks like he's been in the wilderness for months, weeks, years. Oh. Oh, no. Right. Police are trying to ascertain the man's name. He looks like he's in his fifties, sixties. Won't speak, wilfully. Has a deep suspicion of pigs. That would be us, Robin says, clipped. Seems like he knows his way around the bush. Open minds, thudding heart. No Tony, no Tony. Your chest feels too frail for this. For everything. Robin concludes, 'We're talking to him to work out if he saw or heard anything. There might be something. Anything.' Yes, of course. Anything, anything to help.

And then, oh glory and hallelujah, an email. It's back on – the new job. Expect a formal letter of offer early next week. So. It's fine, it's okay. You shut your eyes and breathe out in a colossal exhalation, and bask. The arrow corrects its course, the bullseye is found, the prize is close. The world has righted itself. Almost.

But you just want the offer letter sent now, immediately, so you can sign off on this situation and have it locked in. The wait, the uncertainty, is too distracting; your mind is turbulent with it. Patience, patience.

Phone calls throughout the afternoon with various board members and concerned parents who want to withdraw their girls. Assuaging them. Smoothing. Ironing out. You're good at that, back on track; you've spent a lifetime learning the words and the voice, plus the job email has given you a wave of positivity that sends you surging through your day. You compose a newsletter to the entire school. It takes numerous drafts and once upon a time you would have roped Mig in for a second opinion, but now it's Pup. He tells you to add a little something about faith. Of course. There must be gratitude, yes. You send the text to Alisdair and Yvonne for approval; they'll like that. It duly comes back, your words unchanged for it is note perfect, of course. 'We are in lockstep with the police and rescue services and are immensely grateful to them. I vow to you, the events of this past week will not define us as a community … we will move on from this … thank you so much for your faith-filled care and your loving support … Koongala's strong community remains tight knit, and I am proud of that … our four girls, and our dear Dr Breen, remain in our prayers.' It is sent out to the entire school body at 4 pm on the dot. It is immediately leaked. The media reports on it at 4.18.

All girls have now been extensively questioned. The police repeat that they don't want you involved. They're shutting you out and you're trying not to be offended. But, but. You might be able to crack this in a way they can't. They don't want to know. You tell yourself it's not your place to be at the centre of this. Cin was your project once, but now you must hang back. Detach. Yet you just want to hold her, and hold her.

She is gone from you. The distance between you now is achingly great, where once she would put your wildest earrings in her ears and tell you she wanted to leave her mummy and live with you. 'Because your Christmas presents are better. And I could wear your shoes when I'm growed up.' She made you laugh so much. But now, now, the love feels like barbed wire scraping across your heart.

And where is Tony in all this. Robin calls at the end of her shift. It's good she still calls you, includes you. Why wouldn't I, she chuckles in matey collusion and you tell her how grateful you are. She says the hobo was no good. Nothing came of it, he didn't see a thing. Dead end. Fuck. At 6 pm the three other Cins are dismissed from hospital, to what, at home, you don't know. You will have to wait.

Saturday

Tamsin's mother welcomes you warily into a harbourside house of no books, just as you'd suspected. A lot of glass. A sparkle of sunlight on water, everywhere, too much, on this severe clear day of hurt. Pup has suggested it would be a good idea to touch base with all the families, in person today; you concurred. Good for the school, the board, the narrative.

Tink wears sunglasses. You wish you had. She's thoroughly prepared for the glare of a marble and glass house and you are not, or perhaps she's been crying and is hiding it. Or been hit, possibly, by Hugo, yes. You smile, searchingly, in support. It would make sense. Everything you have seen of her husband, the fragile alpha male who must dominate and colonise and control, must win at any cost. You place your hand in solidarity on Tink's arm, she brushes it off. Thinks better of it. Pauses. Says she's got something to tell you, actually.

A tighter breath. You step closer, as if the walls are leaning in, listening. Is this it. Yes?

A nervous laugh. She says she's asked Hugo for a divorce. Oh. Oh, Tink. You stand square on, holding both her arms. She says these past few days have brought everything to a head. 'Anything I can do?' She shakes her head, she's fine, she'll get through it. 'You okay?' you ask. 'Really?' Woman to woman. 'It's freedom.' She shrugs. 'But ... I lose my daughter.' *What?* 'She wants to stay with her father. With his money and everything that comes with it. All ... this.' Tink assesses the cold, hard surfaces of her obscenely huge house, at the ostentatious lighting and impersonal furniture that looks like it's been styled by a real estate company for an impending sale. She smiles ruefully. 'Maybe I had it coming. Sometimes I'm not a very good mother.' You throw up your hands and say hey, hang on, is anyone? It's a bloody hard job. No mother is perfect. Tink laughs and presses her fingers under her eyes, as if firming away tears. 'I just wish we'd all be a bit more honest sometimes.'

You think of the mother Tink is, among all the types you've seen over the years. She's not the queen of domesticity who proudly changed her surname and now channels all the pent-up energy into rigidly compartmentalised lunch boxes and sparkling shower screens, which her husband never notices. She's not the mother competing with her daughter with the Botox and yoga-toned body while competitively flirting with other parents, in front of her child. She's not the mummy influencer who's made a fortune from Insta photos of her child. Not the netball coach who demands her princess be captain year after year, nor the mother complaining that the school magazine has never, ever featured her babies. She's not controlling and shaping, monitoring test results and tracking movements and going through school bags until the child kicks out in anguish; saying enough, please, go away. She's not the mother doing everything for her child – steamrolling a path for them, constantly saving them – which seems a fertile breeding ground for anxiety. She's not the full-time worker stretched in too many directions and dropping all the balls. She's not the smart one who lost her footing through years of motherhood and now works in admin in a doctor's surgery, brilliantly. She's not the mother actively in love with her daughter, obsessed and wondrous and unable to stop talking about her. She's not the best friend of the child who can't see that it's not wanted and can't bear to let go. She's not the hoverer around the school who will never quite leave, nor the tireless and stoic volunteer. Tink is bewildered and careless but there is love there. Distracted love. Wounding love – but what mother/daughter relationship isn't that in some way?

You both gaze out to the black-tiled pool, which seems to hover over the lip of land, hover over the harbour. Tamsin lies on a sunlounger next to the water in a white bikini resembling dental floss, all long golden limbs and luxe languor. Her eyes are shaded by large mirrored sunglasses. Tink calls out to her that you're here. Her daughter's face is unmoving; an unthinkable insurrection in any other circumstance. Tamsin is not the type of girl to work hard at putting others at ease, she has never been that female, and how confronting and intriguing that is. But you long to hear her cool deep voice again, that timbre like a silk shirt; Cin's, on the other hand, is a flannelette one. 'Tamsin overheard Hugo and I talking.' Tink pauses. 'Well, shouting.' Another pause. 'We didn't want to give her any more stress during this awful time, but … there you go. She hasn't really spoken since, except to tell me that whatever happens, she's staying put. With Daddy.' A pause, a sigh. 'Daddy's girl.'

A shrug at the hopelessness of this turn of events. It's beyond Tink's control. She seems utterly alone, utterly rejected and resolute with it; very thin and breakable. You tell her that you're here for her if ever she wants to give you a call, any time, day or night. She shrugs again; she'll do it her way, and you sense it's likely she'll never confide in you again. You tell her that Tamsin looks ready to get back to school this coming Monday and you suspect that all the girls are. A new email will be sent tonight, in fact. It will mention the benefits of discipline, of focus and routine. 'I could do with a bit of that.' Tink laughs. This is the start of liking her; the chink that lets in the light.

Willa's house is a former hat factory converted into a residence. It has explosively colourful art on the walls. Only one mother is home, Cara, the one known as mama. She says she's been feeding her daughter chocolate bullets all day, in celebration of the miraculous homecoming. Willa lies on the couch and says nothing; just looks, blankly, at the inconsequential small talk around her, barely listening, you can tell. Your future school captain, the one who everyone loves. You don't hang around. Nothing new here, no information scraps. Perhaps the bullets were to loosen her into talk but if so they didn't work.

Elle does not emerge from her room. Beth and Richard say nothing will entice her out. Elle has surrounded herself by a hedge of silence in a quietly despairing house. It's like The Cins are living by the rules of a secret guidebook, a *Manual of Invisibility* that is shutting the rest of you out. You need breezy smiles back, clean of complication. Tamsin especially feels contained, held in, watertight. The perfectionist. There will be no leakage. But Cin. Beneath her jabs of anger there's a new energy that's glittery with sensitivity; as if you went prick! ... with a needle ... she would collapse. Deflate. Something happened out there. Her posture has changed. She's hooded, like she's huddled inside her own world now and is peering out.

Fact: puberty erases confidence in girls. The cruelty of the female condition. Nature or nurture? Nurture, you suspect. The patriarchal conditioning that eases a boy's way through life dampens down a girl's. And puberty is when it hits. Why do we succumb? To that lie of weakness when we are not. Biology, you suspect. A girl's self-assurance is erased as she realises she must be nice and pliant and obedient to succeed the way a man wants her to. The result is a destructive self-loathing, even among the best, as they realise that what is strong in them is not what society wants.

The roar of them. Their vividness, bluntness, honesty. And how you've tried to preserve it, in your Golden Flower most of all. Because the cruellest crime inflicted upon an individual is the crushing of spirit. Yet what happens when the spirit of an entire gender is crushed?

4 pm. Robin's regular afternoon phone call of checking in and touching base. She tells you that Cin, as the perceived strongest, has been questioned again. There is a teacher still lost and police are furiously mining every angle, every possibility, because time is rapidly running out on him. Your girl repeated what she has always said, apparently, maintaining the line; the Sherlocks were satisfied. She's good. You don't want to tell them how good. Meanwhile the media want the girls because the mystique of The Cins is growing. Willa's secret account, which her parents didn't know about, has been infiltrated. Pictures of them are leaking online. Photos in bikinis, on boats and paddleboards in the harbour, in slips of silk at formals and screaming and selfied at pop concerts; the privileged girls' life. Multiple media accounts have been scoured by the tabloid press, not just theirs but those of other Koongala students. It is thorough. Unfair. Out of control. Some girls are loving it, some parents are threatening to sue. You say no to all media access. Large sums are being offered. All parents are refusing except for Elle's, who

hesitate. Then a firm no, on your guidance, though they could do with the dosh. But you must protect the girls at all costs. Their story is argued over across the world, conspiracists and retired detectives are weighing in. Vigilante search parties are rallying. Where is the teacher/what happened/is he alive/were the girls involved.

Elle still hasn't spoken a word so she'd be the least capable of fronting the cameras. Also the least effective as an ambassador for the school. Because, well, let's face it. The least photogenic and severely lacking in confidence, God help the poor little thing. Her bearing doesn't reflect the Koongala world. Beth says that Elle is languishing in bed, staring at a blank screen. As if spelled. Over the phone, a suppressed sob. Beth tells you there's no point in visiting again. It's as if she has given up.

You return to the girls' Insta accounts. Scour the comments for anything missed. Nothing. Elle always looks like she wants to steal a piece of Cin. The gaze, sometimes, is not entirely benign, like she covets the loud, fizzy, outrageous bit. The bit she has always envied, perhaps, and never quite had the courage for. But Cin now feels like a knot of wrong. She was a furious dark scribble in the garage with that furrowed, freshly adult brow. It was as if a cartoon thundercloud of black was scrawled over her head.

You draft an email to The Cins' parents. Under no circumstances will there be any kind of official photo of the recovering girls, despite the media sniffing around for one. It would only make the world want to get at them more. Through the parents you advise all four Cins to take down their socials, or at least put everything that they can on private; but shutting down completely would be best. You caution that they don't know who to trust anymore. A story to consider: of the hunter in America who posted a picture of a deer with three antlers. The most common response? Where is it so I can kill it. You tell all the parents this as a warning. You have read the dark corners of the internet.

You need The Cins back at school, back amid normality. You're not liking where this is heading. The slippage into silence, the closing off. Police psychologists agree this might be a good thing. Get the girls into a regular routine, at school, to loosen them into talk. Because a man might be out there, somewhere in the bush, dying of thirst as we speak. You add to the email that Monday morning, sharp, is the suggested return to school after a restful weekend of recovery. You stress that nothing is set in concrete; the girls will be helped every step of the way and you will be there personally for them. Can just picture Hugo's 'Fuck this'.

Over the years you've been subtly training your Koongalettes as women for the future. To be resilient, focused, punctual, on it. Banned in your preferred orbit are spindly high heels that tip and trip. A full face of heavy makeup that masks and exhausts.

Wheedling and whine. Alongside 'Cope' as the curt mantra is 'Act with audacity.' And 'Use your voice.' 'Don't be afraid to be unlikeable. And don't be afraid of words like questioning and abrupt, abrasive and blunt.' Because that's what these girls are, deep down, until puberty hits and the world tells them to be something else. But in these four girls now is something never seen. It was like being enveloped by winter as you were frozen out in that airless garage, and in that towering glass house, and in that room with its couch covered in sweets.

The girls' new, private knowing is everywhere over you now, like flour.

Your Golden Flower in particular has become a fish hook into your time, snagging rawness; yanking away concentration as you flounder at your desk until late into the night. Finding your Head of English is the number one task, of course, but Cin. Always Cin. Veering your thoughts like a ship pushed off course. Cin in her garage bristling with sweat and strop. Why? They are found and surely it's enough. Yet she feels brittle with unknown hurt.

Tamsin no longer talks at all and Tink wails in a call later that afternoon that it's all your fault. She's never been good at that chitter-chatter thing, you want to snap yet don't. You'd always admired it, actually, in Tamsin. Bubbliness and verbosity can be seen as weakness, lowering yourself; just as enthusiasm is weakness. Tamsin doesn't subscribe. You suspect the likes of Cin and her get what males want from them and don't surrender, deliberately, in their different ways. Because, well, der. It's a dilution of their strength, so why succumb.

Over a meandering chat with Tink you broach various rumours – boys, vodka, boner garages, the party posse. All refuted. Cara rings and again all the scuttlebutt is shut down. Each mother wants to talk through her bewilderment. You let them. Cara sends a screenshot of one of Willa's Instagram posts from a while back, shortly after it was announced she was leaving her old school. A post in farewell with a middle finger raised at the school sign, with hands waving and hats flying and laughter round the edges. A comment from an obviously made-up account: 'Dear Smelly Pillow girl, thank you for moving schools so I never have to see your weird horsey face again. I hope you get run over by a camel's toe and accidently eat a pebble followed by boogers and bellybutton fluff.' Yet Willa kept the post up. Why, you ask her mother. Because she had courage back then, Cara says. The 'back then' niggles but you don't pursue it.

Elle's mother is asked to text as soon as her daughter emerges, any hour. Nothing all evening. Late at night you urge all parents, again, to please consider returning their girls to school sooner rather than later; perhaps they didn't see the email and you want to forewarn them. 'We're aiming for Monday.' Back and forth you go. Hugo the worst, of course. We'll decide this for ourselves is his tone, give them their recovery days, as many as they want. He canvasses the other parents. They agree with him, he has won. Eyes wide blank at the end of it as you stare into the gloom with a cold cup of peppermint tea, undrunk. You forgot to turn on the light at some point yet still sat, utterly alone, in the dark.

10.13 pm. Dot curls in your lap. Holds out her chin for a scratching in the tuck of her favourite spot. You crumble into the warmth, melt into her purr with every inch of your aching body. Soften the brick of your shoulders. Succumb. The Purrminator strikes again. Death by love.

Robin calls. An 11 pm update. Tony remains missing. Silence. Right. This is hard. He's unlikely to be found   alive. Now.   Please God no   not this   this   and after all the exhilaration of the girls returning. No. Your dear sidekick, your chuckle buddy, mate. You will not give up hope. Will not. But if he's not been found alive by now then the conclusion must be, must   that he's

oh God. Help him, please, help   us

and you forgot to ring Adela, damn, and now it's too late. All day you forgot. She's a wall of reproach, it's too hard, you don't have the strength to even text, to be honest. Especially now, with all the implications behind Robin's call. Oh God. Adela's turned from the school and towards the police; accusing you, publicly now, of only being interested in the girls. This is categorically not the case but in her mind it's as if you personally ordered Tony back into the bush. You'll organise a service of gratitude for him, for next week, yes, get onto it first thing tomorrow. Whether he's alive or   or. A service of hope. You make a note in your long list of things to do, your pen digging into the paper. Fear you'll forget, fear your mind imploding with so much. Push yourself, somehow, to write it down. Can barely move after it.

11.47 pm. Robin again. Apologies. Forgot something. There's talk of scaling back the search, although not for a day or two yet. But keep this quiet. There are sensitivities. Adela hasn't been told, no-one dares. It will break her. Robin says a lot of people are now having tantrums over demands not met. Falling apart under the strain. It's like everyone has gone mad out there. The world that was only just holding itself together has been given permission to fracture and it's all going off. Goodness, you say, you can count on me, you say. Calm, measured, quiet.

Not.

The day ends with no advancement and so you sleep, or attempt to, readying for the head whirl of another 3 am wakefulness. Yes, it's back. The torment of ragged sleep, in the armchair you're too tired to get up from. With the cat's heavy warmth curled in your lap and the dog's paws across your feet.

Sunday

The night rings with emptiness. The Cins' silence feels malignant now; it rumbles through your sleep. As does Mig's attack, out of the blue, that you've never risked love. What? Why. No, surely not. Your head is crammed with ex-partners and all your relationship failings, over all the years, as your eyes stare deep into the lonely dark. There was the one who couldn't be slept beside because he was too restless and took up more than his half of the bed – and your life. The one who was silent and never talked. The one whose thrusting during intercourse went on, exhaustingly, for too long. The one who talked over you and never asked questions about your day, your world, your anything. The one who ate too loudly, too carelessly and obviously; you felt an obscene intimacy with the whirlpool of saliva in his mouth and as he chewed in front of you, relentlessly, you knew it couldn't last. Yet just because you live by yourself now, and are comfortable with your own company, it does not mean you do not love. Oh no. You want to ring Mig right now and tell her but don't even reach for the phone, can't; crazed by tired. By uncertainty and fear and grief.

To live alone – organised and lean and wolfish – is the preferred existence now, and you've come to this realisation after years of experimenting with the alternative. Introversion stares into the life you try to lead and it will not let you go. Extroversion is the mask, but after stepping into the world you need to withdraw for a time into the vivid alone, to recalibrate. To allow the too-many people always nudging up close to evaporate. Much of the world doesn't get this charged urge to be alone, to lock yourself away and dive deep into quiet time; 'To make me visible,' as Emily Dickinson once wrote. But your need to ringfence a repairing solitude is very real.

Yet none of this means you do not know how to love, and do not risk it. The obscenity of that. Mig makes you feel wrong, so often wrong. She has a peculiar knack for it. And you are drowning in this 3 am dark. But are you reading too much into her words? Is everything she now says stained with misunderstood meaning – and you cannot ever release yourself into forgiveness. Move on, with grace. Trust. You shut your eyes in a plea of help, softening into prayer, and as you sit there in the poised dark a great calm washes through you and stills you down. Everyone, now, is under siege. Of course. Everyone, now, needs to be forgiven for what they do and say. You're all so fragile in this. Your worst selves, reeling and serrated and exposed. Especially you.

A noise outside. A possum or robber or reporter but nothing can get in, you are safe. A man you once lived with did not check windows or lock doors before he went to bed, then laughed at your 'OCD'. At the fear, a woman's fear, that he had no idea about. You told him women have a different perception of safety and he proceeded to belittle you with uh-huhs and eye rolls then left windows open, 'accidentally'. You could never quite relax. No, you will never live with anyone again. Too hard. If no-one is around you in your home then you don't have to consider them and it's a relief. You spend your entire working existence considering others and your home should be a sanctuary from the challenges of life beyond its four walls.

Mig told you back then that if you loved your chewing man you would have compromised, without thinking; you would have lessened yourself. For the solace of a relationship. The comment felt careless, off. Are you unlikeable for wanting autonomy in your life? Wrong, for requiring order and calm? That's how you had been made to feel in some quarters. Unlikeable and odd, for wanting to live your own life in your own way. Not for the first time you thought: how dangerous is a woman who is happily on her own. How threatening to everyone else. You do not want a man who needs you to do things for them. You are not that woman. And they are so very, very needy. Juvenile, in that respect. And you've already got too many children in your life.

Yet why did Cin call *you* dangerous? Can't scrub it from your head.

6.07 am. No messages. You need this situation tied up with a bow and placed neatly in a box that you can shove under your bed, but a teacher is still missing and it's ragged and messy. You thrive on neatness. It gets things done, it calms your brain. You are not coping.

News websites are trawled. It's now made it into the press that The Cins is short for Cinnamon and Tamsin; other parents or teachers must be leaking it. Everyone knew something was up, the girls were somehow tainted. Excuse me? But they've always been tight and exclusive, rarely letting anyone else in. It gives the girls a strange power. Their indifference is intriguing. The fact they don't care, it seems, about what others think. They are stronger than that. Don't want to belong to anyone but themselves. Intelligence radiates from them.

They never change up the group. You've watched similar dynamics over the years. Note women and girls more closely than boys and it is the same for men, of course; we're interested in our own. It's the familiarity effect. The tendency to develop a preference for things that are easy and familiar, like a reflection in our mirror. The more we're exposed to comforting familiarity the more enjoyable it becomes, and we tend to notice those like us; we empathise, raise up. It's the patriarchy bestowing promotions and pay rises on their own, perpetuating the glass ceiling; it's the label of 'genius' placed on an artist that usually applies to only one gender and skin colour. It results in a thwarting of opportunity for the institutionally ghosted, a muting of ambition when you do not exist within a halo's warmth. You tell your Koongalettes that when the gatekeepers are changed up the conversation changes, refreshingly so. And they must always battle the familiarity effect. Call it out. You are shaping, subtly, your army of girls.

And so to The Cins. Who were attracted to one another like iron filings to a magnet, which was quite possibly an attraction to the forcefield of Cin. It's the familiarity effect writ large and you want to protect them right now; propel them into an uncomplicated future because they don't deserve the unfairness of the attacking internet. No girl does.

Cin is a force beyond what's acceptable; like the witches throughout time who needed to be silenced because of their spark and the truth they spoke. Why aren't women ruling the world? With strength and intelligence like this. As young girls they run rings around the simple, needy, uncomplicated little boy-men around them. Until they don't.

8.07 am. Bathroom mirror. God, the face. Sagging as if it's given up on life. Rogue eyebrows, with what seem like sprouting pubic hairs that have migrated; yet if you pluck them there'll be a gap. New, thick hairs sprouting above your lip and on your chin; hag-white now after decades of bullying black. Every day, new hairs. Plus, jowls. Scrappy, wayward hair. A décolletage that must not be shown to the world and unforgiveable upper arms with an old-lady shelf of breast. Your body is now repellent. Mig used to say you looked mint in your flash daks but you've lost all physical confidence. Attrition, over years. She said as she aged, her heart was growing young, yet you feel the opposite. Your body is a foreign country, it does things differently now.

You extract the pill you've forgotten to take over the last few days. For Hashimoto's disease. Not a grand kind of ailment, not terminal, but life-changing. An autoimmune disorder that triggers an underactive thyroid, which means intense drowsiness and lethargy and quite possibly madness, according to a Hashi mate. She charmingly explained you'd feel exhausted all the time, while watching yourself turn into a slug, and there was nothing to be done about it. You gulp the pill and groan at the saggy morning face in the mirror; it looks like it's melting.

Ah yes, Hashi's. Quite the middle-aged lady thing. Your body is your frenemy now. You'd always assumed you had control over appearance, energy and weight, that what you did with this machine basically dictated how it worked. But now, Lord. No matter what you do your body has a mind of its own, so to speak, and you're not aligned. You saw it in your father's death, when an alert, aware brain was befuddled by a physiology slipping away from him. He was furious and frustrated that his body would no longer do what he wanted, it was sliding away like an errant child who could no longer be controlled.

The confidence of certainty is an aphrodisiac, the rocket fuel to living a good life. It's a firmness that allows you to step strongly into the world and with this battle, you're losing your footing, for what feels like the first time since girlhood. Slimness is currency, power. No matter how little you eat you can't control this new torment. Fat feels like a failure of self-discipline; you can sense it, the perception that you're somehow lesser as your breasts, thighs, shoulders and waist become more, so much more. You hate the helplessness felt as your hormones rage against the dying of womanly might, and give up.

8.32 am. Treadmill. Forty-seven steps. Meant to be five thousand. And … no. Have to wrench your exhausted body into line but aren't sure how to anymore. Doctors, well, you now see the fallibility; so much, too much, feels like guesswork. They've no idea what your exact dose of Hashimoto drug should be, they'll try something and see if it works. It feels shockingly sepia-toned. Your girlhood faith in the certainty of medicine is faltering. There's a border now between the firm country of your old life and this mysterious new one, where a teacher is lost and students are stupefied and your body is a stranger to yourself.

Late morning. The rounds of each household, again. All girls are physically recovered, lolling in bedrooms on screens. Parents report they're hived off even further into their worlds and are not talking to anyone except their group, whether it's allowed or not; it feels like all parents have let go of attempting to corral this, whatever it is. The girls' voices soften when anyone comes within earshot. After gentle prodding the parents now agree it might actually be a good thing to get them back into the classroom. Tink says yes, yes please, eagerly, as Hugo bats his hands in disbelief; you realise this moment is about something else. Tamsin's father looks at his wife pointedly, she shrugs and focuses her attention on you. You tell them, carefully, that the psychologists are saying it would be good to distract the girls with normality. Which would be school. As early as tomorrow. Hugo throws back his head and raises his eyes to the heavens. But you have won, you can detect it. You repeat the line to Willa's mothers. Cara just raises her thumb in amiable agreement; Willa will be back.

Elle is still a problem. Beth wrings her hands as she sees you to the door. 'She's never been the password child,' she whispers apologetically. Ah, the password kid, the favoured baby whose name is used for entry into the computer. 'She discovered that her older brother was it, so then I had to backtrack. Explain that he's been my password forever because, well, you know, I don't even know. Actually. Yeah.' You nod in sympathy. At all the thoughtlessness writ large, for the child who feels too much. The ones flayed by life.

Elle now exists within a cocoon of sullen. Beth wants her back in school but her eyes say nup. You fear her daughter will now join the ranks of school refusers; she's on the way to being gripped by the prison of it. Cin berated you once about even calling it refusal. 'They can't. Just physically cannot get out the door. So call it "school can't" instead.'

You can be indulgent for only so long. A recent decree from the board was voted through, because the situation was accelerating. Contagion. As long as affected girls are enrolled there will be no leniency on fee payment. It's hard to expect teachers to bear the extra workload of teaching beyond the classroom. You're also starting to say no to school refusers from other schools. 'Regrettably the school is full' covers so much. Someone else can have the exhausting complication of these children, let alone the despairing parents expecting a fix.

At the door Beth tells you she is quietly going mad. Her racing mind has taken over her sleeping, her waking, her life. Richard is still working despite being in his late sixties. Second marriage. He should be at home now supporting a traumatised daughter and wrung-out wife; instead he's gone into the office on a weekend. Why do men like this stay on at their jobs, refusing to give way to the younger workers, what are they afraid of at home. Boredom. The blank day. Themselves.

When you visit Mig there's only a whisper of a hello. Your eyes barely meet. There are dark circles under hers. So, she's been sleepless too. We'll get through this, somehow, says her half-smile; whatever this is, is your shrug back. Her daughter was once as open and enthusiastic as a dog, but who she was once is now shut away. Bewilderment unites Mig and you, warily, because neither of you wants to get too close.

You squeeze Mig's arm. A lifetime's history in it. A tiny gesture but it connects. A clean smile spreads across her, releasing you both into warmth. The palm of her hand is enquiring as she guides you inside as if you've forgotten where to go. You don't respond but know she can feel your fragility, your trembling. This is hard. Her head goes to one side like she's just looked inside you, as your top lip wobbles and you can't stop it. Your naked faltering. She smiles again like she's finally ready for a next, tentative step. Your heart races with hope.

Cin is lying on her back on her bed, arms folded across her chest like she's rehearsing for a coffin. She doesn't turn at your hello, doesn't acknowledge you, just shuts her eyes as if she can't bear your presence and goodbye, it's time to rack off. Yes, these girls so need to be back at school. Before this behaviour is cemented. You pull Mig aside and tell her that Cin needs to get back to Koongala, fast, that it's a motherly instinct telling you this. Mig retorts, what would you know about that. Confusion. But it was going so well. Eggshells. She says that some mothers can actually be unmaternal and do you know this? Ah yes, of course. Retreat. Her fist knocks her forehead like something is infecting her too. Your heart contracts. You're not the only one cracking under the strain of this. A silence of too much.

Mig abruptly explains, in apology, that she's just tried to take Cin's phone away but it didn't work because her child wouldn't release her grip. 'She bit me,' Mig says quietly, ashamed. *Bit?* What fresh wildness is this. Once the two of you had laughed together when she bought a safe for Cin's multiplying screens; a rectangular steel box like the ones in hotel rooms because she kept forgetting her hiding places for the devices, until her flat was loud with forgotten iPads and iPhones screaming silently, Find Me, yet she couldn't. But now this. Mig shows you the fresh bite marks on her forearm. You hover a touch in shock.

Cin had worked out the safe's code in ten minutes. Her birthday, of course. She will always be the password child, with the self-belief to match.

It now feels as if the truth is alive and crouching among the girls, waiting to pounce. And that it is something they can never reel back. So they keep to themselves, removed from one another and their families. Each parent is turning their back on you, and on the school, protecting the individual. From what they don't know. But the truth hunkers down and waits.

A call. Robin. Tony's baseball cap has been found by a creek bank. Light-headed with relief. So. You can sense it, he is close. Yet nothing else is found. There are drag marks further upstream as if something large has crawled from the water or been pulled but it's hard to tell what. Forensics are on it. Your chest tightens. A sudden crazy thought: maybe the girls shouldn't be back at school so soon, maybe they need more rest, maybe Hugo is onto something and we need to protect them at all costs. From what? You need to head back to the campsite. To be there. To show yourself. Front up. For the cameras, an impromptu presser. And for Adela, who is still there. You owe it to her. And to your colleague, your friend.

Cretinous tradie utes are dodged on the drive; the pinkie is again waggled high out the window. You yearn to turn off the freeway and drive from all this, right now, to the little weatherboard shack by the sea you can never get to enough. Your real house, your father's that you own outright, huddled in the cleft of a cliff. Made from sun-bleached wood with a rusted tin lid of a roof. It looks like it would be blown over if the wind sneezed but you could live imperfectly in it, quite happily, when the time for retirement comes. Inside is strong. It's where you uncurl. Re-finding yourself in recovery and sleep. You want to be held in its fist right now as you head up the mountain to Adela's eyes; want to be cradled in a simpler life. Because that simple little shack is the only location where you stop trying to be anyone but yourself.

Cin used to sleep in the lean-to out the back. She'd visit you on weekends when you were hers and hers alone, in those days when you were her beloved G. Always there, always reliable and listening; the sounding board who was not her mother. You could talk to Cin about all the things she couldn't with Mig.

She'd natter away while walking along the beach, collecting shells, baking banana bread, rummaging at Sunday markets and buying rainbow Paddle Pops. You knew everything about your little SinsiSin and loomed enormous in her life, in the way your own aunty had in yours. The crackly warmth of the cottage's open fire was the moth-heart of this world. Marshmallows on two sticks made it magical, as did chocolates on the pillow and an old iPhone, just for her, for gaming ('Don't tell Mum'). The long grass skirting the shack flattened this way and that in a carpet of submission to the wind and right now you just want to be rolling in it, in joy, just as Cin used to; puppy delirious at being by the folding, thumping sea, wind whipped and filled up and free of stress.

Can your new position ever be disentangled from the mess of all this? You want the contract signed and the deal locked in right now, to have it safe; want all the corrosive uncertainty to end. Want to be G again, not ma'am, to your god-daughter. The formal offer is yet to arrive in your inbox; this disturbs you even though you were told early next week, of course. Must be patient.

Mig rings as you head up the last stretch of the mountain. Tells you she's been thinking things over and yes, absolutely, Cin should be in school. As soon as possible. Good, you say, the sooner the better. You don't tell her you appreciate the gesture; that it feels like a reaching out. You say that you're heading to the campsite but would much prefer to be at the cottage. She says it's one of her favourite places. In winter, with a cuppa, two naughty sugars. Under the old red and white patchwork quilt, you add. Maybe a hot water bottle in there too, she chuckles, and your entire body softens into the relief of ah, just like old times. Soldering times. Yeah, she murmurs, the old quilt. Is there longing in there? Regret? For that time when your favourite mindset was Together. When Mig would bring Cin to stay in a girly break from stressy city life, to gulp the medicine of simplicity; or gratefully offload her daughter on to you, to make way for an exhibition opening in another city.

She must have found someone else for all that.

Mig hangs up. You breathe deep. Slow the car. It feels like a great force has been pressing down on you, holding you under, not letting up. You crave release. Want the wings of relaxation stretching inside you again, so much.

As the campsite is approached you practise what's to be said to the cameras. Can barely get words out. A smooth assertiveness feels way too trek now. Pardon? Trek? You're talking like a teen and can just picture Cin's eye roll. 'Don't even—' with the palm held flat like a fence.

The media know the car. They swarm so you can't drive through the scrum as you enter the campsite. Microphones are thrust through the open window; your mistake. Are you hopeful the missing teacher will be found soon? (Isn't everybody?) Has it been confirmed that the baseball cap belonged to him? (Yes, but you're not getting that.) Have you concerns about the behaviour of the Koongala girls? (What on earth do you mean.) Their lack of experience, says one reporter, by way of explanation, and your face turns sideways in silent curiosity. (Don't even.) What they do with boys, says another, you know, being an all-girls school. What? Fuck off, the lot of you, you explode as you slide the window up, how can you even suggest that, have you seen what the boys' schools get up to? The little shits.

A shocked silence, then chaos, as they all close in. Sniffing blood.

Yes, you have lost it. And on national TV. Perfect. Right in front of the cameras and just what they want. All jagged, deeply private you is well and truly back and now infecting your professional life and your future prospects. Just great. Nailed it, girl. The reporters let you through in silence and shock. At what they've stoked. You've given them the grab and it's gold for them, of course.

Your shaking hands barely touch the steering wheel as you somehow park. You stride across to Adela with purpose and hold her and hold her and apologise for everything you have done and have not. Your bad, you are suffering here too; can barely hold it together, in fact. She yields to you with a grace you do not deserve. She witnessed your meltdown at the entrance and does not push you off as you cry together, two women stranded in despair and horror and bafflement. And love. For a good man. You know he is. Tony, Tony, my Tony, Adela sobs into your shoulder. He does the dishes, Adela says, he always made the kids' lunches, he gives me the freedom to do what I want. She pulls away and looks straight at you. To be a good mother. To our children. Which is the joy of my life. She says this as if testing you. As if she knows exactly what you think of her. You nod and walk away, saying nothing; walk past the listless gathering of Tony's girls who are coming to the realisation that their father is gone and for good, perhaps. The children of the community that believes people like you have stained the purity of their world, by crashing the future into it.

Robin hurries across. Tells you that the police have negotiated to keep the outburst off the airwaves, for now, citing extreme stress. You shut your eyes in gratitude then raise your thumb in thanks to this hugely capable woman who's got your back, it's all you're capable of. But you just want to lie flat in the dirt, your arms wide with your face to sun. With relief. You are saved, as is the school.

Someone leaks the footage anyway. X goes off. The chicks are closing in to peck the bleeding one among them to death. Not long now, it feels. Hugo will find the clip soon enough. And possibly your new bosses, in your new position, but they're all ex-educators so will perhaps understand and recognise that it's time for a battle-scarred old warrior to pull back from the coalface, to an office job. You hope.

After an hour at the campsite your forehead is twisted into what feels like a permanent knot. You knead it with your fingertips, surrendering to the urge to just piss off, away from all this. Tony will not be found; the girls will not speak; not everything in the world is tied up neat. You excuse yourself and head out, driving straight to the beach shack fast. Because you can no longer stomach the thought of the silent house waiting for you on the school grounds. All the eyes, questions, stares in Koongala's hallways and offices and classrooms. Need a hit of the sea. Salt air flushing you clean. Ring Pup from the car and tell him you'll be driving straight up from the coast tomorrow. He says of course, no worries, get some rest, Sarge. He says a leader's job is to prioritise and you do not need to act on everything – delegate or ignore. Have you ever loved a man more? You tell him this. 'Aw, Sarge. Can't have you unravelling on us, can we.' You suspect, from his tone, that he's seen online the campsite outburst.

Unravelling? You accelerate. Thoughts galloping, can't focus, mind grabbing at everything, skittery and flittery and swamped. They are back tomorrow, tomorrow, and you need to plan. You are dangerous on the road, not driving properly, weaving across lanes and pulling up abrupt and chancing it. You dream of embracing the glory of No in your life, no to everything and everyone but uh-uh, not yet. You stop at a supermarket for supplies. Get stuck leaving the carpark, can't angle your way clear of a concrete post as you reverse, you are wedged, it will not work. Where is Tony when you need him; he'd get you out of this and you'd both have a laugh. But now. You sit there in your car, half in and half out, and weep. Refuse to ask for help, don't know what to do. Then abruptly reverse with a sickening crumpling sound and a huge scrape. To escape the nightmare. Escape everything in your life.

Tony is your friend, your *friend*. You josh like he's your little brother. Exchange Christmas gifts on the last day of the school year. His to you is always chocolate, because he knows the addiction that gets you through; he gets crazy socks in return. Elf on a Shelf, Homer from *The Simpsons*, Trump. You never see him wearing them but you both have a right old laugh. You call him Boss Cocky and he loves it. And as you've bantered together recently you've thought, well, actually, this one's on the way out, his species of rigidly binary and blinkered masculinity; the world is leaving them behind. Yet he's so damned handy to have around. Who ya gonna call? Tony. He's a huge loss to the school – and to you.

And ... exhale.

The shack is as rough inside as a handmade mug but your shoulders soften as soon as you step inside. You push up the rattly old windows to a vitalising blast of the sea. Dinner is cheese on toast followed by an entire packet of Chocolate Montes and you couldn't care less. You flop on your back on the twangy springs of your dad's old dipping bed and spread your arms wide in exhaustion. Close your eyes, for a moment, breathe deep, and still. You awake God knows when in a velvet dark that cups you in the palm of its hand; you have slept deeply at last. Outside, the thwump of the sea, a solace.

You turn and slip out a pic of your girls from your phone case. It's a crumpled Polaroid of Mig with Cin, your dear, precious girls. A halo of sunlight behind beach-wild heads. You curl around your father's pillow like it's a lover spooned. The hot tears come, and come.

8.48 pm. Your phone pings. Ah, back to reality. The media outburst is gaining traction. Pupils and parents will be devouring it by now, WhatsApp groups going wild, fingers flying; she's gone mad, they'll all be saying. You place the photo on the bedside table, switch off your phone and clamp your father's lumpy pillow over your head. Need more rest, somehow. Removal from the regular world. Anxiety is now sabotaging your life. Oh, for it to stop. Everything. Just stop.

Untangle from these days, you pray. Undo the knot, you implore, straighten and smooth because you just want to lie back and bask in a lovely, releasing forgetting; somewhere else, in a brand-new life. You curl like a child in your father's bed and pray with white-knuckled hands clasped under your chin as if you're clutching on for dear life. You pray for help.

And then, and then, a small hand of stillness on your back. Like now. It'll be okay, it seems to soothe; trust me, it sneaks through you; ssshhhhhh. Firming you forward, alone in the dark. And so you pray. For Cin and the other girls, and for Tony most of all. For the superpower of normality, all over again, if you're ever again allowed the   grace   of it.

Monday

3 am. Grabbing at fragments. Stop the world, you want to get off. But you pull yourself together.

Text Pup at 6.01 am that you will see him at 7.00, on the dot, as usual. *Righto Sarge*, he responds instantly; so, he is up too. *Glad you're back, mate.* You speed into the city on empty roads. Straight into the office.

7.15 am. A briefing from Robin. Searchers have given up hope. Sniffer dogs and helicopters are all for show. For Adela, who you must not forget in all this, for the school and for the world. Amateur sleuths are still arriving. Robin says it's now about crowd control. We don't want mass disappearances at this point. There's a distrust of the police, Robin says, because Tony's Christian, perhaps, and God-botherers don't trust the police anymore. The oddness of that. How the world shifts on its axis. Sovereign citizens are rallying, they have their theories.

The letter of offer should be coming today. Not long now. The verbal assurance – their word – the only rock of certainty in this sea of toss.

All Cins are returning to school today, except for Elle, whose situation hasn't changed. Beth has gone quiet over the phone. As if she just wants the world to go away.

You hope there will be no bullying. The girls have tipped into vulnerability under the feral exterior; it attracts. You hope the form doesn't exclude or ostracise. You see the damage from exclusion again and again, every day within the school and every night on social media. The sleepover, party or concert a girl isn't invited to; the triumph of the cruelty on social media. Sometimes unthinking, sometimes not. When someone is perceived as different there's the need to crush them, to make them go away. And so often that's the child who shines with individuality or talent. Bullying is envy, after all. And what are The Cins now? Famous. And damaged.

8.21 am. Cin, Willa and Tamsin walk through the school gates in lockstep, arms linked. Strength in numbers. Collusion. A knot of togetherness. You stand inside the grounds, in readiness, holding yourself in, pushing down the emotion of having them here, among you, united and strong; you just want to hug them but of course do not. So wonderful to have you back … here … with us, you say, you falter. This feels like a misstep. The Cins nod, politely, receive the words in silence and continue. Impregnable. Rehearsed. There is a strange glittery allure to them as they walk among you all, the unbreakable trio. Other students, teachers and parents fall silent or step back as the mysterious phalanx passes by. Waiting, watching. For what? You're nervous, you lick your lips. How to approach this. A public containment is in the set of their faces, their lockstep and linked arms. It's almost as if they'll be contaminated by you. By the school. By all the watching.

They all wear sunglasses. Which are banned. As if so what. Cin's plan, no doubt, it's the energy of *Wife beaters are so fucking hot.* You remember again that Orpheus glance back on the fateful morning of the vanishing. The lengths we go to, for attention.

Cin is uncharacteristically tidy today. Perfection doesn't suit her. She's the child who grabs something uniformish off the floor, crumpled and stained, and when her mother protests she retorts that she'll pile her dirty clothes together in a heap and spray them with deodorant to clean them up, okay? That girl, that singular girl. When you tried to wake her one morning at the beach shack years ago she proclaimed, eyes still shut, please don't disturb me I'm busy doing mind yoga. You chuckled and she got away with it; always, always, you'd laugh. But no laughing now.

Fearful. Need Cin whole. Need her to escape this unscathed. Awe rolls you in its paws when it comes to her; Mig too. Her fierce feminism shaped the child and now, oh Lord, it feels like you're all reaping the consequences. The world is turning, the media pressing in; so many commentators and keyboard warriors do not like the Migs of the world. The female who is not submissive. Who cannot be corralled.

'Why would I trust something that bleeds once a month and should die,' was a comment in a chat forum last night. Some*thing*. Ah, not even human. Your heart cracks to think of it; of your girl, bewildered, amid that. They have no idea what's out there, in the big wide world. What awaits the girl with a voice, a strength, a questioning will.

Mig is parked down the road. Hovering, expecting the girls to run back, perhaps. It looks like she drove them together yet their homes are scattered to the east, north and west so it must have been a task; over several hours through morning traffic. What was discussed?

Attempts at connection are rebuffed as the school lawn is traversed. The Cins have a strange power over knowledge, notoriety, secrets in this place. The more sinful and silent the group seem, the tighter and more powerful they become.

A headache is coming on. You can feel it congregating above your right eyebrow, its faint insistence that will intensify over the day; it cannot be stopped. You retrieve a Coca-Cola from the office fridge. Medicinal. Sometimes works. Only Pup knows of this habit. And Cin. She used to head straight for the fridge and grab a can in the days when she'd have the roam of your office; on weekends, when she was still in primary school. She'd put her legs up on the desk and laugh with the glee of ownership. Taunting, challenging. Playing God. 'Naughty days!' She'd raise a toast.

Today is a day of observation. You've told staff at a morning meeting to be ready to move in at any moment, yet to give The Cins latitude. Who knows what fragilities are lingering. They've made it clear, on this walk into school, that they just want to get to their lockers and have a normal day. You all fall back into the routine of school life. Mustn't overwhelm.

A detailed report at recess, from your spy network: throughout classes The Cins are speaking to no-one but themselves, shutting the school out. They're largely mute. They refuse to answer questions in detail. Curt, monosyllabic answers; shakes of the head; a unit of silence that refuses to engage with anyone else. The discipline it must take to be this.

Ever since kindergarten Cin's reports have despaired, in a fond way — 'chatty', 'lacks focus', 'disruptive' — but this new containment is something else. It would take a will of steel to crack it. You don't know how.

When asked specifically about Dr Breen, by anyone, teacher or student, the answer from The Cins is a blank and uniform 'no idea' or 'don't know'. Dead-eyed. The girls look to their leader often with sly, questioning glances, whenever a query is thrown. Cin can answer this, do this. Like the others don't quite trust themselves. You need to carve her off.

Mig is rung straight after recess. She tells you there's nothing to crack, the girls are in shock and exhausted, and this is a mother talking, okay, a mother's instinct. Do you detect a touch of snark in the tone; no, surely not but heat sprints across your face. 'Just let them be,' Mig says, 'back off.' Right. Got it. A bulldozer of warning in her voice. Like you are a person apart.

You start organising an assembly of gratitude, for Tony, for tomorrow morning. It will not be a memorial. It may well be a celebration. Because anything could happen in the next twenty-four hours, anything good, or   or   horrific.

You venture down the Year Ten corridor in the next period change. Cin is at the end, opening her locker to a tumult of school gumph. It falls out. She stuffs books, papers, tampons, pads free of their packaging, broken sunglasses, a sports shirt, a still-knotted tie and a boxing glove back inside, any old how, then turns her back to ram the door shut on the mess. You glide up next to her. She laughs, grabs your hand and places it squarely on the metal to hold the door shut while she secures the padlock. 'Thanks, Sarge. Team effort.' You draw back as if scalded, not welcoming the abrasive familiarity, not liking the glare of adulthood that is freshly about her; the glare of being an equal in this. It's wrong-footing. Plain wrong. There's something too upbeat and faux-casual to it, to her pretence that everything is okay — and it's back to business as usual — when it's so not.

Yet, yet. Cin is talking, engaging. How to use this. Can she possibly, perhaps, suggest a way to help her friend Elle, to get her back to school? She lifts her head back, observing: what is this. Says no. Why not? It's complicated. You tell her to come to your office immediately.

Once inside the expansive room you order your girl to sit on the couch. Instantly the feet go up on the coffee table. You swipe them off. Bring out another Coke for your gathering head. Where's mine, Cin taunts. Sssshhhh, conspiratorially, as you hand one across, trying to read this new shardy edge to her. Her eyes light up at the Coca-Cola; it's a glimpse of the old Cin, the old relationship. This was your ritual; the fairy godmummy secret when she was young and far away from the iron grip of Mum. But there's no chuff in Cin now, no childish glee that you're back doing this evil thing together. She's on guard. A bristle of spikiness fences her off. The crack of the cans opening in tandem. You clink them together and sip.

    Old times, but   not.

You're sitting on opposite couches. You ask Cin to help you with Elle. Silence. Come on. Please. I need you for this, you're good at it. Cin is knotted, says she can't. She's tried, nothing is working. Why? Because. Why? She says Elle is in shock about Dr Breen and is blaming herself. What? You lean in. Cin is not looking at you, staring at the Coke can. You lick your lips, stop. Why does Elle care so much, you ask. Because he went in after us, Cin says, and then it happened. Bingo. Your breathing shallows. What happened, you say casually, calmly. Cin looks up. Pauses. He vanished, she says. He vanished, because of us. Because of our stupidity in getting lost.

You sit back. Standoff. Round One. Cin has won.

The headache presses in, right through your eyebrow in this turbulent quiet. Everything is wound down, watchful, still. So, what did Elle think of Dr Breen as a teacher, you finally ask. You can feel her thinking, what to say, how. Cin shrugs off your question. 'It's just not relevant.' End of. Right. But not. Why, you ask. Why would it be, she says fast and not quite comfortably; nothing to see here. You sit back, another slug of the Coke. What's going on, Sinsi, you sigh. 'Nothing, it's what we said, he got lost.' She is speeding up the talk, emphasising the 't' in lost as if this will make you go away, make this go away. Takes another sip of her Coke, leaves you hanging. Cinnamon. It's the name she hates, the one she gets when she's in trouble. She seems so young all of a sudden, a child. I have to ask these questions, you say, come on. Why is Elle in so much shock about Dr Breen? Cin looks at you odd, scowly with hurt. Aren't we all? We're all reacting differently here. It's just how it is. What was Elle like with him, in class? He never noticed her, she snaps, dismissing you, dismissing all of this silly talk. 'No-one did. There's nothing to see.'

You ask what Cin thought of Dr Breen but she's clammed up, refusing to talk any further. She gets up to go. Come on, you cry, opening your hands wide, give me something. Sinsi, you plead. 'We all want attention,' she says at you, into you, and you start. 'Someone who cares. Notices.' This is suddenly adversarial; it's as if her hand is reaching into your brain and scooping out your thoughts. Your confusion, guilt. Cin knows you never quite knew Elle's name. That you used to privately joke about the too many Amelias/Emmas/Amelies in the Koongala world. She stands across from you now, glaring, caged by unwanted knowledge and careful with it.

You dismiss her. It's no use. Too soon. Grab the half-empty can from her hand as she leaves. It was good while it lasted, Sarge, she laughs in response, a chink of the cheeky girl of old in that moment. You want to reach out to the kite soaring off, reach out to tug her down, to safety, to the known. Instead you bolt to the bathroom and vomit up the Coke in the toilet bowl. Your migraine has you well and truly in its grip and there's a whole day to get through.

11.44 am. Mig texts with a screenshot of a snippet she's found from Cin's diary. The journal was strewn among bedclothes in the world's messiest bedroom. Dated yesterday. *All those girls who ask me to go KYS well fuck them sista. It's like they want something broken in me. Something has turned super-quick like this is all my fault whatever this is. So <u>unfair.</u> Fuck this. Just back the fuck off.*

Mig cannot unravel it, neither can you.

A call from Beth. Present, at last. Like she's finally woken up. She doesn't know when Elle will be back or when she'll leave her room or when she'll have the courage to talk to anyone. There's something so final about it, she says, like she's been stolen. Panic in her voice.

12.30 pm. Lunchtime. The huddle of Cins look up at you expectantly as you roam the grounds, hovering; just checking in, says your mask of a serene smile, nothing to worry about. You are practised at soldiering on through a headache, the world cannot stop for you. And you've become the supreme queen of hover at Koongala; pacing the grounds, the classrooms and corridors, offering kind words, checking up. As all history is wiped but this, the most cataclysmic event in the school's existence. Whatever happened to The Cins is like a dampening shroud upon you all. The Cins' defensiveness is in their rounded backs as they sit in the garden in a tight circle, not letting anyone else in. No-one approaches. No-one dares.

You are yoked to them. As is Adela. Must call. Suggest a meeting. Too hard, too soon.

And the awfulness of that KYS. So. Cin is also dealing with requests to unalive herself, as they say, because the word 'suicide' is policed. Right. New. Plus, Mig's horror about this, alongside your own. It's like the collective can sniff blood, some fresh weakness, and the problem now is that any humiliation is public. In the old days, if a boy didn't like how you looked, he might say it in private for your own secret agony but now he writes it online for everyone to thrill over. And with Cin they can discern a turning. What do they know. That she is tainted, yes, and she must have been hoping for a hand, just a single hand, reaching out to her at this point. But no.

1.15 pm. The end-of-lunch bell. The penultimate period. Cin is the only one of her gang who's in the Advanced English class; the rest are STEM girls. Your god-daughter has an astonishing way with words, a singular writer's voice already. It has been noted. Her Year Seven English teacher sent a short story of Cin's to Tony once, to marvel at, to give her the gift of creative confidence. Your Head of English told you privately it was extraordinary. But Mig told you a year or so afterwards that Cin never heard back from him. She knew Dr Breen had it, the other teacher had told her, and she repeatedly asked for feedback, acknowledgement, something. Waited for weeks, months, for his comment of validation – yet it never came. Ah, disempowering through diminishing and ignoring; a move from the patriarchy playbook, of course, and then the episode was overtaken by the passing of time. But Cin remembered, Mig told you. She said that Elle, her sounding board, got the frustrated brunt of it at the time. The audacity of Cin's creativity comes swiftly and naturally to her. There's a clean truth in it, a fearlessness. She's unafraid of honesty and it is power, like an incendiary device inside her, waiting to explode.

You hover near the classroom door.

Cin walks to English slowly, stark with aloneness. Her separateness now feels intense and wrong, almost violent. She was never this. Her presence in the school is an uneasy volcano; it is as if the earth is breathing and breaking up beneath her and she is holding it in, mightily holding it down. Her eyes are focused on a meandery nothing until she catches you waiting by the door. For her. She veers away without speaking, like she doesn't want to have anything more to do with you, with anything, with the grown-up world, thank you very much; like she just wants to curl up far away from everything here, a caterpillar silking a leaf over itself. You retreat. Leave her to the bloody hands of Macbeth and his lady.

1.28 pm. Adela in the office vestibule. Unexpected. Her face is drawn, her hair unbrushed, her clothes slightly askew all of a sudden; everything is taking its toll. You recognise her slippage. It's hard to live around an absence of calm, both of you. You usher her into your sanctuary like a secret. She says Tony is gone for good and it's the first time she's articulated it. Her prayers are unanswered, God is giving her nothing, she doesn't know what to do. You stumble through all the possible explanations, all the hopes that have been swirling in your head – Tony's an experienced bushman, he'll know how to survive, he must have fallen, hit his head, twisted his ankle, is unable to walk – until you peter out and just hold her and hold her, once again, because it's all you can do anymore. You tell her you're not giving up hope; the shake of her head tells you she has. No, no. You hold the frailty in her spine, hold her weight.

Media queries, still. You're allergic to this world now; the baying collective. Fuck off, you growl to the last request for an interview then put your head to the desk in mortification. Pray it doesn't end up in a gossip column. Need to learn how to be human again, you have forgotten, have tipped over to the other side as the pain presses further into your right eyebrow and down your cheek. Loneliness, too, is vining its way in. You all wait now for Tony to be found, in any state, wait for the storm to break the back of this unbearable heat. To escape the relentless calls you pace the corridors again like a governor in a jail. Snail a fingertip close, closer to your girl as she walks from her English class; slowly, not drawing attention, just wanting to connect. To her own private hell that she is going through, alone. It's as if a vessel of bruises is deep inside her. You can smell it as you pace, hovering over them all; your four broken little chicks in this world.

A fragment of memory; of Mig, Cin and you braided together into a single thread of strength. The high glee of the three of you at your beach shack, on the verandah anointed by late winter sun, stretching your feet into the light, side by side, for their licking of warmth. And inside, on the kitchen windowsill, a sprig of jasmine that Cin had picked, sprightly in a jam jar, ballooning its sweet fragrance. It will never happen again. The relationship is gone. Mig accused you the night they returned of ruining Cin; spat that she should never have gone to your fucked-up school of fucked-up little shits. She's upset, all over the place, of course; you all are. You need to find the circuit breaker but haven't a clue what it is. You lurch to the toilet bowl; it comes over you so suddenly. Throw up again. Can't keep anything down.

Back in your airconditioned office, your forehead is pressed against the cool glass of the window. Cin has never been this lost and all the mothers of the group are reporting something similar. You now dread your girl will be one of those who slip through the cracks of life; all promise disappeared, like water into sand. The shock of this new iteration. In all of them. The start of a different, retreating life. How to head it off at the pass. Perhaps it's not possible to.

You call Tamsin into your office as the afternoon stales. She arrives crisp, ready, neat; the girl who'd always play Centre in netball. You ask how her parents are coping. Fine. Silence.

Dr Breen is still missing, is she worried? Silence. Is your family? She says her mother wouldn't care because she hates practically everyone and always hated Dr Breen especially. Oh. Why? Because he hated people like them. Who? Rich people. 'He'll never be found,' Tamsin blurts, reeling you back. You nonchalantly pick up a notebook, waiting with pounding heart for her to go on. This is it. 'Will he, ma'am? Will he?' Oh. Tamsin starts crying, just; wipes her eyes, blinks, then resumes control with a deep steadying breath. Like it's a technique learnt.

They're giving you nothing. Not even worth calling Willa in. They're good. Tactics will have to change.

After Tamsin leaves, Gaden puts his head around the door and enquires about the service for Tony, as if he knows now that he'll never be found. You all do but can't quite say it. Claimed by the bush, by mystery. And so you all must put it to bed and move on, yes. But no. Hang on. Too soon, for any of it. You tell Gaden there'll be a chapel service of gratitude at a date to be announced, soon, yes, of course, but more immediately a speech for Tony at tomorrow's special assembly, he'll be the focus. Because it may help. All of you. Get through this. Yes. Because you all need help.

Another text from Mig, another screenshot. She's going thoroughly through her daughter's room and has discovered a scribble on the side of Cin's crappy Ikea wardrobe, which is usually covered by a cluster of hoodies hanging on hooks. 'Love Mum but do not like her/love Mum but hate her/says I'm her only reason for living but she's the only one who makes me cry/why.' You ring. Tell Mig children were put on this earth to break our hearts. What would you know, Mig shoots back. Do not respond. 'You used to say they were put on this earth to make us laugh,' Mig says, quieter, and you understand it's her clumsy way of apologising but still you do not respond to your former friend. Spent. Wrung out. Sick of trying to entice her back, over so long; of always walking on eggshells now. Bankrupt.

A standoff of prickly, hurting silence. Both too afraid to launch. Mig finally says she's searched all day and has found nothing to explain anything. Cin is like a submarine slowly sinking from sight; ever since she came out of the bush she's been cold and hard and steely grey, under the horizon of life – but inside it's all burning, you take over, all churn and throb and furnace. Mig agrees. She's hurting, you want to scream, she's a complete fucking mess; she's yours, yes of course, but she's mine too, my girl, my responsibility. But you don't dare say any of it. What would you know. The unmothered, the barren, the apart in all this. All you say, very quietly, is that you're worried. Mig sighs. She is too. She tells you she got an air kiss from Cin this morning, just one tiny acknowledgement, and it was like an explosion of blossoms in her chest. 'Not that you'd know.' 'What?' Here we go again. 'Forget it, Kick. Nothing.' You ring off, flat-footed, have never been good with the rapid comeback. Text is your thing, not the quickfire response of a verbal lunge. And with Mig you don't want any of this.

Back to work. To your screen. You refresh your emails again, and again. No offer letter. You pray, you trust. It *will* come. Must. This can't be slipping away. Fuck. Everything so wrong.

The Cins gather in the locker area between final periods. There's the slap sting of indignant words, from a distance, but you're too far away to make anything out. Is their solidarity starting to fracture? The friendship feels like it's now strewn with shards of broken glass and they're all treading carefully. Not touching, and not trusting anyone else.

'Fuck off,' Cin yells across then catches you looking. 'We're not saying anything.' 'Just checking you're okay,' you respond in a cold voice of authority. 'We care, Cinnamon. About you, about all of you.' She's thieving from you now, thieving calm. You feel loyal to no-one anymore but this fragile, unpredictable creature of wonder before you, yet can't show it. Something or someone has schooled her to retreat from the world, to question and distrust. She used to teach you another way of being and it was instructive; you'd never been as assertive as this when young. And she was so good at banter, all the teachers commented, she was a joy to have around.

Robin confirms in a quick phone call that there's still no sign of Tony. Or his body, which is more likely now. Body. You gasp at the nakedness of that word.

'The bush is on their side,' Tink says in a call you make to each mother before pick-up. 'What do you mean by that?' The woman giggles, veering into panic. 'No idea, babbling, falling apart here.' Aren't we all. You're instructing each mother to collect her child personally, if she can; the girls are a little too wobbly and need a net of protection over them. It's been a big, disconcerting day and you're no closer to anything. Tell your girl you love her, you plan to say to each woman, and she'll drink it up like she's nourished. Because, well, teenager. They're basically cats, you plan to say, indifferent and scornful and enigmatic but oh Lord they need to know we're there for them – and occasionally, beautifully, they'll reward us by rubbing up close.   Might.

Tink says she's lost a daughter and a husband in the space of a week and could cuddle a vodka bottle right now, cuddle it to sleep, but won't, nope, will absolutely not. 'I need help to do that.' These past few days are the deepest this woman has ever spoken to you; she who sometimes jogs near the school but never lingers, never slows down, with anyone. She's always moving forward, ever faster, ever skinnier, as if she's afraid to talk. Afraid of what might be unearthed. But now. You always respond to honesty and vulnerability, to the courage in both, the hand reaching out. On a spontaneous whim you invite Tink over some time, for a coffee. Really, she responds, wow, I'd love that. You sense the smile on the phone and smile back. Two lonely people, recognising it. Two lonely people crying out in the dark.

Maude starts wailing as soon as she hears your voice; she's lost her baby girl too and possibly forever. We'll get her back, you soothe. All the broken people. The advice, now, to all the mothers: we need calm, patience. To ensure the best possible entry back into the world. Today has gone as well as it can. Everyone is understanding. They think their girls should go back tomorrow, gently. A sense of fragility is hovering in the air. Baby steps from now on. This feels so hard.

And now Mig. You take a deep breath. Two wary women, circling each other, and there is no pleasure in talking to her now. You've nothing left to say to each other and after the perfunctory checking in there is none of the old connection left. Mig's voice is reserved, she is not coming to the table; no, this will not work.

You feel plumed by tears as you hold your phone to your ear; your eyes are prickly and raw. Your dear bestie, your oldest through decades of mutual milestones, has driven the friendship to this withered point. Why, why? It was as if Mig was trying to … what? Break you. And she did. You began to question everything. How had you offended? What was *wrong* with you? This was loss through magnificent, triumphant silence. And when times were good for you, no less, when you were accelerating into a dazzling career; yet you were losing a friend in the process as well as a faith in who you were. Mig wasn't a stayer. And so, perhaps now, you must pack up and leave. Divorce from this. To protect yourself.

But no, Mig's not done with you yet. You recognise it. And so into the arena you must tread. She's going back, and back, and back, worrying at the wound. Is it that she's not satisfied with your professional decorum, your measured calm through this ordeal of the lost; does she demand a more primal response? Something unhinged and loud and honest.

Here it comes, here it comes.

'You've never been really, properly reckless, have you?' Mig crashes into the waiting silence. Bring it on. 'Impetuous. Or stupid. Or just plain … wrong. You're so fucking … tight.' Ah yes, all the anguish of the last few days is now spewing out. 'Well, have I got news for you, girlfriend. Reckless can be really healthy, actually. Because life for most of us is messy. Especially with kids around. And if you could just let go for once, and seize, I don't know … looseness, life, love, all of it, you might be really fucking surprised by what's on the other side. You need to get out in the world, Kick. Risk. Get a life. Because perfect is really hard to warm to.' On it goes and on and you know through years of experience that your role is to listen here, and not remonstrate, to give the venter space. Because that is healing, repairing. 'You have no idea what it's like as a mother. What this brutal, obsessive, irrational love is.' Okay. Gently you put the phone on speaker and place the phone on your desk, gently you press the tears in, pushing down your eyelids so nothing will escape. 'The truth is, you can only help so much with this, Kick.' Right. And there it is. Is Mig telling you to back off here, that you're unqualified to go deep? Is she pushing you away from her girl to protect her? From what is going on. From what you might find out. You don't know what to think anymore. She's scrambled your thinking and everything now feels like a stew of attack and paranoia, a stew of slur. But is it all in your head? Everyone is so fragile here, in their own particular ways.

A considered sigh, the one school parents get after a revealing little outburst. Mig doesn't see you. You have been judged and found wanting but are too tired to fight it. You are what you are and sick of being made to feel wrong. This feels too much like a concerted attempt at felling, reducing, cutting down. Yes, the fault lines run deep but yes, before you is a lioness raging over her cub; forgive her, she knows not what she does. 'You don't know me at all, Mig,' you rasp quietly. Glary with hurt. Cursed as the woman who feels too much, and buries it.

A pause. 'Fuck it, no, actually, I don't,' Mig responds with a laugh, at herself, wrong-footing you. Is this an admission, an apology, a chink of light in the portal to old times. 'I'm sorry, Kick. About everything. All this fucking shit between us.' But no, it's too late; you're backing off. Do you even want to be braided together again, now, the three of you back together. You're not sure. You are pinging with hurt.

What happened to us, Mig, you dare the asking. A pause. I don't know, she says, either not wanting to go there or genuinely not knowing. And neither do you. 'I was always kind of jealous of you,' you blurt. 'Well. Yeah. Right back at ya, sista,' Mig retorts. 'I never wanted you to triumph *too* much. You could do well, but not too well.' 'Yep.' And so it is said, and what follows is a mulling silence that honesty has wrought. It feels like there is nothing more to say in terms of the friendship now, and a recognition of this end point from the two of you. You both have to face it. This is the death of mateship. It happens, life has taught you this; you're always telling the Koongalettes that not all friendships are meant to last. But the humiliation. The brutality of failure. That you can no longer make this work. You don't ever want to be alone in the car with Mig again yet you spent decades driving each other to and fro. Merrily tooting the horn as you picked each other up, and at the end of the night hovering by kerbsides until the other was safely inside. Yet if Mig died now, honestly, you'd feel relief; good, she's gone from your mind. You've come this far in the span of your friendship and now, on this wretched shoreline, you have nothing left. It makes you enormously sad, and grateful, that you had a Mig for so long in your life.

Yet there is one more question before you hang up, before you curl on your office couch and cry, and cry, over everything; but on mute so the office staff can't hear you. It's about something that's been snagging at your thinking all this past week. Why on earth did Cin embrace that awkward, dumpy, pimple-smeared little Elle, the girl who everyone forgets? Mig hesitates. 'Because ... I dunno. Kindness. Maybe? Like, Sinsi saw the girl with no friends and ... yeah ... maybe that. Perhaps.' Kindness. Ah, yes. Which you never give Cin credit for. And which two old friends cannot manage at this point.

A gruelling day brittles into hardness. You bite the skin around a fingernail, tear off tiny strips. A bad habit that leaves a bloody mess. A Band-Aid will be needed to hide the finger from the world; it looks unbalanced. And your headache hasn't lessened. You've vomited into the toilet bowl three times now. You no longer want to talk to anyone and convey this to Pup just before you deliver The Cins to their parents at the school gates. It's like you're being infected now, but with what. Guilt, despair, loathing. Uncertainty. What have you done.

Willa's father, Jay, is at the gate to pick up his girl. Maude and Cara are at work. He's the gay dad, the sperm donor who takes his child every other weekend. He clutches his laptop bag to his chest like a white-collar shield. Grandparents pay the fees, which is the case for almost a third of the girls in the school. Jay's face is worn as he catches sight of you; conveying here we go, this is too hard, too fucking hard, but he's trying not to show it. We've lost our girl, his face says, help me. You cannot. You smile in acknowledgement at a gentle father, a good man, standing before you in his cloak of unconditional love. It is a gift, this deeply maternal sense of caring and tenderness, and not all women have it; is it even gendered, you wonder. Well, no.

At one minute to Close of Business the formal offer lands in your inbox. At last, at long last. The vast chuff. You wiggle your fingers over the magic words on the screen. It is done. Done. Done. The new life, the release. Onward. Blossoms in your chest. Thanks Mig, tipping the hat, and once she would have been the first person to be told.

You visit Adela again in her pin-neat home of chain-store furniture. Leather couch, tiled floor, clear plastic over dining table. She repeats in a tic she can't shake that Tony always does the dishes for her, yes, right after dinner. It's the little things, her voice trails off. She says you don't know him. He's an unfashionable man, she says, but that doesn't make him a bad man. She pauses. Although of course it does in the eyes of … of. No, please, you shake your head, please Adela, nothing is black and white. You loved him too. 'Love him,' you correct. Adela looks at you like you wouldn't know how. 'You lot are so quick to judge,' she snaps, then apologises. 'I do love him, as a colleague, and as a … friend,' you say quietly. Hurt hovers in the air. Adela suddenly smiles, just, in the silence. It is all you both have left; a tentative hand again reaching out.

6.45 pm. All mothers report in. It's a new pact to keep in touch. All are worried. Screens kidnap their girls, sucking away talk, vanishing their inner light. You want to take their new energy and hide it in a place where secret things lurk; a forgotten corner, a safe; lock it away like a depth charge waiting to be lit. While you work out, somehow, how to diffuse it.

The police do not need to know any of this. You're now circumspect with Robin in your evening check-in. It was a tough day, it'll get better, nothing to report. Certainly no leakage. Robin tells you that the rescue mission will soon be entering a 'search and recovery' phase and you don't dare broach the specifics of this; can guess. You're asked if Cin, the ringleader, was any different today. No, you say breezily. Why is she even the ringleader, you enquire. Robin doesn't know. Just a hunch. You do not tell her that no-one saw the real Cin today because she's iceberged. Hidden is her new currency. She's lost confidence and it's like someone has told her she's wrong, a wrong human; they've got to her finally, whoever 'they' are. And she believes it. The queen is felled at last. The world has won. It has beaten her down, vanquished her. Finally. She was gazing at her shoes at pick-up, not at the sky, and she was never dulled and broken and stopped like this. Her strength was all in the stance, once. She was the perfect, open, curious Koongala girl. Once.

It's an unspoken truth that parents send their girls to this school for the way they'll one day talk and walk. With confidence. For the way they'll one day enter a room. With confidence. The parents are buying into a luxury brand by choosing this establishment. Your school wraps itself around their offspring like the smooth purr of a Mercedes or the beautiful cut of a Chanel suit. Private education is worth it, for all this. For peers, networks and the self-assurance that will buoy its students through life. But now, over this catastrophic week, all those advantages feel wiped. Exhibit A: your very own Cin. She is derailed. Something malign has entered her world, all their worlds, and you're unable to collect it and lock it back in its box. The darkness is out. Did Tony make that happen? Did any of you?

So, a new approach, new tactics. Worth a try. Who would crack, spill, leak, out of the three of them? Who hates you the most. Tamsin. You will call her to your office tomorrow, yes. Then think, actually, all three have never been questioned together. Remiss.

You always thought difference would be hard to live with. It needs courage, you told Cin once, wondering if you didn't have enough of it yourself. But Cin's careless, carefree difference was like rocket fuel – it gave you strength in your own life, that this little girl didn't care a jot what anyone else thought of her. It was a superpower. Yet this can be a dangerous trait too, of course. The loneliness of the different. You never consider that enough.

9 pm. An endlessness of emails, deep into the evening. Hostility is now crowding the narrative, jostling to be heard. Parents are complaining on all fronts. The Cins are too soon back to school. Tony is still missing, it's taking too long. Their child's mental health has to be considered. Their child has to share a class with 'those girls'. Not enough kindness. Not enough counsellors. Students should be allowed time off around now/students should not be allowed time off around now. The media huddle cannot be controlled. Rumours have been heard. All the new ruptures between families and the school, fuelled by the worried-well parents of the unscarred. Lucky them. To be so uninvested in this.

You pity high school principals the world over, because as their students are going through all the hormonal upheavals of puberty their mothers, often, are going through the menopause; with all its exhaustion and depression, paranoia and strop. It's perfect timing, the perfect storm. The lioness with her cub coupled with the mind no longer under control. They know not what they do, you have to remember this again and again. Because you're going through it too. With all the anguished, attacking emails you resist the urge to answer back but it's hard. You want to blast them out. Silence them for good by letting off a full panoply of shots.

The fact that school fees are paid makes parents feel they have a right of ownership over you, that teachers are servants to be bossed around. You add tonight's offenders to the mental list of parents who may well be punished some day; a grubby little game that gives you satisfaction on this harried evening, even though soon you'll be leaving this behind. You stare at your hectoring laptop, feel glittery with darkness. Serenity is mauled. There is no going back. But oh, the complexity of us. You're not evil, or wicked, surely. You're just a woman. A complex, impetuous, passionate, angry, exhausted, fragile female. All contain multitudes, all have untidy lives, and all need an understanding for the complexities carried within. You bow your head at your desk, your hands propping your forehead. Snap up. Delete the parent punishment list. It's ridiculous, and you're better than this.

The days ends with a weight upon it. The atmosphere is sultry and heavy; a storm needs to crack the heat; crack the tension of this unknowing. Oh, for out. For the great tumult of a southerly buster, flushing you all clean. And so to bed, restless bed, on this unsatisfactory night. You lie on your side with a pillow clamped over your head. Dot picks her way across the valley of your torso and settles on the ridge. You meld into the thrum of her presence, into the slab of her warmth.

Tuesday

'He'll never be found.' Tamsin's words are a mantra rangy and ragged through your sleep. How does she know. Unless she knows.

You gasp awake. Headache gone. Freed from its grip and the relief washes through you.

5 am. New zing. What is this freshness, obscene, within you; a zealous energy roaring back. You clean the house; thinking, thinking as you sweep through the hoarder's lair that's become a haven for clutter and dust because no-one sees it anymore, except for the reception room. Because you had dismissed Nell, the cleaner; too embarrassed by the smallness of your life. You felt seen. Didn't want the judgement. But now, glorious energised now. Out, out, damned blot of cat fur and cobweb, out, out, taunt of loneliness.

Cin is key to this. The slow fuse will be lit. Because healing starts when a person is listened to, of course; when they're given the grace of silence, and space, by the listener. The Cins need to be spoken to, collectively, at some point. You need to explain that secrets stunt our development while using your sorcery to spin a fairy tale of a spider's web. If you can. Lure them into talking with story, a tale of the kind you used to weave long ago, with Cin, when her eyes would close in anticipation of impending magic. One upon a time …

You must somehow slip to the girls that honesty is release. A disruptive power. A currency that firms. The Cult of You has always been strong with this lot. Poised as they are on the cusp between adulthood and growing up; that point where the world wants to tip them into being quiet and unthreatening and reduced. And God, the violence of the crime of quietude inflicted upon young women, the violence of affronted testosterone pushing for them to be something else. So. How to mobilise the Cin army, your footsoldiers arcing their way into a brave new world like arrows to a target. This setback must not thwart the trajectory. You will not have them stopped like women are always stopped. You will extract the truth and deal with it. You've been demented by uncertainty, broken by sleeplessness and stress and you need to be put back together. Somehow.

Hair is swiped back and notes jotted on the speech for Tony's special assembly as you speed through rooms with wet wipes and broom. The kitchen suddenly. Why? The spare room. Can't remember getting there. Daisy and Dot look at you expectantly, wanting food. Ignored. Not the allotted time. Work to be done.

Margaret Thatcher said that by the age of fifteen she had nothing more to say to her mother; they'd moved so far apart in intellect, perspective, connection. You will not be that to these girls, ever. There's a subtle disparagement among your Koongalettes of the mothers who don't work, the ones who exist as housewife, surrenderer, doormat; those quaint women of the past. Did the girls get this from you, the school, the world they live in? There's a faint embarrassment among those who don't have a strong, working female role model in their lives. It's Tamsin with Tink, Elle with Beth; it's the flinty acceleration of the next generation into a new era. A flicking off as they move into other, shardier worlds. You dread the sour whiff of irrelevancy as you age. Can sense even now the creeping chill of invisibility, like a bath slowly turning to cold. You feel seen by these newly adult Cins; detect the faint dismissal of the sad, lonely, crazy cat crone in their midst. And you will fend it off by fixing this. For them.

So to work.

How to soften your girls into talk. You had recently mentioned to the Year Twelves a work strategy: if your back is against a wall, pay a compliment. That's it. There will be a subtle recast, yes, for Koongala's magnificent qweens who survived their ordeal out bush. These girls are an advertisement to the world;

they're the warrior women of Koongala, the crème de la crème who triumphed. There will be a recast and they will be lifted high. Celebrated. Yes.

An early morning call. Beth is apologetic but it's final. Elle won't be back. They've tried everything. You tell Beth the school fees will be waived until Elle returns – no, please, you talk soothingly over her, it's the least we can do. She *will* come back, you affirm. You don't believe it. Elle is your ninth school refuser. There were three more, freshly yesterday, and now her today. Who will be next because you know there'll be a next. It feels like a copycat complexity and its tragic. You don't have an answer for it; nothing, with so many of them, seems to work.

Beth laments that Elle doesn't read anymore and she was such a reader once. Is it phones, fractured attention spans, the competition from streaming services? You tell her that barely any of the girls read anymore and it breaks your heart; you yourself have a pile of unread books on the bedside table. The school librarian has suggested her world go completely digital, to, quote, 'free up space'. The present is a foreign country, they do things differently there. Cin has stopped reading and once she gobbled up books. Fairy tales, pony stories, holocaust narratives, gay boy romances, then it all just died out. You have no answer. Cin still gets her As by listening to the audio book on double speed, or just jumping ahead to the set text's last chapter.

But Beth's phone call is good, it gives you an excuse for the recast. You'll gather The Cins on the pretext of sorting Elle out; it's always flattering to be asked for advice. You'll get your head around this once the assembly, scheduled for 11 am, is out of the way. Parents will be asked permission for a celebratory tea later in the week, and at the Gate House, yes, good. You'll soften with kindness in the enchanting dwelling no student is ever invited into, except Cin, secretly; she used to be slipped in on weekends. Long ago. Before she got old and knowing and dangerous.

Parents text their assent instantly. Everyone is hovering by phones, exhausted by the endless unknowing, you all need this sutured and every ping could mean release. You'll get back to everyone on a date once this morning's assembly is out of the way; meanwhile you're working on getting Elle to join her girls. Beth texts back: *Good luck with that.*

And in the midst of it all you wiggle your fingers once again over the letter of offer – deep breath, and release. Soon, soon. It is the magic elixir into a future that's fresh, the blueprint for the escape route. You feel like a child as you stare at the affirmation, squeezing your cheeks in silent glee. Later in the day, when you can snatch a moment, you'll return to this secret treasure box and open all the attachments and reply. The response needs careful thought. Not too eager or quick or gushy; gratitude and grace. You do not have the time or head space for it now.

A breakfast meeting with Robin in your café. Checking in on each other, in person, before the day swallows you both. You sit up the back in the shadows. The media is finally moving on but you never know with that lot; you're wearing your bucket hat just in case. Robin says it's baffling that Tony has vanished without a trace, alive or— Dead, you jump in too quick. You stare at each other, trapped in pause, grim. Nothing makes sense. You keep your voice casual as you ask why the homicide squad isn't looking into your colleague's *friend's* disappearance.

'Disappearance?' Robin slowly cocks her head. 'You haven't used that word before. Or homicide.' Oh. Really. You accidentally tread on Daisy underfoot. She yelps. 'Don't know what I'm talking about,' you blurt in a rush. 'Haven't a clue, of course.' Clumsy. In that moment a glass screen has slid up between you. Oh no, not her too. Robin explains, with a new formality in her voice, that according to the police's Standard Operating Procedure – known as SOP – the homicide squad is only alerted if it suspects a murder. And it does not. Nothing's been found to raise suspicions; the girls' scrappy stories are consistent. You ask Robin what 'suspicious circumstances' would be. 'You tell me,' she retorts. A divergent path widens. Wariness. In a sudden hot flush you feel the rage rising, at everything, all the frustration and fury and you don't know what you're saying anymore; you're barely catching the conversation as if it's over there, in another room. 'I just – I – I'm – it's so, too much –' You're laughing, touchy, snappy, wrong; needing to leave yet not wanting to lose your ally and taking it out on poor Daisy as you push her from under the table; she growls in rebuke and you instantly regret it. You make your apology to Robin, tearing up – haven't slept for a week, sorry, just feel … helpless, it's all getting to you. 'Hey, no worries. It's getting to all of us,' Robin says in the grace of a softening. A nod, a smile, yes. She's a good woman, better than you, and she has retrieved this. Through all the exhaustion you both want this relationship to work. You feel a primal need for connection right now, for friendship wherever you can get it. And Robin and you had made a good start.

A brisk walk through the school grounds, close to bell time, ignoring the greetings from congregating girls eager for scraps of talk; eager to be the chosen ones, drawn into the halo of your attention. Parents and media still need to see your presence, the comfort and concern from the top at the school gates. You ignore the odd sneakers instead of school shoes on one girl, the hair not tied back on another, the skirt too short that's rolled up at the waistband because yes, you know all the tricks and may actually have done that one, once. The girls sense the veered focus. This is never you – gaslighting isn't your style. You're immersed in the minutiae of the Koongala world and your brand is to live and breathe it. But not today. There's work to be done. Not least, Tony's assembly. Your dear, dear man. Once he'd be arranging this type of thing and you're acutely feeling his absence.

Your head. Swirling with the day's tasks and with the gathering of The Cins at some point. You'll give them Tim Tams, yes, show them how to bite off the corners and dip them in hot Milo and suck; teach them the naughty trick then jump casually into the assumption that Dr Breen is not coming back. Yeah, girls? You'll get it out of the way fast. Need it ruled out, or in, one way or the other. What they know. To protect them. Just in case.

Maybe a writing exercise. New pens and three Koongala-monogrammed notepads. To keep. Special. Did any of them have a motive, possibly? Because of what Tamsin said about Dr Breen not coming back. How does she know, unless she knows. It's too insistent in your head.

You jot down your suspects. The tomboy at the top and you almost can't bear to write it. But Cin is the most likely and capable out bush, your strongest and handiest with a rope. A knife. There's a big dose of testosterone in there plus a chip of ice and it's a ruthless combination in a young woman. But, but. No motive that you know of. She's the odd one out among the privilege. Fierce and fatherless and from an uncushioned background and Tony relates, surely, yet kept clear of her. He said once she was defiant and you remember apologising, appalled; defiance is not a good look in a student. You told Mig later and she flared up. 'We want our girls defiant! It's how the world changes. You should be proud of it. Back off, sista.' Yet,

yet, not enough of a motive. Plus Cin is a man's woman, she gets on with them, banters, flatters, teases. The ease possibly stems from primary school when she was constantly mistaken for a boy. Her only black mark would be signing up the entire form for the Click Club, yet Tony acknowledged in private that it was genius. She is a man's woman but not Tony's type and he knew it; knew she didn't care for his ilk. Dismissed the dinosaurs and worse, laughed at them. The ultimate diminishment.

Suspect number two. Tamsin. Tony hates the thoughtlessly rich. It's tied up with envy and misogyny and a chip on the shoulder, from childhood; the wealthiest are to be subtly punished. Tamsin felt the slight sneer, she has told you this. Tony resents people like her for the oblivious cushioning of a privileged life. Plus your netball Centre would be good at cleaning a crime scene – you're shocked that you're even going here now. But Tamsin has a desire for perfection and organisation; she gets things done. The type who plays Annie in the school musical. Does everything with seriousness and success, possibly even crime. The opposite to the ditzy parents, thoughtlessly existing on their unearned family money. The ones who are always late because they can afford to piss others off. They do not see those who exist differently; they have the nerve and carelessness of those who've always had a cleared path. Tony is aware of it.

Suspect three. Willa. With all the complexity of her own sexuality. Hers plus her family's. The knot of it for the deeply

Christian Tony, whose spirituality is not your own. The visceral disgust he must feel for Willa's world, which borders on the weirdly personal as it so often does with men like this. Abused, as a child, or suppressed. Who knows. But his type always seems obsessed with young people's sexuality; when the kids, now, couldn't care less. Willa would have loathed him ever since the Click Club incident. Children that age hate with such simplicity, purity and focus. But is it all enough of a motive? Any of it? And why are you even friends with Tony, anyway? You've always seen through him. His sense of entitlement, his lack of insight, his bewilderment in this new world of women; to him, nothing makes much sense anymore. He is an unreconstructed Aussie bloke and by rights you shouldn't have anything to do with him. But everyone contains complexities and contradictions; everyone is flawed. And despite everything, you are friends. You enjoy Tony's company. You get on. There is chuff there. Joshing affection. It is what it is. Nothing is simple, nothing black and white.

There is one other in the suspect mix. Elle – well, Elle's forgettable. Does Tony even know her name. Being ignored is not a reason to be involved in someone's disappearance. Yet, yet. Turtled. Refusing to come back.

So. Four little warrior feminists who've absorbed all the lessons threaded through their growing up; taught to call out the cruelty of men. Let us examine, girls, the slur to 'Get back to the kitchen where you belong' and deconstruct the power differential in it. Let us look at the lengths the insecure man will go to. You have told certain trusted Koongalettes to always have their Insecure Dickhead Radar on alert, because these are the men who want to dominate, flatten, destroy. Reduce the strong female to their own level of insecurity. Break them. Let us examine the fear in men who expect the female to soften and shrink, you have said. It is the fear of us. Of what we'll do, collectively, to them, if we're not contained.

One ace to play. Attention. The most focused form of love, an unlocking generosity. Attention to lure The Cins and your goddaughter in particular. You can sense the rangy hunger of the child still in her. You'll break her with kindness.

You have dressed carefully. A black Bella Freud pants suit over an orange vintage shirt; collar tips pointy, cuffs below the sleeve. It's in the style of Nick Cave but only a few will get the reference, Cin most definitely. You usually impress in speeches by speaking entirely unscripted, spelling a web of enchantment to new parents especially. It's a party trick that never fails to impress. But not today. You'll read from the page, don't trust yourself. Your head is swamped with too much as you walk from your office to the assembly hall through the school's centenary garden, a beautifully manicured sanctuary that was your idea. Flowers as tonic and benediction, a medicinal circuit breaker amid the toss of life. You come here often, outside school hours, for necessary stillness; come to the symphony of this little place that marks the heft of the seasons in joyful bursts. Year after year there are the camellias and then the jasmine, the gardenias and frangipanis followed by the crescendo of flowering gums with their blazing red bursts nodding happily in the breeze. But today your head is bowed, your brow furrowed; you do not note any of it.

A pause before entering the hall's discreet side door. Deep breath. You shut your ears in momentary prayer, in a plea for calm and strength. You hear them all inside, the entire school body; the shrill energy, restlessness, speculation. The teachers will have lined the sides of the auditorium by now, keeping an eye on specific charges, all adults on edge. The school leadership will be in a row of seats across the stage, an empty chair for Dr Breen, which you have requested. Too stark? Too late now. Your fist presses into your heart to quell its frantic beat.

As you open the door you catch Pup's eye. He's been waiting for you. He winks. You've got this, you'll be okay. You want to cry with the grace of the noticing. Straighten your spine, steel yourself and walk strongly into it, among them all. The hall hushes in expectant silence.

This is not a eulogy, most definitely, girls, but a note of appreciation for one   who is   who is   ah   *lost* among us. The room is poised, breath held; what freshness are you going to impart, what viral snippet. You don't dare look up, not trusting to remain stoic and on track. Don't know who might have a phone, who might be secretly recording. Head down, focus, keep to the script.

On you read and on, the words bending and shimmering through tears threatening to erupt. A drop balances on your nose, it's flicked off. Dr Breen is a man who's very precious to our Koongala world, yes. To paraphrase the Muppets creator Jim Henson: students don't remember what a teacher tries to teach them, in the end – but they remember what they are. So. What was Dr Breen? A servant. To all of us. Twenty-three years he's been serving us. He's been a father at this school, has been – excuse me, *is* – an inspiring teacher. Leader. Colleague. And friend. To me, to us, and at this point you press your lips together, you dare a smile, a looking up.

But   the faces. Oh.

Stares. Stony at you. Mouths agape. Arms crossed. Bodies in slouch. A gulf of   difference, a wall of no. From them, so many. You're confused, look down at your speech, have lost your place, look up again; your words are not with them, not carrying them. No. This never happens, what is going on. You recall in that moment something Cin said once, about people who 'manage up' and treat those below them differently and that everyone knows it except the boss; but you wouldn't have any idea of that, would you, she said in a challenge like it hurt, 'because you are the boss'. And you forgot it until now. You slide into silence. And stare. Back. Through the invisible wall of no. You've never done quiet like this before, in a school assembly, you're in uncharted waters; the spell of your teacherly authority is broken and for the first time ever you are unmoored and uncertain   and then   then   shocking

a scream.

Near the front. A scream of   what? Who? Wild in it.

Oh God. Those girls. Her. Tamsin. Hands on either side of her head as if she can't bear this anymore, any of it, she has turned into something else. Hands tight over her ears to make this just stop   make *you* stop. Then a low thrum as others pick up on it. Join in, so many of them, seizing the moment in a collective screaming of   what   rage fury grief, you don't know, can't read it; all these girls wild with anger like a throng of cicadas beating their totem in a high summer heat. It is tribal. Obscene. Unloosed.

You panic, look around, don't know what to do. How to stop it. Cin is not joining in, not with them but apart; she looks at you coolly as if assessing what you'll do next. You glance helplessly at the teachers clustered around the edge of the room – at Pup, Gaden, Helen Venty – but   bewilderment. What is this? Someone, help, explain. Make it stop. Is this some huge generational fuck you. At men, at what men do to them. Is it a cry of release. Is it about the way the world is slamming into these girls, the compromises they'll be asked to make. The way in which the female spirit is boxed in, muted, othered. Is this grief, a breaking, a cry of *stop everything, get me away from this*. All of it or none? What? You cannot read it. *What?*

The screaming suddenly falls into a raggedness and then stops, as if an unseen conductor has dropped their hands into quiet. What hesitates into the void is something fragile and stunned. You grip the sides of the lectern. What to do.

The assembly somehow continues in a lopsided, uncertain way; everyone shaken but no-one daring to dissect what has just happened, no-one understanding, perhaps. As if it's too secret, too animal and mysterious and dangerous. Where, where   was I, you stumble. Girls, yes, girls, you try to get the words out but they won't come and then you   you   just   stop.

Look around. In a silence of too much.

You must take control. Steer the girls back. You walk off the stage, make your way to Tamsin up the front, next to Willa and Cin. Firmly you take Tamsin's hand and lead her out of the hall with your arm protectively around her shoulder, clamping down her fragility with your fingertips pressing firm, holding her up. I've got you, girl, it's alright. You indicate to Cin and Willa to follow, firmly you tell the assembly that Mr Delaware will take over and you stare at Pup but he is momentarily discombobulated, in shock, then leaps to attention. Of course, Sarge, yep, got this.

Everything is stopped and wrong as you lead The Cins out. Away from all this. Whatever it is.

None of you talk. Four of you, in a tight phalanx, you very much enmeshed in the group. Tamsin trembling under your touch. You gather The Cins into your office vestibule and gently, tenderly, tell them to sit, to wait and relax while you sort some quick things in your study. 'And then let's get out of here,' you say, 'to the Gate House. Why not, yes, for a cup of tea – or something stronger if you'd like.' 'Vodka tonic,' Cin leaps in, being Cin, but it barely raises a laugh. 'I could possibly rustle up some Coke,' you say, then jump in before Cin beats you to it again, 'a-Cola.' She laughs, too loud and too harsh. The others are subdued. You must be careful, so careful with this. Not sure where it will end up. But now is the moment; something has begun.

As you gather some paperwork you can hear the girls unwinding in the room next door, their voices threading in and out. They check phones liberated from pockets, exclaim over messages from home, 'My mother is *so* annoying,' and express muted wonder over the Gate House at last. No talk about what just happened, although a shush from Cin at one point in a conversation scrap you can't catch. They toss around the secret nicknames they've always given each other – Fungus, Maggot, Booger – you've never known quite which is which. The talk circles back to the Gate House; will there be cobwebs, candles, dripping wax, what's it *like*. Cin's not letting on she knows it already. Good girl. Always thinking, smart.

You brisk through the door. 'Right, let's get some food into you. Tim Tams, sushi, Milo sandwiches? I can get the canteen to rustle something up.' The girls smile at the lame attempt at joking, they grant you a soft laugh. They look so young, suddenly, like they just need a hug. 'We need a celebration, don't you think? Because you've all been magnificent, you know. You came back. In one piece. What a feat.' They nod, yes, so much more swirling underneath.

Your sudden shiver like a horse as you all walk to the Gate House. The girls are muted, tense. Winter's clench is here. In you go. To the forest, the oven, the magic house.

Heads crane and mouths gape at gargoyles on gabled roofs and carvings around doors and sandstone fireplaces the length of beds and dragons in stained-glass windows. You settle them in the sitting room, the book-crammed sanctuary of the house. A silver tray of Tim Tams is pounced upon and in a moment of raw teen hunger there is a glimpse of old selves. The carapace is slightly cracked, in comes the light. Just. 'Go for it,' you softly laugh, 'you deserve it. And okay, outside of school maybe I'm not *quite* so virtuous.' Tamsin cocks her head as you pluck a biscuit for yourself.

The Cins settle into deep white couches that threaten to swallow them up. They seem so small in them, limbs askew; they do not yet perch like adults. You say they're allowed to eat chocolate on the pale cushions because you trust them, unlike those grotty Year Sevens. 'Which you all were once.' A pause. 'But you lot are civilised, of course. Responsible and, quite possibly, chocolate-addicted. Like me.' They laugh, they're allowed to be here, they're treated as adults. 'Not completely responsible,' Cin throws across, 'I am seen.' 'Watch it, madam. Behave.' It is the rhythm of banter of long ago and you both fall into it now too easily. The others are silent, what new dynamic is this, what history swirls beneath. Tamsin looks sharply at Cin.

Four Coca-Colas in colourful vintage champagne flutes are quickly produced. You raise a toast to The Cins' safe return; the panther, nonchalant. No mention of what went on in the assembly hall, that can wait, perhaps forever. Maybe they couldn't articulate it anyway. And if you freshen the wound by attempting to dig out an explanation they might shut down completely and all will be lost and you're treading carefully, so carefully, with this.

The girls are asked what they think their future might be now they're back. They look at one another, hesitant. You tell them – quietly, conversationally – that they can trust you, your talk will go no further than this room, you just want to help. This is a special place, a safe space, the cone of silence is sacrosanct. A collective withdrawing. The anemone is poked.

Dot's melting softness is scooped up and briefly held to your cheek then placed gently on Willa's lap. The Purrminator settles and thrums. Your Cin wilts into it, tickles and strokes; Dot stretches out her chin and closes her eyes in ecstasy. It releases something in Willa. She tips back her head and shuts her eyes and a single tear rolls down her cheek. As if everything is all, suddenly, too much.

A room poised. Everyone on watch. The weight of these tense days settles into the stillness. A prickly quiet exposes each of you on your own lonely path. What's wrong, you gently ask. Willa's eyes stay shut, then, then. 'I don't know what my future is anymore. Everywhere I go this'll be hanging over me. Forever.' What? 'Oh yeah, the bush girl. One of them.' Willa says she won't be able to do anything now, her future has been stopped. Tamsin blurts out indignantly, 'But nothing happened!' and it's like a shield to the talk; she is speaking to the girls rather than you. A silence now, wire taut.

Tell me what happened.

Cin breaks the dam of silence, eventually. Picks her way through spiky words. Says that hang on, even if something did happen, somewhere out there, and you knew, well then how could they ever be with you every day now for the rest of their school lives. If you knew anything, if this bewitching cone of silence really did exist, but they had to look at you every day, at school. Yeah?

You ponder what would happen if the spell was broken by a hard spotlight of truth. Do you even want it. Is it too hard.

What's going on, you ask, blunt.

Derailment. Withdrawal. What to do. You sigh. So. It has come to this. Honesty's potency, which they need a lesson in. This is hard. Okay, here goes. You lift your arms and remove the pins from the back of your neck and place them carefully in your mouth. The girls are intrigued. What is this. You lift off your fiery red wig, revealing greasy grey tufts underneath. Lift away your flamboyance, charisma, dazzle, and present to them your naked vulnerability; you become honest. 'This is me,' you say. 'And it's really hard to show you. Because I don't show anyone. But there you go.' You tread carefully through the shock; not even Cin knows of this; both hands are at her mouth. You tell them that a famous writer once said that everyone has three lives: a public one, a private one and a secret one. And this is your secret one. And sometimes it's good to reveal a hidden life. To connect. Because that hidden existence can be vining and suffocating; and it's better, cleaner, lighter, to live more honestly. And no, they're not allowed to take out their phones. They laugh. You tell them that secrets are releasing. Honesty is a bridge. It extends a hand. And if we reveal our truth, bravely, we often realise we're not so different from others after all.

'What about Cin?' Tamsin blurts. 'Where is she in this? Who is she to you?' You smile, ah, the netball Centre has clocked it. 'For Cin, yes, I would do anything. To have her back.' You pause. This is it. 'My girl. My   god-daughter.' Tamsin looks at you both in hurt astonishment. Your voice cracks because you've come to the realisation that love should not be meek and muted; the attention in love should be, must be, generous. You are breaking through the confinements of cowardice in this moment. 'But this is not just about Cin. I'd do anything to have you all returned. To what you are. Were. So … magnificent.' Your squeeze your cheeks, holding in tears; mustn't allow emotion. As headmistress it's not your thing. But Cin. Just sitting there and grinning at you like she's five again, like a hat flying off into the sun.

She holds her flute carefully in front of her, as if she's a child with a communion cup. Says firmly, deeply thinking, that her mind is made up over something. Says it's all good. To all of you. Tells the girls she's known you for a very long time, all her life actually and you're okay, one of them, it's alright. The relief washes through you like a dam released. So. Back on track. Tamsin pulls Cin to her. It's okay, your god-daughter repeats and extracts the fingers dug into her arm; I'm good at this, Cin assures you. The grin again. And as she looks at you, you can glean the little girl with the huge heart, flung wide; the little girl who just wants to be loved. To be noticed, for who she is, despite the world telling her she has to be something else. The others hesitate; this is going too fast. Cin tells her friends you're an old family friend. Something like a fairy godmother. And that she can make this work, she's got it. What does she mean by that; but you catch the ball and run with it. You are walking into a dark wood yourself. Yet persist.

You sense something uncurling in Cin, the wings spreading hesitantly inside her once again and her spine straightening at the prospect, so close, of release. Perhaps. You want it so much. You shut your eyes and pray for it, shut your eyes in a vast receiving. Of hope.

'One upon a time …' Cin says, soft, soothing, just like when she was six. She says imagine all of them, all your girls – a rise of protest from the others – but Cin does not stop, she ploughs on. One upon a time, she repeats, testing the waters and you nod, yes, yes, go on. Just imagine that all the girls, well, there was no particular 'one' in this. Gasps, from the rest of them, gasps of no. But yes. Together, yes, and Cin nods, matter-of-fact, conducting this.

Tamsin crashes down her flute. The spell is broken, Cin falters in the telling, she looks at you. 'Don't be afraid of the truth,' you say. 'Never be afraid of honesty.' Cin is still. Finds her firmness. Tells the others that it will be alright, it will set them free. All of you. I've got this, she says. You take a deep breath. This close. You say that honesty is a woman's secret power, it is passed from woman to woman, treated sacredly and understood, a seam of secret knowledge. 'And kept?' Tamsin asks. You look at Cin. Choke up. Her eyes flit from you to her girls. 'Fuck you, Cinnamon, if you fuck this,' Tamsin growls deep and low. 'Then we're all cunted. Every one of us.' 'I won't.'

Your barely breath.

Cin takes you by the hand. Says trust me, I've got this, to all three of you. Starts talking then they all do and it's just a hubbub of voices, all protest and refuting and admonishment and you can't listen, can't get a narrative straight. All you can glean is that Cin had nothing to do with it – but the rest of them did. Maybe, perhaps. 'No, we're all in this together,' Cin insists. 'All. Together.' The others are muted. 'This won't work … unless, unless it's all of us,' Cin says into the vortex of the quiet at last. 'Because it is.'

She looks at you. 'Strap yourself in,' she says, 'for The Story of The Hole.' Willa and Tamsin let her proceed; defeated or trusting at last, you can't tell.

In the womb of this room, an expectant silence that is flavoured with so much. Cin sits with her legs wide, elbows on knees and hands clasped under her chin; you sit very still, very straight. 'One upon a time,' she says, her voice now darker in tone. The heel of your palm pushes into your chest. What game is Cin playing at, *you* were the one meant to be spelling everyone. 'Close your eyes, Fairy Godmummy.' You do, for she has taken over. 'Imagine a man, G.' Distracted by the name from long ago. 'He's lying peacefully in the bush. He's nowhere, he's anywhere. Perhaps.' Cin speaks in the cadence of the stories you used to tell her once. 'He's on his back. His arms are folded across his chest. A crown of flowers is around his head. The birds are above him, chitter chattering. And he is free. At last.' Cin speaks as if seeing this. 'We don't know where this man is,' she continues. 'We can't say exactly what happened, because we don't really know. But no-one will ever find him. And that feels like the only certainty in this crazy mess. This is a fairy tale, after all, G. A story we tell ourselves. To understand, and to make things less … less …' Cin's voice trails off and you open your eyes to see her looking at you, for help. You nod. 'Hard. We tell ourselves stories,' you pick up the mantle, 'to make sense of the world. To understand, and to warn. And to absolve. Sometimes. Yes.'

So it begins. Measured, calm. A story of the four of them at a secret infinity pool. An Insta-famous place, shut off to walkers because it's too dangerous; people have had accidents in the past trying to get the viral shot. It's a small, love heart–shaped waterhole, a secret rockpool that's a resting place for rushing water before it tumbles over a towering cliff. And the only thing separating visitors from life or death is a metre or two of shallow, slippery rock on the lip of the plunge. Tamsin knew about it, she'd done her research, as she does. She had told Cin days earlier, had said she wasn't brave enough. But Cin was. Of course. For the secret Instagram shot, in the place that had been closed off.

It is ridiculously simple. Cin carves her girls off, lagging behind the main school group. She knows the gate to look out for, the fire trail that many miss. It's easy to slip behind, as stragglers, to slip from the teachers' sight. Vodka is in their fashionable water bottles. No teacher will know. Elle wasn't meant to be included but got wind of the plan and tagged along. As she does. Always wanting to be part of the group and Cin let her, of course, as she does. Your god-daughter didn't want any distraction as they flitted through the bush.

Beyond sight and sound of the excursion group, on the way to the love heart pool and taking frequent sips from their water bottles, the girls get talking about virginity. That pesky encumbrance they all want gone. Tamsin before eighteen, when her mum lost hers, and that embarrassingly mature age has to be beaten. Cin says that maybe, perhaps, she's already lost it, maybe she's actually done it. This news electrifies the group. They pull and wheedle the story from her.

Cin says it was a boy who gets the bus with her every day. Two years older. He noticed her, he noticed. Dr Breen's nephew, in fact. He made her breath skip, to think of him, her stomach dip. It was just once, she says, and she wanted it. Well, she thought. At the time. She gave consent, she thinks, takes another sip. Perhaps. They were at a party, he was noticing her, she felt cool, and grown-up, and wanted. She was peeled off to a bedroom. He held her by the hand. In ownership. Cin's voice gets quieter, another sip, your shallowing heart.

A finger gesture is what Cin remembers the most. To some of the mates in the main room straight afterwards. And then into a phone held up. It was only then that Cin realised she was being filmed by another boy, by the door. Oh, your girl. Your beautiful girl. To this.

And did she really, actually, want to do that precious, life-changing, dreamt-of act here, in this sour-spirited place. Yet she went ahead. Because it's what girls do. She was humiliated. Hurt. The shame of it. That she did it, and that she felt … lesser … from this point. Later that film would be uploaded and shared among boys and men under the title Fresh Little Pussy. It is very hard for Cin to say this bit. Now. And you can hardly bear   bear to   hear   it.

The girls arrive at the infinity pool but barely clock it because they're so absorbed in the story. Cin tells them it was quick.

That she remembered thinking, Oh, that's it, after all her years of craving this. The attention of the boy on the bus had made Cin feel mature, ready. Until that bleak and lonely Saturday night when it didn't. And a gesture to the lads is Cin's one scalpel-sharp memory. That moment when the boy turned to his mates and raised his middle finger with a smirk of triumph. It was a blunt signalling. A private 'got her' moment. Between males, not Cin, oh no, not her at all. Where was she in this? Nowhere. Because this boy she had liked on the bus wasn't doing this for her, at all. He was doing it for his lads. This was triumph, for him. She was just a hole. Just that.

Your god-daughter's voice has gone very small, very quiet. Your hand reaches to hers still balled; she bats you away as if burnt. I felt so alone, she says, I didn't tell anyone, didn't tell my mum. Tell me now, you say. So. What Cin recalls. An utter absence of tenderness and of anything approaching an orgasm. A feeling of grubbiness. Worthlessness. Wrong. And of the boy's total sidelining of her wants, which felt intentional and immoral and completely normal. Yet Cin had just given away one of the most precious, complex things she had; the deep, secret kernel of her. Her tightly private sexuality, her secret self, alongside her nakedness, which she'd never shown to anyone. She'd tossed it all away freely, for what? She wasn't sure. She wondered in the stony aftermath why she didn't feel better, older, more confident; why she just felt reduced. Plus, there was an utter absence of the thing Cin craved most. Tenderness.

On that lonely night Cin realised a startling truth. She was just an object to this boy. She had been erased in all other aspects. At no time did he ask what she wanted, at no time did he consider her pleasure. It didn't enter his thinking. The boy threw across to his mates afterwards, in the lounge room, 'On a plate, mate, on a plate. Why wouldn't I? Just look at her,' as he put his hands over Cin's breasts from behind, in ownership.

Silence. From all the girls at the waterfall. Then an explosion of fury, of horror. 'Why didn't you tell us?' 'I lost myself,' is all Cin cries by way of explanation. 'I was ashamed. I'd wanted it so much.' 'Fuck that dick.' Elle punches fists to the sky. 'He choked me,' Cin continues. 'Slapped me. Rammed his fingers up me.' Of course. Because so much sex now is about humiliation and degradation, and how did it come to this. Porn, of course, at a teenage boy's fingertips. Which he's learning from. You've preached to senior Koongalettes, urgently, that sex must be about beauty and generosity and tenderness, that most of all. Yet Cin has allowed this, this, abomination, this annihilation. Willingly. Because, well, because she wanted to be loved. Oh God, you shut your eyes again. She wanted that gift of attention. You thought she had wanted to disappear, to not be seen by you and you let her, for years, but all she wanted was to be found. By someone who noticed. Who made her safe. Who wasn't … dangerous.

At that moment, at the rockpool, Dr Breen shouts from a distance. Tamsin holds out a palm in a furious stop of silence – God not him, of all people, now – just as Elle yells out, 'Over here, Doc D'mean, this way,' then looks at the girls like yeah, so, der.

Because every teen, of course, wants to belong.

And she wants Cin's love. And she sees it. The teacher who ghosts the brilliant ones and Cin especially, by ignoring her. Tellingly. The English teacher who doesn't want to engage with her words, reads her work and feigns indifference. Because, ah yes, failing to engage with someone is a power. A way of diminishing. You've seen it with teachers of mediocrity confronted by the brilliant student, which forces the mentor to face up to their own insecurities. You've seen it with the girl group confronted by the precociously different; the girl's triumphs and courage and audacity are not commented on, as if this will make it all go away. You've seen it with the men dealing with women who are forces of nature; who are strong and dangerous and uncontainable and therefore must be neutered with a studious failure to engage. And this is Tony Breen. Dr Breen. Working in his high school and belittling the best and brightest among him who might have a chance to actually fly further than him. So he ignores or diminishes the precocity, to quieten it. Crack the confidence. Clip the wings. Make the talent disappear. He wants a muse not a rival, and Elle sees it.

To her, to them, Tony is a man of the Old World. Who mansplains and manspreads and removes a girl's pockets. He is the police officer who takes twenty-four hours to respond to the domestic violence call – then arrives to find the woman dead. The GP who tells the woman with endometrial pain to have a baby and get over it. The male gynaecologist who insists on the unnecessary examination. He is the tradie who tells a girl in the street to smile, love, come on, it's not so bad – but it is. He is the airconditioning that's a setting too cold. The elbow claiming the plane's middle armrest. The men's shampoo and deodorant that are cheaper than women's – yet guys earn more. The drugs designed for male bodies. He is the car safety features tested on men and men only. He is the judge diminishing the sexual assault case. The jury that doesn't believe her. The bloke who chokes and slaps and shocks. The one who controls. Who ghosts. Who diminishes. The one who cannot get a girlfriend and taunts women online. Who randomly punches women in the face. Who sits right next to them on the otherwise empty bus. He is testosterone, the hormone of competition and dominion. He is the insecure alpha as opposed to the confident beta and the boy with the raised finger and the man who will not stop, will not rest until he's colonised and controlled and triumphed. And Elle sees it all.

'Fuck him that fucking cunt,' Elle says, battle-ready. Willa goes to say something but Elle is edged, cusped, wants to do something, what, they can smell the spark of her. And yes this is the girl who wants to belong to the group, who'll do anything to belong and who loves, deeply, her Cin. 'Dr Breen! We're stuck,' Elle yells out again. 'What the fuck are you doing?' Cin asks. 'Nothing,' Elle responds, 'but our headmistress would be so fucking proud of us.' You feel a frisson of fear and guilt; this makes you culpable. Elle smears mud on her cheeks, laughing, then they all do; ah, your Cins, your women of the future, your warrior army readying themselves – but what on earth is coming next. Your teeth dig into your bottom lip. Cin is not looking at you as she talks.

Dr Breen arrives. Can't find the girls. They're all silent, giggling softly in the bush, it's a game. He gets angrier, and angrier, he calls them out. But they're good at this. Thwart the man. Fuck him over. Laugh at him but silently because as Margaret Atwood says, men are afraid that women will laugh at them, yet women are afraid that men will kill them.

Cin looks up. 'That's it,' she says, abrupt, breaking the spell. 'We hid. He crashed away. And we never heard from him after that. He vanished.' A pause. 'Or we did.'

What? No. *No.* Can't stop there. You insist she continue, come on. 'Don't do this to me.' Want more? Cin asks in a soft taunt. You nod. Please, you can't bear it. Really? Cin holds off. 'Don't do this to me, Sinsi.' Okay, okay. I'll give you more, G. Here goes. One upon a time.

There was a girl who became someone else. A new person. Why are you so awful to us, she jabbed at the weird man. The girl is pumped up with a strange power she has never felt before;

it is bold and bolshy and strong. You'd like her, G, she found her voice. She forces the man into walking backwards at all her questions, his hands out in front of him, with his back to the plunge. He's suddenly splashing, laughing in shock, he's splashing and stumbling in the shallow water of the rockpool but this is not a game; he's suddenly edging backwards to the slippery rocks. To the green waiting algae. Laughing then not. Then. Then. In a flash of a moment the man stumbles. Slips. Calls out but no-one moves forward except Cin, too late; he is swept over the edge by the whoosh of the water and is left floundering, injured, at the bottom of the waterfall. Just like that. So quick. Leaving four girls in shock. In silence.

The man has hit his head. He is bleeding. Furious. He is shouting at them. This is the girls' fault, all of this. They will pay for this. Big time. Parents will have to be faced. Police. They will be punished. Expelled. This is assault. They're going down, all of them, every single one, and Daddy's money can't save them now, their future is over. They watch silently. Then. Then. A rock hits the man square on the head. Another rock lands, and another. Another. Another. Until all that shouting about expulsion and jail and stupid fucking spoilt little cunts is is   stopped.

'There was no me in this,' Cin whispers finally into the shocked quiet. 'Just you.' What does she mean? 'Maybe it was all of us,' she whispers. 'Or none. Maybe we all did it. Or none. Maybe, as I said before, we just went quiet and he vanished. Our game.' She shrugs. 'Our silly game. Or maybe ... he never even got to us in the first place. Your choice, G.'

You sit back in your chair. So. All for one and one for all, yes, she's part of this, a musketeer, a Spartacus. As are you. 'You wanted to hear this.' Pardon, what? 'This story. I told you, to help.' What. Who. 'You.' Cin smiles calmly, serenely, like the teacher who's just explained the way of the world to the confused student. 'And maybe, G, the truth is exactly what the cops think it is.' What. Which is. 'A man got lost. And four girls didn't. And no-one quite believes them, because no-one ever believes the female. They always think the worst of us. Don't they? You taught us that, ma'am. Remember.' And with that switch back to 'ma'am' you feel seen. Implicated, as teacher and colluder in this. Cin smiles again, watching, noting, saying nothing; like she is reading you precisely in this moment.

You laugh, don't know why; this is so wrong, crazy, mixed up. Information is power, of course, and the question now is what you do with it. But confusion is also power. Wrong-footing, blind-siding, flurrying up. You know that chaos can also win when you don't know what to believe, and that maybe, possibly, you just have to surrender here. Give in, for peace.

Yet Tony. Your confidant, your mate. But Tony, the chauvinistic dick. Your Swiss Army knife, your accomplice who keeps your hands clean. But no, no, your Koongalettes see it differently, of course. Only last week he mansplained inequality in the newsletter marking International Women's Day. His voice was platformed over all the women on staff because he had pressed for it and you let it pass but your acolytes had noted, as they do; they had thought, critically, like the good girls they are. And they do not let it pass, they call it out. But how far does calling it out go, and what of the absent Cin who found her voice. You shake your head; a shiver of confusion. You have no idea what's just happened, what's fiction and what's not – and don't want to know now, perhaps.

'Love you,' Cin barks as a challenge. You jump. What are you to do, say. 'Love you,' Cin repeats, jabbing with her wilfulness. The hungry demand, 'love you, love you', keeps coming as you sit in shock, in silence; 'Love you,' Cin pelts into you with insistent violence until you eventually say it back, beaten down; 'Love you too,' and the ice is finally broken, and … relief. Of letting go. You stand, in wary silence, your shoulders like rock; you stand looking at each other across the gulf of a generation and in that moment Cin's a small and deeply sensitive child, who just wants love, and you can feel the roar of it.

So. So. You are trembling here, exposed. What to do. Head reeling, all over the place. Cin nods to her waiting girls. It is done. 'Well,' you say to them, robotic and flat and not even sure why because nothing is decided here, nothing, not a thing worked out or tied up. What to believe, which version. Three faces look at you now with that familiar, studied blankness of the past few days, of stories locked. Then your beautiful, brave, fragile Cin suddenly blinks, a touch too long, as if everything hurts; a goddaughter on the precipice and about to be swallowed up, and in that moment you feel the terrible weight of the love and in a rush of emotion you hold out your hands, to all of them, don't know why; you reach out and all four of you clutch tight in a circle and it's as if you will never stop the holding, in that moment, ever; saying nothing and saying everything, trembling and squeezing and vulnerable and stopped.

All the stories we tell ourselves. To understand, soothe, forget. Cin has spun a tale of a prince and his posse and you're not sure if it's the truth or not, you'll never be sure. But you do know one thing. Only one. The reality of a finger gesture to a group of lads and your beautiful girl at the centre of it; the reality of suddenly realising you are nothing but a hole to them. From Golden Flower, with all that audacious promise, to this. And you just want your girl to wear sunshine again, somehow, in a radiant blast.

You usher The Cins out of the room and away from your house in careful silence, barely knowing what you're doing. Need to think. *Think.* 'Honesty, yeah,' Cin whispers in farewell. You chuckle in confusion, in shock; your head hurts. Because what you have here, quite possibly, is a deluded cult of obeyance, yes, and it won't go down well. Your mind skips ahead to Hugo briefing the defence. Quoting his daughter's indignant words back to a court. 'We were inspired by her. We did this for her. We were devoted to everything she said. Because, well, *her.*' You see the contemptuous jab of the finger at you and the police psychologists picking apart that very female desire to please. And they're so young, little girls underneath, and you always forget this; their brains aren't fully developed. Yes, of course, a cult of obeyance. Which you encouraged. But. But. Did you. Elle declared their headmistress would be so fucking proud of them – yet was that all part of Cin's elaborate tale of flattery, or the truth. What did they do, if anything. Your arms wrap around your torso, your fingernails dig in.

You watch The Cins leaving the school grounds, walking through Koongala's gates without looking behind them. As they depart the campus they laugh, throwing back their heads at some private joke and draping their arms loosely over one another's shoulders and waists. They do not look back, even once, it is all forward propulsion. Cin raises a finger in a huge fuck you to the sky and it is just like the audacity of old times; like they've shrugged something off as they walk into the possibility, again, of an untrammelled future; walk into a world where everything, actually, might be alright, and your heart lurches at the sight.

You head to the desk in your home office. Sit, carefully, as if it's mined, all senses alert. What just happened. You are calm as you ring Mig by reflex then hang up before she answers. What are you doing, you're not thinking straight; no, that section of your life is over, you need to sort this out by yourself. Need to fence off everyone else. You are calm as you think about what might happen if the world jumps to the conclusion that The Cins are somehow responsible for this. All supposition, of course, but you know the impact an accusation would have on them, even if found innocent. The gruelling court case, oh yes, and trials by press. The social media trolls and the worldwide infamy and stalkers and incels stewing in their caves; all the rumours and questions and hate that would dog them for the rest of existence. Jail, possibly. Ruined lives. You know all this, oh yes. And you know what to do.

The blade of knowing.

You arch back in your chair, stretching clenched muscles in your torso and shoulders. In this moment you just feel like disappearing in a puff of smoke, from this entire clusterfuck; all jobs present and future, all the uncertainty and pressure and stress. In this moment you just want to disappear into your lair by the beach that's ringing with light, shedding burdens as you go, and live a vanished life. Because you need the balm of a simpler way and you're suddenly ready, so ready, for a surrendering into a quieter, more observant life. You want to stride into the third trimester of living in vivid peace. But no, not yet. There is work to be done. Always work to be done. It never lets up.

You're not afraid, as your girls sometimes say, to alive yourself. Your heart is growing young as you sit and think, and think. Of your beautiful, broken Cin, and all The Cins who need to be repaired here. Put back together, winged with love. All the girls. See, you want to say to Mig now, I can be generous too; by God, I know how to love. To love well, and to risk it. But nothing will be said, of course, it is all in the doing. God answered your prayers and gave your girls back and now ... now you must protect them and guide them, steer them into firmness and shield them from attack, from slander and scuttlebutt. For their survival. Something has been cauterised; this is your path. Because these girls need the gift of attention. Yours. Here. Now. The panacea of love. The tonic of confidence. To bloom. This is your job. And Mig's, and Tink's, and Beth's, and Cara's and Maude's and all the other mothers in this world; it is your job to pull back the bow for them, to set them free.

You know what to do. It hurts, so hurts, but you're used to that. You straighten your chair and turn to your emails. To the offer letter. Your fingertips dance over the sentences yet again, slower now; your fingers hover over the words known off by heart that had so recently floated you in bliss. You hone and shape your response, to a third draft and then a fourth, removing the first and last sentences and a rogue 'just'. In three crisp sentences it is done, the decline regretful and elegant.

And ... send.

You stand and look out the window, gazing across the centenary garden to the Koongala gates. Thinking of those girls, all those blazing girls. They do not know how much older women have freighted in them as they watch them arrow into their future in a beautiful brave arc; as they watch them, breath held, soaring into a future accompanied by the weight of repetitious history; as they watch them arcing up and away from them, hopefully free, perhaps, who knows. We can only hope.